# Driving Into Darkness

IAIN CAMERON

ISBN: 978-1503335004



To find out more about the author, visit the website:

www.iain-cameron.com

For Andrew Brown Sinclair (1923-2014), an inspiration to all who knew him.

# ONE

Decisions, decisions. It would be the most important decision of his life, but he was focused only on the road ahead.

Having just endured a long and fractious meeting with engineers and technicians, there was no way he could drive the straight and boring A23. He needed something more challenging. The B2117, a narrow country road with plenty of sharp bends and several long straights would do nicely.

The bike's big Ducati 900cc engine responded with a beautiful deep-throated burbling and a mid-range whine, a superb blend of high-tolerance engineering, top quality components, and the finest lubricating oils that money could buy, making the aural experience every bit as pleasurable as the ride itself.

If he was thinking like an engineer, it was because he had spent most of the day with them, although the engineers in his company worked in more microscopic realms than could ever be found in an Italian bike factory; but he was sure the principles employed were just the same.

In the mirror, a Subaru Impreza was coming up fast. On another day, when he didn't feel so tired or preoccupied with the incompetence of a new supplier who couldn't deliver parts when they needed them, he might have delivered a quick puff of Ducati exhaust before disappearing into the distance, but today he eased over to let him pass.

The Subaru moved alongside but made no effort to overtake. He glanced over. The driver was alone, mid-thirties and sporting a baseball cap, dark glasses and a chin that hadn't seen a razor for a while. Despite the fading light, his sneering disdain for bikers was obvious, and when the driver indicated he wanted to race with a regal pointing of a finger, he nodded his approval.

Before he could react, the Subaru surged forward. He gunned the bike and was soon hugging its rear bumper, determined not to lose him. A long straight started after the bend and he knew he could take him there. The Subaru sailed around the tight corner as if on rails, but he stayed with him, the fat tyres of the Ducati almost on their sides. Before the road straightened, he eased the bike upright and wound up the power.

He moved to the right, shadowing the Subaru's rear wing and trying to get a good look at the road ahead. Sections were barely wide enough for two cars, never mind the number of overloaded tractors and lorries that used the road regularly. With a subtle dip of the elbow, he pulled out and accelerated hard. The speedo touched ninety-five and when they were level, he looked over and gave the insolent prick his middle finger.

Before his hand regained a firm grip on the handlebars, the Subaru swung towards him. For a split second, he was caught in two minds: brake or accelerate? Before he could do either, the Subaru made contact with the front wheel and in an instant, the bike shot over the carriageway and into woods at the side of the road.

He crashed through rhododendrons, brambles and holly as if they weren't there. He gripped the handlebars with all his strength, trying to reach the brake, but the bike was shaking so violently it was impossible to feel anything or to see through the wildly shuddering visor. For an instant, his fingers touched the brake but before he could pull it, the front wheel hit something solid. The bike stopped dead and he shot high into the air.

For a moment he felt weightless, ethereal, the ground racing by in a grainy, green and brown collage. He was falling, falling when he slammed head first into the trunk of a 500-year-old oak tree.

# TWO

Detective Inspector Angus Henderson opened the car door and wearily climbed out. He knew it was a stupid idea to go out boozing in the middle of a major investigation, but last night the temptation to let off steam had been too great. He stopped for a moment to let his brain catch up with his tired body, before gulping a lungful of fresh air and popping an extra-strong mint into his mouth. He walked towards the house.

A young copper stood guard at the place where the front door used to be. It looked as though it had been attacked by a medieval mob looking for witches, or rammed by a bulldozer in the course of extracting an ATM machine. The wooden frame had been turned into an ugly mess of splinters and bare brickwork, with the door hanging open and a large hole where the lock used to be.

'Is Mrs Frankcombe inside?' he asked PC4367, who came from God-knows which police station as he was having trouble remembering which part of Sussex he was in.

'Yes sir,' he said, a touch too brightly for Henderson's liking, 'she's in the living room with the

FLO, Mrs Wilkes.'

Only an hour before, Henderson had been in bed, comatose and enjoying one of the deepest sleeps he'd had for many months. At some point in the future he would forgive Detective Sergeant Carol Walters for having the temerity to wake him up, but not yet.

It didn't help that the sanctimonious Miss Walters was behaving like a card-carrying member of Alcoholics Anonymous. She'd reeled off all the stupid things everyone had said last night in the car on the way over. This had included the boorish and sexist behaviour of many of her colleagues, conduct supposedly banished by successive government decrees and the directives of righteous Chief Constables. Walters had left the pub before closing time, and unlike the rest of the crew who ended up back at his place, she'd gone straight home.

It wasn't difficult to locate the living room, as every door in the house was thrown open to allow Scenes of Crime Officers to dust for prints and search for traces of hair and fibre. However, if the other three cases in this inquiry were anything to go by, they would find diddly squat, and if it wasn't for the spectre of another *Argus* headline berating an incompetent police force for not doing enough, Henderson would send them home now and save the taxpayer a few quid.

The opulence of the house hit him like a slap, as had all the other houses he'd visited in the course of this investigation. With antique-stuffed hallways, bespoke fitted kitchens, and enough hi-tech gadgetry to keep a geeky 16-year-old in rapturous ecstasy for many years, there was way more valuable stuff inside the house than languishing outside on the driveway or in the garage. However, it was his job to catch the criminals, and down to the psychologists, sociologists and psychiatrists to understand what motivated them to steal cars.

The Family Liaison Officer, Madeline Wilkes, looked up and smiled as Henderson and Walters entered the room. Madeline's smiles were so warm and inviting that someone with less resolve than himself could get into trouble with the pc-police, or her rugby-playing husband, if her natural friendliness was misread. That aside, she was a skilled FLO and her attendance at crime scenes such as this was always a source of comfort to traumatised victims and their families, and made his job very much easier.

PC Wilkes was perched on the edge of a cream-coloured sofa, holding the hand of a woman Henderson assumed to be Mrs Frankcombe, slight in build and almost engulfed by the large matching armchair.

'Good Morning, Mrs Frankcombe, good morning, Constable Wilkes,' he said extending a hand. 'I am Detective Inspector Angus Henderson of Sussex Police and the Senior Investigating Officer on this case. This is Detective Sergeant Carol Walters.'

'Hello,' Mrs Frankcombe said. Without rising from

the chair, she moved her trembling hand up to shake his.

'May we sit down?'

Wilkes got up. 'I'll wait in the hall, sir, until you're finished. Call me if you need anything.'

He took her place on the settee but didn't reach for the hand of the victim. Gestures like this weren't his style and in such a pc-age they could easily be misinterpreted.

'I'm sorry to bother you at such a difficult time, Mrs Frankcombe,' he said, 'but as you are no doubt aware, this is the fourth such robbery of an expensive car in the area over the last few weeks, and if we are to have any hope of catching these people we need you to try and remember as much as you can about the incident. Feel free to take as much time as you want.'

'I will.' She sniffed. 'I want these bastards caught and no mistake. They beat up my husband and put him in fucking hospital. Yeah you bet I want them caught.'

Henderson was slightly taken aback by her foul-mouthed outburst, not that he hadn't heard a woman swear before, but it seemed incongruous from the mouth of such a well-groomed and well-heeled lady. However, he knew stress and fear could cause even the most restrained individuals to drop their guard and eschew social niceties, albeit for a short period.

It was hard to estimate her age, especially as her face was streaked with tears and make-up, but he guessed mid-forties. From the look of the expensive hairstyle and smart, elegant clothes, not all of their money was spent on the house and the car. She was slim and sun-tanned, no doubt from holidays in warm, sunny places and not from lying on the patio recliner out on the terrace, visible through the French windows, as it was late March and the pleasant spring weather promised by Brighton Meteorologists had yet to materialise.

'Please start at the point,' he said, 'when you noticed something was going on.'

'Ok. I woke up about two-thirty, although it's only a guess as I'm sure I didn't look at the clock until later.' She paused, as if distracted by a sudden thought.

'Did a noise downstairs wake you?' Henderson said, trying to cajole her along. 'There's substantial damage to your front door and I imagine there must have been a lot of banging.'

'No, it wasn't that. I'd had a few glasses of wine during the evening you see, and I took some sleeping pills as I find it hard to sleep after I've been drinking. I was well zonked when it happened. Alan woke me and told me he could hear something strange going on downstairs.'

'What did it sound like?'

'We're at the back of the house so it was bit muffled, but it was a constant thumping, a sort of boom-boom-boom. If I hadn't known it was the middle of the night, I would've thought it was the builders. We're always having work done.' She paused to take a sip of water.

'Where was I? Ah yes, Alan got out of bed and said he was going down to see what was going on. The noise changed, and I could hear lots of banging. I found out later they were pulling all the drawers out of the hall table and dropping them on the floor. Didn't the fucking morons realise it was an antique, a 1760 Chippendale?' Her face was red with anger.

'So Alan went downstairs,' Henderson said.

'No, I mean yes, but he didn't go willingly. Someone came into our room and scooped our mobiles from the bedside table, then dragged poor Alan downstairs. By the time I got to the top of the stairs, they had him on the floor and they were kicking him.' She began to sob. 'Big boots into a man who's nearly sixty, I ask you,' she said as she raised her tear-stained face to look at him. 'What sort of animals would do such a thing? He's in hospital now with broken ribs, concussion and God-knows what else.'

'You have my sympathies,' Henderson said.

He waited a few moments until she recovered.

'What happened then?'

'A few more kicks and punches and he told them where the keys to the car were. He had to otherwise I think they might have killed him. They grabbed the keys and a few seconds later they were out of the house.'

‘How many people did you see?’ Walters asked.

She looked up at the ceiling. ‘Four. Yes, there were four men in the house.’

‘Was it obvious they were men? Did you hear it in their voices, or was there something in their size or demeanour?’

‘I don’t know.’ She paused a moment. ‘No, not voices. I suppose it was their build. You see, they were all wearing black clothes and gloves and with a balaclava sort of thing over their heads. I didn’t see their faces, if that’s what you mean.’

‘Did you hear them say anything to one another?’ Henderson said. ‘For example, did they use names or phrases, anything you can remember?’

‘No, I don’t think so. They didn’t say much. In fact, other than to demand the car keys, I don’t believe I heard them say anything.’

*

After saying goodbye to Mrs Frankcombe, both detectives walked out into the cold March morning. Henderson spent a few minutes looking at the damage to the door while Walters wandered away. When he finished looking round, he found her standing in front of a large, open, oak-framed garage, wide enough to house three cars.

Her casual position, propped against an upright, shoulders relaxed, hands fiddling with something in her pockets, bore all the hallmarks of a seasoned smoker. She had kicked the habit four months ago, but it was clear some practices were proving harder to break than others.

He walked over to join her.

'It's not much protection for a high-value motor like a Porsche, wouldn't you say, sir?' she said.

'I suppose not, but good enough to stop the rain from besmirching an expensive paint job, and keeping frost and snow away in winter.'

'True, but I can see another advantage.'

'Which is?'

'Most people keep a load of old crap in their garages, like old beds, kids bikes, and boxes, but this open style forces even untidy scumbags into keeping it tidy.'

'You could be right.'

He now knew they were on the fringes of Henfield, a large village to the north of Brighton, and he could see why the Frankcombe's house had been targeted. It was large, five bedrooms, several reception rooms and a swimming pool, all set in five acres of land. He had experienced the long drive up from the B-road, and from the four corners of the house all he could see were paddocks, lakes, woods, and farmland. No other houses, no streetlights and no neighbours.

They came for the car. This one, a three-month old Porsche GT2 RS, worth around one hundred and seventy grand, fitted comfortably into a thieves' shopping list which already included a brand-new Ferrari California, a Lamborghini Gallardo Spider, and, his personal favourite, an Aston Martin DB9.

The sweet daydream of exotic cars came to an abrupt halt as they walked to Walters's car, a 5-year-old Golf in much need of a wash and a thorough spring-clean. Before they got there, he heard another car heading up the driveway. As soon as it stopped, Rob Tremain, the chief crime reporter for *The Argus* jumped out.

'Inspector Henderson, good to see you,' he said walking towards them. 'Heading back to the office now, are we?'

'Morning Rob. Yes we are.'

'What can you tell me about this one?' Tremain said, thrusting an electronic recording machine towards him. 'Would you say it follows the same pattern as the other three?'

'Pretty much. The door's been smashed open with something heavy, possibly the same sledgehammers the gang employed in the other robberies. Mr Frankcombe was beaten until he told them where he kept the keys, and they disappeared with the car a couple of minutes later. At this moment, we have a team of forensic experts working inside the house. If the gang left anything behind, a fibre, a bit of DNA or a cigarette butt, we'll find it.'

'All very reassuring, but there's not much chance of that happening is there, as they found nothing at each of the three other robberies? These guys have been professional so far, but is there anything you've seen at this house which gives you confidence this might be the place where you'll find a vital clue, forensic or otherwise, that'll help you track them down?'

A tricky question as Henderson would be damned with a 'yes' and damned with a 'no'. 'Let's wait and see on that one, Rob, but forensics are only one strand of our investigation. We are also looking at car dealers and CCTV cameras, liaising with other police forces, a whole range of things. If I may, I would like to ask your readers to report any unusual activity they see around a garage or a lock-up in their area and if they're offered an expensive car at a knockdown price.

'Where do you think the cars end up?'

'Not in Sussex, I'm sure. Re-badged, re-plated, and shipped to the Middle East or Asia is my best guess. It's much easier to sell a stolen car in those places than it is here in the UK.'

'Thank you Inspector.' He made a play of switching the recording machine off. 'So, if I can ask you, off the record. This is the fourth such high-value car robbery in our area, how many more will it take until you stop them?'

'C'mon Rob, how would I know? These guys are in and out of the place in minutes; they don't talk much, they don't leave anything behind and they disappear with the car. There's not much left for us to work on.'

'I know you don't have a large squad on this one. Is the Chief Constable giving this case sufficient priority?'

A few weeks ago, Tremain wrote a scathing article about inadequate resourcing levels in the county, leaving the Chief Constable and his ACCs seething in anger. It wasn't the usual jungle chant about wasting taxpayers' money, but an attack on the spending priorities and judgement of the Sussex Police senior management team.

Henderson gave him the standard line about the need to prioritise scarce resources, but no way could he admit that this case was different from any other. On a typical murder investigation, there was always more to do than was possible to achieve with the limited number of personnel and restricted budget at his disposal. On this one, there was so little for them to get their teeth into he was hard-pressed making best use of the small team he had. Now if Mr Tremain could put a positive spin on that one, he was a better man than the DI.

# THREE

Davis was still talking. William Lawton tried to concentrate on the man's gruff, Bradford inflection and weasel-like features, no doubt cultivated to frighten and bully his staff, but Lawton's mind was wandering over to the blueberry muffin and the aroma of fresh coffee emanating from the tea trolley. None of this lot would make a move until he did, and even though he liked to keep them waiting, the temptation was too strong. He rose from his chair as Davis was hitting his stride.

It had been a fraught morning at chez Lawton. His 19-year-old daughter, Haley, would soon be going back to university in Manchester after the Easter break and the thought of it left her as tense as a high-voltage electricity cable. It didn't help that her younger brother Ben was baiting her non-stop by telling her a Polish language student had been lined up to take over her room.

His wife Stephanie had started to chew his ear for burying his nose in the *Daily Telegraph* while World War Three raged all around, and then he was berated by his daughter for not defending her honour against the boy-devil. Moments later, Ben blamed him for not taking his side against the two witches. In disgust, he'd dumped the remains of his toast in the bin and headed off to work. No wonder he often felt sharp pains in his stomach after eating, probably the start of an ulcer or something more serious.

'And therefore I think this would be a fantastic project for my team to undertake,' Davis said. 'It will give them great experience of–'

Lawton could take no more. 'Yes, yes Graham, I hear what you're saying,' he said, picking up his customary 'Malaga Beach Bum' mug and filling it with hot, fragrant coffee. 'If we had limitless buckets of cash, but we don't. We need to see a payoff and after reading your report, I don't see one in this instance.'

It stopped him dead. Ah, if the Chairman could see him now, he was a chip off the old block. William Lawton was Managing Director of Markham Microprocessors, a company founded by Sir Mathew Markham thirty years ago. Sir Mathew was still de facto chairman but played little part in day-to-day operations, and was reaching a point in his life when he was considering severing all remaining ties with the business.

Sir Mathew started the company in the early eighties with twenty grand borrowed from a favourite uncle, and filled his head with as much information as he could find about the embryonic science of semiconductors. With no more business sense than the average hobbyist, he blagged a contract to make the central processing unit for a new home computer and set to work.

His genius, although he would say it was a consequence of his impoverished circumstances, was in hiring two clever programmers to develop the software. He was unable to offer them additional money, people, or development tools, and in this monastic atmosphere they produced a brilliant piece of computer code, frugal in its use of computer memory and power but devastatingly effective in the way it executed commands.

This software was incorporated into the first Markham microprocessor, called 'Suki,' after Sir Mathew's beautiful, socialite daughter. It was seized upon by a rapidly growing personal computer industry. However, the company's fortunes changed forever with the introduction of battery-powered devices, particularly mobile phones and laptops. Famed for their low power consumption and heat generation, Markham products soon cornered the market.

Nowadays Suki, her siblings and children were incorporated into millions of phones, laptops, tablet computers, and other portable devices, turning the business into one of the most profitable companies in the UK. However, Mathew Markham's parsimonious ethos still burned within these four walls and no one would be profligate with money while William Lawton occupied the Managing Director's chair.

‘Moving on,’ Lawton said. ‘There will be no Financial Update today as David isn’t here, but I assume you’ve all got the Flash Report that his deputy, Jon, managed to put together this morning.’

The assembled business heads emitted a communal sigh, disappointed not to be told by David Young, the Financial Director, what a great job they were doing; he would have reported yet another sales increase with profit way ahead of target. This usually led to a noisy bout of mutual backslapping and much drinking and merrymaking in the pub or restaurant afterwards.

Like an actor picking up his cue, Lawton would always try and singe their cloaks with a warning that it could all go up in smoke if there was a cataclysmic shift in technology, or the development of a revolutionary product. He encouraged every member of the senior management team to allocate part of their day to ‘blue-sky’ thinking, and, if necessary, make use of the two rooms specially designed for this purpose. The fear of failure kept him awake at night and he hoped it did the same for them, as he was not the fountain of truth, enlightenment, and happiness many of them believed he was.

He looked at the paper in front of him. ‘There is one remaining item on the agenda, Any Other Business. Do we have any?’

‘What’s the latest on the takeover?’ Alan Thomson asked.

Lawton sighed. 'Can I remind you all that what the Chairman has put on the table isn't a takeover, despite the term being used by reputable newspapers who really should know better, but an expression of interest. The Chairman is asking anyone who is interested in buying the company to come forward, and we will judge whether their offer, in terms of money, technology and ambition, is good enough. On the other hand, he may decide not to sell at all if no one can come up with the goods.'

'So, how is the 'expression of interest' going?'

'Another four companies have contacted us since the last time we spoke, but so far we don't feel any of them have either the financial muscle or the intellectual capacity to move us to the next level.' He glanced around the room, making sure there were no interlopers. 'You see, we are treading a fine line here. On the one hand, we can't tell them about Kratos as we don't want the information to leak out into the public domain, but on the other, we need to assess if they've got the money and the technical know-how to make it the world-beating success we believe it will be.'

'I think we are betting too much on one horse,' Didier Beauchamp said in a deep, French-accented voice, 'it is, after all, untried technology.'

Lawton had a choice to make. Such a comment could start a bun-fight between the believers and non-believers, and with twelve in the room, it could be a noisy and at times belligerent affair. Sure enough, a few moments later, voices were raised.

'Hold it, hold it,' he said putting up his hand to quieten them. 'We've all been here before and quite frankly, I've got better things to do with my time than talk about what may or may not happen. Now, if there is nothing else...' He looked around at all their faces, daring anyone to speak. 'Fine. I'm bringing this meeting to a close. Thank you all for coming.'

He gathered his papers together and rose from his seat as they were starting to bicker again. He left the room and let them get on with it. In the quiet sanctity of his office he scanned the Post-it notes his PA had stuck to the computer screen, and after moving the mouse to re-activate it found another forty-odd emails had arrived in his inbox since leaving for the monthly meeting some three hours before. A quick glance told him there was nothing that couldn't wait until morning, and after picking up a file from his desk, he headed out.

The desk of his new PA, Jules Carrington, was located outside his office and the poor lad jumped when his boss made a sudden appearance. He tilted the screen of his computer away from view. Facebook, Twitter, or the odd computer game were about tolerable, but even though the business was situated in Hove, next door to the unofficial gay capital of Britain, Lawton would not countenance any boy-boy stuff, no matter how many Minority Rights or

Equality seminars he attended.

'Jules, I'm off to see Sir Mathew. Knowing how the Chairman likes to talk, you can count me out for the rest of the day.'

'Right-oh Mr Lawton.'

Today Jules wore a bright yellow V-neck and flowery, patterned shirt. The word 'subtle' did not exist in the boy's vocabulary.

'The usual rules about calls–'

'I know, I know,' Jules said holding up a small, dainty hand to silence him. 'Only put them through to your mobile if they are from one of our main customers or suppliers. All others, take a message.'

'Very good Jules, you're getting it,' at last, he almost said. 'I'll see you tomorrow.'

It was often a relief to be heading down the deep, carpeted stairs. It had been an exciting challenge helping Sir Mathew run the company when they were growing rapidly all those years ago. Then, the signing of each new contract was a triumph, and 12-hour days were the norm. These days, growth had slowed down to regular but unspectacular single digits, and almost all of the major mobile and laptop manufacturers were their customers. It was hard not to see his work colleagues as a bunch of over-paid, squabbling kids who needed the occasional boot up the arse to wake them up.

On the ground floor, behind a smoked, glass-topped desk, sat the immaculately coiffured Mrs Carla

Roberts. She represented the modern face of security, replacing the stoic, tattooed ex-army sergeant-major. While her repertoire of skills did not stretch to a punch in the chops or a forearm lock, her faultless diction and impeccable sense of style would dissuade any feckless intruder from chancing their arm.

'I'll bid you farewell, Carla. I'm off to see Sir Mathew.'

'You're not coming back to the office this evening, Mr Lawton?'

'I'm afraid not. Bye.'

'Goodbye Mr Lawton.'

He stepped out of the building, walked to the car park at the rear of Markham House and climbed into his car. It was a short, effortless drive to Holland Road, but the same could not be said for the climb up to Melanie Shaw's flat. It was on the fourth floor of a restored Victorian building without a lift.

When she opened the door, she greeted him as she always did, as if she had not seen him for weeks, and gave him a long, sensuous kiss. If his hormones and everything else had been dulled during the last management meeting, with all the dreary descriptions of project milestones and coding problems, they were alive now and jigging with delight.

'Hello William,' she said, her hot breath wafting into his ear as her beautiful, even, pearly-white teeth nibbled at it.

'Hello Melanie, it's good to see you.'

'Did you have trouble getting away?'

'Oh no, the old faithful, 'I'm going to see the chairman' never fails.'

'Ha. How long have we got?'

'I'll need to be home for seven.'

'We've no time to lose, then,' she said as she walked into the bedroom.

Lawton loosened his tie and followed her leisurely, swinging rear. It reminded him of his grandmother's antique pendulum clock, but there was nothing old-fashioned about the way Melanie performed between the sheets.

# FOUR

DI Henderson rushed out of his office clutching a slim folder, now late for his next appointment. He was due to chair another meeting of the Operation Poseidon team, the inappropriate name the police computer had allocated to the inquiry into high-value car thefts; a moniker that should have been reserved for a boat nicking scam, or drug shipments smuggled aboard cruise liners.

While the car thieving case was an annoying thorn in the side of Sussex Police, it had not yet reached the level of a major investigation. It was unlikely to do so in the light of the number of more serious crimes on Henderson's plate, and on those of his senior colleagues, and so his small team of eight could easily fit into Meeting Room 4, a small pokey room without any windows.

It had been a long day. He had been seated at his desk by seven, an hour earlier than usual as recurrent toothache had kept him awake most of the night. He couldn't see the point of spending any more time lying in bed or moping around his flat. On those rare occasions when he made it in before the rest of the team, he often got more done as there were fewer phone calls and even fewer interruptions; but what had started out as a promising day work-wise had rapidly degenerated as his diary had filled up with a succession of meetings.

By nine-thirty the first of many visitors had trooped in and out his office, offering updates on their progress, or the lack of it in the case of the car-jacking investigation. After lunch there had been a major get-together of senior officers and the Chief Constable, where they listened to his latest thinking on Community Policing and improving relations with the local population. Few things in life were as insufferable as toothache, but this had to be one of them.

The meeting over-ran and he didn't get a chance to go outside for a walk in the fresh air, or enjoy a chat with the smokers hanging around the front door of the building. He now he felt agitated and restless. All he wanted to do was go home, swallow a couple of paracetamol tablets and sit watching the TV with a large glass of Glenmorangie in his hand. Providing those bastards the other night, some of whom hadn't left his flat until gone three, hadn't got there first and finished it.

Whenever he walked into a team meeting, Henderson harboured a fantasy that his presence would cause the cackle and burble to cease, or at least quieten to a murmur, much like it did when any of his former schoolmasters at Lochaber High School in Fort

William came into the classroom. In fact, his appearance was barely acknowledged at all, except for the odd nod or wave; but then he didn't have a thick leather tawse nestling under his jacket, or a propensity for throwing chalkboard dusters at the heads of unruly miscreants.

'Ok,' he said, scraping his chair towards the table, 'let's make a start.' He looked around the room but instead of the expectant, animated faces that often greeted him, all he could see now were tired and listless expressions. He knew that would change the instant a breakthrough was made, but it wasn't going to happen today.

'By now you've all had a chance to digest the theft of the car from the house in Henfield on Monday, and the attack on Mr Frankcombe, and hopefully you've made some progress on your enquiries. Let me start with you Phil, how is Mr Frankcombe?'

DC Phil Bentley cleared his throat and removed a sheet of paper from the pile in front of him. The youngest member of the team, he had spent a year on the beat in Crawley, and another two at Worthing. It came as no surprise to his bosses when the bright 24-year-old, who unfailingly volunteered for extra overtime and carried out the crappiest duties without demur, requested a move to CID.

As always, Henderson was willing to give opportunities to young talent, but their value to the unit would be judged not only in the cases they helped solve, but also in their reaction to the inevitable setbacks. To date, the tall youngster, dressed in a light polo shirt and chinos even though it was still early spring and the weather outside damp and grey, had yet to put a foot wrong.

'Mr Alan Frankcombe was admitted to the Royal Sussex with a broken arm, broken nose, three broken ribs, and extensive bruising to the front and back of his torso and legs, consistent with a good kicking with heavy boots. None of his injuries are life threatening or will leave him disabled or scarred, but the doctors think it will be at least six weeks before he can return to work, and a couple of months after that before he gets back to normal.'

'That suggests to me,' DS Walters said, as she doodled on an A4 pad, 'their violence is escalating. If anyone resists, they'll beat the hell out of them until they tell them where the keys are.'

'Even to murder?' Sergeant Tony Haslam said. A little smile played on his lips as he tried to catch her eye across the table. He had been seconded to the team from Traffic Division, as he had an encyclopaedic knowledge of cars, but Tony also had a soft spot for the feisty sergeant. Unfortunately for him, Walters did not reciprocate his admiration or welcome it. As much as she regretted shunning the attentions of any eligible and attractive man, in her book dating a guy from the office was taboo.

'I don't know if they would go that far, just for a

car,' Walters replied, 'but you have to admit they don't stand any nonsense and hand out a pasting to anyone who gets in their way.'

'True,' Haslam said running a hand through thick, spiky black hair, 'but it's different from many of the gangs operating in the Midlands and Surrey, as they only use the threat of violence and are in and out of the victim's house fairly quick. This lot seem to be taking things to a whole new level.'

'So, Tony,' Henderson said, keen to move things on, 'any news about the car they just nicked, or any of the other three on the list, for that matter?'

'The car they took from Henfield in the early hours of Monday morning was a Porsche GT2 RS with only three thousand miles on the clock. It fits perfectly into the profile they've established so far. High quality marque, top of the range model, full spec and not long out of a dealer's showroom.'

'Could someone in a dealership be giving them the nod?' DC Seb Young said.

'I think it's unlikely, Seb as each car was sourced from a different garage.' Haslam rifled through his folder once more. 'Ah yes, here we are. The first car, taken from a house in Brighton, came from Samson's in London; the second from Cuckfield, was purchased at Dales in Shoreham; the third, at Petersfield from ALS in Eastbourne; and the last one, the Porsche at Henfield, from Callans of Worthing.

'As for finding where they're selling them,' Haslam

continued, 'Sally and Seb are still looking through the small ads in car magazines and checking various websites, but so far none of the cars have shown up.'

'Thanks.' Henderson looked at Pat Davidson. 'Pat, the crime scene. Make my day and tell me they've left something behind this time.'

Crime Scene Manager DS Pat Davidson was in charge of the SOCO team which had dusted and combed every surface of the Frankcombe house for any clue, no matter how small, to help them trace the people responsible, but Henderson wasn't hopeful. Witnesses reported the gang always wore leather gloves and balaclavas, and so far they'd left nothing behind but a few wool fibres from a garment widely available in BHS or M&S stores.

Davidson took a large slurp from a can of Fanta orange before shaking his head. 'Sorry boss, nothing much yet, I'm afraid. They didn't even take their gloves off to beat up poor Mr Frankcombe. I'm telling you, these modern criminals have no sense of fair-play.'

A similar story came from DC Sally Graham, in charge of house-to-house enquiries, and DS Harry Wallop, working with Tony Haslam in trying to identify who the buyer might be among known criminal gangs. It didn't help that the house was isolated, so they didn't have the benefit of street CCTV cameras or witness sightings from nosey neighbours. Henderson was about to move to the next item on his short agenda when Sally Graham spoke.

'Sorry to interrupt, sir, but there's something I forgot to say before.'

'Go on.'

'I don't know if it's significant, but when we were taking the neighbours' statements, a man called Doctor Robert Masters, a retired paediatrician who lives further up the road from the Frankcombe's place, said he was awake at three in the morning as he needed to go to the loo. Afterwards, he went into the kitchen to fetch a glass of water and saw a large white van drive past. The reason it stuck in his mind was it looked like one of those chilled food delivery vans which calls into the local shop in the village, but they don't come around his neck of the woods until at least seven-thirty in the morning.'

'If I could give a doctor a bit of advice for a change,' Harry Wallop said, 'if he didn't drink so much water, he wouldn't need to get up in the middle of the night to take a piss.'

A collective groan went up but Henderson ignored it. Could this be the little nugget they had been waiting for, the veritable needle in a haystack, the result of hundreds of man-hours, or the ramblings of an old man with a brain befuddled by too much whisky and Temazepam?

'Enjoy this moment, people,' he said, 'this could be the first time we've ever had an eye witness to anything in this case. Then again, it might be nothing.

There could be a dozen reasons why a large white van was driving past his house at that hour of the morning.'

Haslam was searching through his papers once again. The man took more papers into a meeting than a government minister. 'Tony, have you got something to add?' Henderson asked.

'Hang on a sec, there's something of interest in here.' He pulled out an enquiry sheet, peering at it over his glasses. 'It's on this page somewhere. Ah, here it is. This,' he said, holding it up for everyone to see, 'is the report on the theft at the O'Conner house in Cuckfield when they took the...' He looked around the table for help.

'Lamborghini Gallardo Spider, the second one,' Walters said without looking up.

'Yes, dead right. Thank you Sergeant Walters, I owe you one.'

A ripple of bawdy laughter encircled the room, causing Walters's face to crumple in disgust.

'Listen to this,' Haslam said, oblivious to the mirth his comment had caused. 'A neighbour of theirs, Margaret Draper, said more or less the same thing as DC Graham's Doctor Masters. She says, 'I saw a large van driving past the window and moving slowly as if it was in low gear, or was just starting out and the engine was cold. During the day I wouldn't give it another thought, but at two-thirty in the morning, I thought it a bit odd."

‘Could be a coincidence,’ DC Graham said.

‘You’re a detective,’ Walters said, ‘since when did you believe in coincidences?’

‘Sally,’ Henderson said, ‘I want you to re-interview both Doctor Masters and Margaret Draper and see if you can tease out any detail that might tie the two sightings together. Then we’ll decide what we do with it. Well done, it was a good spot.’

‘Right-oh, thank you sir.’

‘Now listen up. We need to change the direction of this enquiry. I’m not dissatisfied with any of the work done, far from it, but I’m not convinced the breakthrough will come from forensics, our car thieves are being too careful for that. It will come from the sales side of the equation, the buyers and sellers of these stolen cars.’

‘Before you make a change,’ Haslam said, ‘be aware the thieves who nick the cars could well be a different gang from the people who sell them. The sellers are probably buying the cars at a fixed price from the thieving gang and selling them through their own channels. If that’s the case, the two groups will communicate with one another through a single contact. Nicking the sellers, or ringers as they’re called, might not stop the thefts.’

‘I realise that,’ Henderson said, ‘but when I look at the similarity of the raids, high value cars only a few weeks old, it makes me think they’re being nicked to order. If so, it must be the ringers who are pulling the strings and the car thieves are doing what they're told. So nicking the ringers will stop the thefts.'

'Yeah, maybe for a time, until they find another buyer.'

'That's a chance I'm willing to take.'

For the next ten minutes Henderson outlined his mini re-organisation, shifting the emphasis from what was becoming a fruitless search for the gang, to spending more time in trying to establish who the buyer might be. He left the meeting feeling only partially uplifted but confident he was doing the right thing.

He had to do something. The lack of information was driving him nuts and there was a review scheduled with his boss in a couple of days' time and Chief Inspector Harris, as always, would want results, not lame excuses.

# FIVE

He slumped down on the settee. It had been a crappy morning. The DSS were playing silly bastards with his disability money, and despite loads of notices posted around the place telling 'clients' not to abuse staff, if it hadn't been for the security screens he would have jumped over the counter and carved the ugly bitch's face.

Rab McGovern was a thin, wiry Glaswegian who at times was jumpier than a rabbit thanks to all the dope he took. His body contained more tats than the Illustrated Man and he had a predilection for getting into fights due to an argumentative nature, particularly when drunk or high on dope. He bore the ugly marks and scars of numerous street fights and prison attacks, most visibly a ragged scar on his right cheek.

However, he could usually get out of fights with profuse deployment of his trademark tools: an open razor and a serrated hunting knife. The scar had been given to him by a bloke more than twice his size during a fight at Saughton nick in Edinburgh, when he was forced to defend the honour of his hometown against a bunch of arse bandits from the east coast. In telling the story, he always saved the best bit for last: his assailant had not got off scot-free, able to go where he pleased to maim more of his compatriots from the west, as he now moved around with the assistance of a wheelchair and crapped into a colostomy bag.

To be fair to the DSS, he wasn't disabled, other than having a long razor slash on the right thigh, given to him by a mad druggie who was so high on some crap he missed slicing the side of his face, but he could fake a limp better than most. If there was any doubt in their minds or they wanted verification, he didn't bother producing a doctor's note and instead dropped his trousers. That was often enough. It was an ugly thing running from a point close to his balls to an inch or so above his right knee, and looked debilitating even if it wasn't.

It was ugly because at the time, McGovern was also out of his box on dope and didn't go to hospital right away. When he did, he was so abusive to the doctors at the Southern General in Glasgow, he was sure they had employed a leather worker with bad eyesight to stitch him up.

He pulled a beer from the fridge when he heard the thump-thump of the stereo system from the flat above. The owner was a former bond trader, now a crack addict who cruised the streets at night getting his fix and slept most of the day, hence some days the music didn't come on until late in the afternoon.

McGovern had warned him before about playing

his music too loud but the prick didn't listen or didn't take his warnings too seriously. He hauled the door open, ran up the stairs two at a time and banged on his door. When he opened it red-eyed, hair needing washing and wearing crumpled clothes he had probably worn in bed, he said, 'Where the fuck's the fire?' McGovern grabbed a handful of t-shirt and head-butted him across the bridge of his nose.

He walked over to the stereo, a neat B&O system that must have cost a packet, and pulled it off the shelf, the connecting wires popping out as he did so. He dropped it on the floor and stamped on it. As usual, he was wearing heavy boots and after only three whacks, it was turned into a heap of broken acrylic and a mess of electronic circuitry, with the added bonus it had stopped playing the techno crap the prick had been listening to.

Damien, as the druggie was called, was bending over holding his face and trying to make sense of the pain in his nose. He would only realise he had nothing to play his CDs on later, when the effects of the drugs wore off. McGovern walked up to him, his finger pointing at his face with the rigidity of a steel blade.

'You stupid fucker. I told you to turn it down.' He kicked him in the nuts and smacked him in the face with his knee, knocking him backwards where he banged his head on the wall. 'Next time,' McGovern said, leaning in as close as he dared to avoid receiving a puff of rancid breath, 'I'll decorate your face with my fucking razor.'

McGovern walked downstairs to his flat, grabbed his jacket and headed outside. He wandered around Clapham for a while, trying to ease the anger out of his system. He was meeting the guys in ten minutes and they needed him cool and business like.

In a building two streets away from Severus Road where McGovern lived, he entered a flat on the second floor. As usual, the large armchair was left for him, a position where he could see everybody and keep an eye on the door to make sure no one was standing out there and earwigging, or trying to stick a surveillance camera through a gap under the door.

The gang were all there, his gang. Stu Cahill, a good looking bloke and an expert at cutting telephone lines and neutralising house alarms. Even better, he gave them access to a database that told them exactly where they could find a nice new motor.

Jason Ehuru, a tall, well-built guy who could strike the fear of God into the most resistant 'target.' A cool man in a crisis, driver of the getaway car and an indefatigable handler of a sledgehammer.

Brandon Rooney, another big guy, fearless and a genius at driving and fixing any motor, no matter how complicated. Ehuru had brought him into the gang and the tall Jamaican had proved his worth time and again when they were stuck inside an unfamiliar car, unsure how to start it, never mind drive it.

It was McGovern who had pulled them together

and drilled into them the standards he demanded. If anybody screwed-up or tried to be clever, he would be on them like a rash. No matter how big they were or were, or how indispensable to the operation, he would take them down. They did things his way because his way worked, and in time they would all be rich, not stewing their arses in some piss-smelling prison cell. No way was he going back there; no fucking way.

'Stu,' McGovern said, 'get a move on, I don't wanna be here all fucking day. People to see, balls to break.'

'Sure thing,' Cahill said. He lifted a sheet of paper and peered over it, like an actor about to deliver his lines but the thick bastard couldn't remember what he had for lunch, never mind trying to memorise a few lines of a play.

'The next take is a Maserati Quarterport Sport GTS. Bloody silly name for a motor, if you ask me.'

'It's *Quattroporte*, ya dickhead,' Ehuru said. 'It's Italian for four doors.'

'Thank you mister smartarse, have it your way. Next on the list is a four-door Maserati, ok?' He picked up a computer printout. 'The last one sold in the south was to a guy in Warninglid, near Gatwick Airport, three weeks ago.'

'Is the motor on Benny's list?' McGovern said.

'Yep it's there.'

'You sure?'

'Of course I'm sure, Rab. I doubled checked.'

Cahill was a handsome bastard but he had to be

watched; he would rather try to get his mitts up some bird's dress than do the needy on the car lists. With short black hair, a face devoid of marks and scars and the right amount of pecs to get noticed, he was washed, scrubbed and wearing his best t-shirt and jeans. This could only mean one thing: he was on the pull. This did not please McGovern as Cahill's little lady, Jena, was vital to this enterprise. He didn't want her getting messed around. He would need to have words.

'You been there?' Jason Ehuru asked as he pressed back in the chair, his bulk causing it to squeak in protest. To those that didn't know him, the big Nigerian with close-cropped hair and arms like a heavyweight boxer was a menacing presence, larger and stronger than anyone else in the group, but to those that did, he was a pussycat unless crossed.

'Yeah, I've been there,' Cahill said. 'It's a big gaff, well away from neighbours and with fields all around. I couldn't see another house for miles.'

'Course it's a big gaff,' Rooney said. 'You don't think somebody in a council flat in Clapham's got a hundred and fifty grand to splash out on a motor, do ya?'

'Yeah, yeah.'

'What's access like?'

'There's a quiet road at the end of a field, then it's up a long, narrow farm track to their place. No neighbours and no fuckin' gates.'

‘You sure?’

‘Of course I’m bloody sure. I know what fucking gates look like.’

McGovern nodded. ‘Good. We can be in and out of there quicker than last time.’

‘This motor, gents, this Maserati,’ Rooney said, ‘it’s a bit downmarket for us, yeah? Ain’t it a cheap Italian sports car made by Fiat or somethin’?’

Brandon Rooney, a solidly-built, half-caste Irish-Jamaican didn’t do weights like the other guys as he worked on a building site carrying bricks all day, the only one of the four to have a ‘real’ job. He had shoulder length Rasta-style hair and a genial face, which some said made him look girly, but this belied a sharp brain, nasty temper, and a deft ability with a flick knife. Having the jumpy fucker in the same room as him made McGovern uneasy.

‘Rooney you fucking prat,’ Ehuru said, ‘you might know what’s going on under a car’s bonnet, but you know fuck-all about cars. This motor’s got a four thousand cc engine, costs over a hundred grand and sounds like a sports car should. The fuck you care? We get paid even if we nick a scooter or a Peugeot 208, right Mac?’

‘Yep, Ehuru’s right but listen up, we need to crack on and yak more about the gaff,’ McGovern growled. ‘It looks like an easier take than the last one but I still need to make sure you fuckers know what you’re doing, I don’t want any fuck-ups this time.’

# SIX

A well dressed man stepped out of Markham House and into spring sunshine. Normally he 'acclimatised' before moving out of the sterile, air-conditioned atmosphere of the building behind him, but today he was in too much of a hurry and the sharp blast of cool air swirling up from the seafront made him gasp. For once, William Lawton's reason for leaving the office early wasn't a lie. This time, he *was* going to see the chairman.

The drive to Ditchling was always pleasant in the Aston. It offered a good mix of road conditions to keep him awake, even after a hard day. Driving through Hove was a pleasure for different reasons, as he could admire the smart houses and the attractive girls, before picking up the by-pass where the car's six-litre engine gave him a thump in the back as it left everyone else for dead.

His progress came to an abrupt halt at Coldean Lane, which, as usual at this time of the early evening, was choked with traffic. Ten minutes later, the long straights and beautiful scenery of the Ditchling Road beckoned, restoring his good mood once again.

Ditchling was a quintessential Sussex village with

rose-covered thatched cottages, narrow streets overhung with oaks and silver birches and quaint pubs selling real ale. It possessed a colourful heritage dating back to the days of Alfred the Great.

The sting in the tail for all beautiful villages of this ilk was in attracting thousands of tourists. It was not unusual in mid-summer to find the centre of the village at a complete standstill, clogged with cars, delivery vans, and buses, along with tourists so intent on reading the blue plaques and looking at old houses, they were unaware they were standing in the road.

Stavely House, on the eastern fringes of the village, had stood for over three hundred years, but having been modernised and re-modelled numerous times it now took on the air of a new house trying to mimic an old style. With six bedrooms, numerous reception rooms, a tennis court and a swimming pool, it was now too large for one man. Sir Mathew Markham was divorced and his children had all flown the coop, so it was no surprise to see a 'For Sale' sign had been erected in the front garden.

Lawton knocked and was slightly taken aback when Sir Mathew open the door. 'Hello Mathew,' he said, putting a friendly hand on the old man's shoulder, the chairman didn't do 'man-hugs'. 'Is Mrs Hodges off for the day?'

'Hello, William, come on in, come in. No, she got a call this afternoon to say her mother has taken a turn for the worse. It's lung cancer now,' he said leading him into the library. 'They don't expect her to last the month.'

'How awful.'

'Well if the old bat had given up the ciggies when Kate told her to, all those years ago, she wouldn't be in the place she is now.'

Markham eased his large bulk into his favourite leather armchair while Lawton sat on the bright but comfortable flower-patterned settee, and placed the folder he had been carrying beside him. The chairman had already started on the whisky and was reaching for the bottle to top-up his glass. This was a bad sign. Booze clouded his crystal-clear judgement and brought out an argumentative nature that always seemed to be bubbling below the calm, studied exterior.

The chairman offered him one but Lawton declined, and in the absence of the redoubtable housekeeper, headed into the kitchen and made coffee.

When he resumed his seat on the settee, he opened the folder.

'How did the monthly meeting go on Monday?' Markham asked.

'Fine, Mathew, no burning issues to report.'

For the next few minutes Lawton briefed him on recent software developments, sales levels, new ideas and what the senior management team were up to, with particular reference to wives, girlfriends, divorces, and children, as he liked to hear all the personal stuff. He then moved on to the three main items topping their agendas whenever they got together: company accounts, the proposed sale of the business and progress or otherwise on Project Kratos.

'I'm a bit light on the financials this month I'm afraid, but what I've got is the Flash Report, sent out last week by David's number two before the numbers were finalised. It's ninety-five per cent accurate and fine for our purposes.'

'Oh. Where's David? Is he away somewhere?' Markham asked, reaching for his coffee cup. The whisky was on the back burner now as there were more pressing issues to discuss.

'David wasn't at the meeting. We haven't seen him at work since Friday. When he didn't make an appearance this morning, I asked Jules to call round at his house. When no one came to the door, he called his home number. He heard the phone ringing inside the house but no one answered. I'm getting no reply from his mobile either.'

Markham sat back, stroking his neatly trimmed beard. At one time it was black, giving him the air of a television presenter or a West End actor. Twenty years ago it turned silver to match his thinning hair and he now resembled the esteemed professor of Egyptian hieroglyphics at a Cairo research facility, a pose he cultivated.

'How odd. David's never gone AWOL before,

especially at this time of the month. You know how he likes to have a go at the poor sods for spending too much money.'

'I agree but–'

Markham's hand shot up. 'It's more important than that, William. I'm in the middle of delicate talks and if word gets out that our Finance Director has suffered a heart attack or a nervous breakdown, it could all fall apart. You know what it's like with those Koreans, trust is everything.'

Trust? Koreans? What the hell was the old fool babbling on about? What talks with Koreans? Was it in reference to the sale of the company? If so, nine companies had stuck their oar in; two Japanese, three Americans, three British and one Russian, but no Koreans.

'Find him, William. We need David back at his desk pronto.'

A bewildered Lawton talked him through the financials and other major software developments, but by the time they started to talk about Project Kratos, normal service had been resumed. He handed Markham a two-page paper summarising the development team's progress over the last four weeks, and it was obvious he wanted to read it in full, as he sat back in the chair, holding the document out in front of him.

After a few minutes he put it down, took off his glasses and rubbed his eyes. 'This is fantastic,

William. I never believed we'd get this far. Good God, it looks like we could have a working prototype inside a couple of months.'

'Yes I know, it's terrific news.'

Markham Microprocessors, in common with most of the companies in their field, had grown frustrated with the batteries of mobile devices as they were struggling to cope with the huge loads being placed upon them by high-definition pictures, games, videos, software applications and music.

With the proposed rollout of a 4G network across Europe promising a whole host of new, unheralded but power-hungry services, it was now widely recognised that battery technology had not kept up with other developments in the electronics industry and a crisis was looming.

A Markham software engineer called Gary Larner, a maverick who walked the thin line between genius and madness, was obsessed with the idea of extracting electrical power from radio waves, and given the parlous nature of battery technology, Lawton had given him his head and a large budget to find out if he could do it.

He couldn't but using his basic ideas and concepts, the current development team took it much further and now they believed they were on the cusp of producing a working prototype. If successful, mobile devices would never need to be charged from a power socket; a Markham microchip buried inside would charge it with energy extracted from radio waves in the air. This would not only annihilate one of the major aggravations of modern life, but also turn the company into one of the biggest hitters in the business.

'How are Marta and Sanjay doing? Are you looking after them?'

'They want for nothing. They're working all hours on the project as you can imagine, staying late and coming in most weekends, but everything's fine.'

'Make sure it is, we don't want them going off the rails like our Mr Larner, do we?'

He nodded. 'Of course not.'

Their discussion came to a natural conclusion ten minutes later and Lawton rose to fix them both a whisky. He handed a glass to Markham, and, trying to sound as calm as he could, said, 'Who are the Koreans you've been talking to?'

Markham peered at him over the top of his gold-rimmed glasses. 'Didn't I tell you, William?'

Lawton shook his head. 'No, you didn't.'

'I must be getting forgetful in my old age. It's the Han Industrial Group, a large conglomerate based in Seoul. They'd heard of us through the Korean shipping group we use to ship the Medusa chip set, Crown Transportation.'

Lawton nodded.

'Yong Nahm's cousin is the MD of the Han group and they got talking. He mentioned he had been looking to buy a high-tech company for several months.'

'How have these talks progressed?'

'They've been more like negotiations than talks, to tell you the truth.'

Markham looked embarrassed, as well he might. Lawton knew he had kept it from him deliberately, knowing he wouldn't like it. 'They would be a good fit for us as they have a growing electronics division and huge amounts of money to invest. They like us because we're cutting-edge and they think we could turn their mobile phone business into the world's largest.'

Markham babbled on for a few more minutes, about the work Han did assembling circuits and building laptops, but Lawton couldn't concentrate. He knew a lot about the Han Group, as he had travelled to South Korea many times. They were an aggressive buyer of companies, keen to build additional revenue streams away from the core industries of oil and forestry upon which the huge industrial conglomerate had been founded, and which provided their large cash pile.

In their approach to acquisitions they adopted what had become known in business circles as the 'Cisco Model', but with a little twist of their own. Whilst they followed the American networking company by insisting an acquired company adopt their procedures and systems wholesale, no matter how good or expensive they were, they also insisted on putting a Korean management team in place, including a new managing director.

Lawton shuddered in fear. What the hell was he going to do at the age of 54 with no job and no income? His wife said she always wanted to retire to Spain where they owned a villa, but to do what? Improve his tennis serve and his golf swing, or catch a better suntan?

How long would it be before a 'golden parachute' payment sank, deflated, into the Med and his savings ran out? How long could he stand listening to his wife's constant nagging about his swelling paunch, complaining about his underperformance in the bedroom or moaning about him getting under her feet whenever she tried to clean up; a belligerence heightened by flinging too much cheap Rioja down her neck? How long would it be before he would find it all too much and there he would be, bashing her over the head with his new five hundred quid Titleist driver and chucking her lifeless body over a cliff?

He knew all of the main companies in the microprocessor design business and none were looking for people of his calibre. In any case, many of them had branded him Sir Mathew's poodle, with no real ideas of his own. His determination to make Project Kratos a success was designed to prove all the doubters wrong, and if successful would turn him into one of the most influential and important men in the business.

However, a working prototype was still several months away, too late in the day to stop this curved ball the old man was bowling. He made it sound as if Han were now assembling their troops, ready for the onslaught. Perhaps it was worse than that. Maybe they were already inside the compound.

He needed time to think, to plan, and deploy his defences, but of one thing he was sure: stopping the Korean takeover had now become his number-one priority.

# SEVEN

DI Henderson walked into the Shakespeare's Head in Chatham Place to be greeted by Maggie behind the bar like a long-lost relative. His flat in Vernon Terrace, in the Seven Dials district of Brighton, was only a few streets away and while he wouldn't describe the pub as his local, the familiarity of the bar staff suggested otherwise.

He took a seat at the back the bar and lifted the newspaper lying there, but didn't read a word as his mind was still on the call he'd received from CI Harris just as he was leaving the office. It wasn't an enquiry about his team's progress on Operation Poseidon, there hadn't been any, but instead Harris wanted his take on a surveillance job in Worthing that had gone belly-up.

It wasn't one of Henderson's jobs, but he had bags of experience in this area, firstly for the Football Intelligence Unit of Strathclyde Police, attending football matches and watching the crowd while they were concentrating on the game; and secondly, with the Strathclyde Drugs Unit, mounting long-term surveillance on gangs, trying to catch them with their hands on the merchandise.

Harris was collaborating and canvassing the opinion of a 'seasoned officer', as the good book told him to do; but in reality, the man had little practical experience to draw on and he was more likely filling in gaps in his knowledge. He had been 'fast-tracked' into the Chief Inspector's job following a first class Psychology degree from Durham University, a post-grad diploma in Criminology from Cambridge University, and a bag full of brownie points after participation in a successful joint operation with the Metropolitan Police and Customs, involved in smashing a gang trafficking modern-day slaves from Africa.

It emerged later that perhaps the Chief Inspector had not been the active and resourceful participant in the investigation as he had led everyone to believe, but by then it was too late and the job was his. Rapid promotion was at the heart of his problem. He had missed out on all the street craft, locker-room banter and gut-wrenching experiences an apprenticeship in uniform would have given him. While he excelled at administration, budgets, and office politics he was crap at all the other stuff that most coppers believed was important.

Henderson was nearing the end of his first pint when Rachel arrived. She looked beautiful as she sailed through the door, looking as if she owned the place. A journalist with Brighton's daily newspaper, *The Argus*, she wrote a weekly column on the environment and rural affairs, and when her editor let her off the horticultural leash, made occasional forays into profiles of prominent local people.

She worked more regular hours than he did and would have been home by six, which would have given her an hour and a half to get ready. He had been waylaid by the call from his boss and didn't get home until seven, only enough time for a quick wash and a change of clothes. The grooming and styling results spoke for themselves.

On leaving university with a degree in English, Rachel had wanted to become a motoring journalist, but life in Brighton was way too much fun. She had been working for the local paper for six years and he couldn't see her moving. They'd met nine months ago at one of DS Hobbs's regular dinner parties, and the fact that she was still here and putting up with his odd working hours, black moods and sartorial shortcomings, was testament to her legendary tenacity. Or perhaps a sign that she really liked him.

She was wearing a light blue dress, brightening up a dreary, cold evening and revealing enough of her tanned legs to remind him of their late summer holiday in Cyprus together. Her black hair had recently been cut short, giving emphasis to the roundness of her face and highlighting deep green eyes that often shone with mischief and affection.

'How's the carjacking case going?' Rachel said after he placed a drink in front of her: New Zealand

Sauvignon Blanc, chilled, large glass.

'Has Rob been talking to you?'

'Rob Tremain? No, I hardly ever see him, he's never in the office.'

'Fibber. He's frustrated at getting nothing out of me, he's started using you.'

'I hope you're joking.'

Her face looked stern: a boss reprimanding a junior member of staff for a serious indiscretion.

'Of course I am, but I wouldn't put it past him.'

'Well there's no need to question my ethical integrity. Rob might not value his, but I value mine.'

He had been joking but nevertheless he was careful what he said in front of her. She might believe in Chinese Walls and professional ethics, but there were plenty of people she worked beside who didn't, and who were expert at teasing facts from reluctant witnesses.

'The gang left the house they robbed cleaner than a doctor's surgery. Knowing our luck, we'll find a bit of DNA or a fingerprint and I bet it won't be in the database.'

'It was a Porsche they took this time?'

'Aye they did,' he said, lifting his pint, 'a GT2 RS, whatever the hell that means.'

She frowned at the bare-cheek of the thieves or perhaps in sorrow for the loss of the car. 'It stands for Gran Turismo Rally Sport. It's a cracker and the one I would go for out of the lot of them. It's aggressive and fast, but still a car you can use every day to drop the kids off at school or do the Sainsbury's shop.'

He gave her a reproachful look as he resettled his beer glass back on the mat. 'I think your little Seat is fast enough.'

'It is, but it doesn't stop me wanting.'

A few months back, she'd been badly injured when her Mazda MX5 hit a people carrier coming out of a driveway. He knew the accident wouldn't dent her interest in cars, but there were times he wished she would set her sights a little bit lower.

'Where do you think they sell them?' Rachel went on. 'I've never seen any of them in the magazines I read.'

'Our researchers are doing the same thing. Maybe you should all get together one night and swap stories.'

She gave him a playful punch on the arm. 'Don't be silly, I do it for fun.'

'Is that what you call it? If there's a degree course going, you could teach on it.'

'C'mon, tell me, where do you think they end up?'

'My best guess is the Middle East or China. Give them a set of new plates and a new colour job and their new owner wouldn't give a monkey's where it came from, especially with forty or fifty grand knocked off the price.'

'You do know why they wanted the keys so badly?'

There it was, the petrol head journalist trying to

get behind the wheel once again. 'Tell me,' he said.

'It's nigh on impossible to steal a modern car without them, due to the clever way the key communicates with the ignition system. You see, it will only allow a car to start if the correct key is presented. Thanks to this little innovation and better alarms, gone are the days of returning to a car park only to find your car's been nicked or the side window's been smashed and all your CDs have been stolen.'

He nodded. 'Tony Haslam told me as much.'

'Yes, but here's something he might not have mentioned. Thieves are now able to steal just about any car fitted with the keyless ignition system.'

'The cars you can start with the key still in your pocket or your handbag?'

'Yep, those, although it's not what you would call a key, more like a signal emitting fob.'

'How?'

'When the owner gets out of the car, the thieves jam the door-locking signal, making them think it's locked when it isn't. They open the door and plug a laptop into its diagnostic port and make a new fob. They can then use the fob to disable the alarm, start the car, and drive it away, as the fob doesn't need to be plugged into the ignition as a normal key would.'

'Ingenious.'

'I think so too. Are you any closer to catching your thieves?'

'I would love to say we discovered a cracking lead today and we're hot on the trail of the criminals, but no. We seem to be going nowhere with the case and it's getting harder geeing-up the troops in the morning, and sometimes that includes me.'

'Poor thing,' she said rubbing his arm, 'because I've had a good day. With summer coming, I've got loads of country shows and events to plan, and my boss in all his wisdom has given me an interesting piece to do about energy. You know the sort of thing, where our region gets its power, how much we're contributing towards government targets on renewables and all the other stuff.'

'It'll make a change from eating goat's milk fudge or drinking dandelion and nettle wine. Give me the genuine article any day. When do you start doing this?'

'Next Monday I'm off to Shoreham Power Station, just me and a photographer, so expect to see me in a boiler suit and hard hat, hanging on for dear life and trying to smile from one of the chimneys 70 feet up. It's probably too late to tell him I don't like heights.'

'I'll look forward to it and make sure I keep a copy of the paper and show it to you every time you slag me off about what clothes I'm wearing.'

She paused for a moment, looking coy. 'I hoped I'd catch you in a more positive mood this evening Mr H, as there's no easy way of doing this.'

'What's this, the brush-off? My mother warned me

about women like you.’

‘You don’t get rid of me so easily.’ She reached into her handbag pulled out a copy of *The Argus*. ‘It’s the latest edition,’ she said as she handed it to him. ‘Hot off the press as we used to say.’

He turned to the sports section to see what Brighton and Hove Albion were getting up to. He didn’t often get a chance to read a newspaper but before he could look at anything, a manicured hand slid across the page to stop him.

‘No, Angus, we read newspapers from the front. Look what it says at the top.’

Beneath the newspaper’s title ran a bold taster banner: ‘Car-Jack Victim Speaks Out – Criticises Police - See Page 5.’ Beside it was a small picture which he immediately recognised as Mrs Frankcombe.

He looked at her, puzzled. ‘What’s this, ‘criticises police’? Is Rob Tremain playing silly buggers again?’

‘Just look.’

He turned to page five as instructed, and there on a two-page spread were pictures of Downs View, including the shattered front door, their stolen car and a tired-looking Mrs Frankcombe standing in front of the garage. She was in much the same position as Sergeant Walters a couple of days ago, the garage still empty but for the little Micra Mr Frankcombe used for driving to the station.

He skimmed over the bulk of the text, most of which had been in the paper after each of the other raids, but he looked closer when his name appeared.

*'The senior investigating officer, Detective Inspector Angus Henderson, arrived late to the scene as by then I had seen plenty of other policemen, and the fingerprint people were packing up. He looked dishevelled, as if he had just got out of bed, and I'm sure his breath smelled of alcohol. He left me with the impression he didn't have a clue who has stolen our lovely car or put my husband Alan in hospital and as a result, I don't have the confidence to say this won't happen to some other innocent family.'*

# EIGHT

They travelled in Cahill's souped-up Peugeot to the Right Place, a large pub in Clapham. Way back, it used to be a traditional street-corner boozer with loads of dark wood, a floozy barmaid and a place where you could still find London Porter, but it had been transformed by new owners into a happening place with great music, a superb choice of bottled lagers and shots, drugs and plenty of gorgeous girls. It had now become one of the main hangouts for young black kids in this part of South London, as the DJs were from Jamaica and played all the stuff they liked with none of the techno-electro crap they were playing in the white-boy clubs.

They pushed their way to the front of the crowded bar and after getting drinks, stood and watched the dancers. Rab McGovern sipped his beer and let the music, bright lights, heat, the smell of alcohol and sweat, wash over him. He could do this all night. There was something beautiful and majestical in following the gyrating hips and swaying bums of voluptuous Caribbean women dancing to a rhythm, making them appear as if they were making love to an invisible deity.

McGovern had spent a large part of his 27 years inside some institution or other, first at reform school, then at a Young Offenders Institution, and finally an adult prison. Like a replicant in *Blade Runner*, he devoured his time on the outside like a new arrival. If it made him seem like a man who thought his time was limited, as he would soon be returning to prison, not a bad assumption given what he did for a living, it was misleading. He wasn't going back, no matter how many people he killed or maimed in the process.

There was no need for talking, nigh on impossible as the music was loud, attacking the body as well as the ears, and anyway, he wasn't big on chitchat. The only time he talked much was in the meetings when they were planning the theft of another car. They knew the drill, but he needed to keep them in line and make sure Rooney was taking it easy on the rum, Ehuru on the weed, and that Cahill wasn't messing around with other women.

By one in the morning, he'd drunk only four beers and danced for a bit before finding the girl he was looking for. He had spoken to her a few times before, but tonight he turned on his best patter and now they were outside the pub and walking back to his place, stopping occasionally for him to put his tongue down her throat and slip his hand inside her jacket to feel those beautiful titties.

They continued walking until they came to Severus Road and a few minutes later they turned into the building where he lived. For a tough street kid with tats on his arms and scars on his torso, he refused to live in a dump, and even though Jasmine had been boozing all night and could barely walk straight, her exaggerated outburst when she first saw how clean and tidy it all looked sounded genuine enough. It took some time to persuade her that he didn't share the place with his mum.

He'd seen enough of her gyrating body in a silver dress to know he wanted to see it for real, and without much messing about, he was an impatient man, he took off her clothes and she did the same to him. She stood there naked and for a moment he was caught in two minds, to stand there and gaze at her beautiful body with full thirty-eight inch D-cup breasts, trim and flat belly, broad hips and thick, muscled thighs from playing hockey or dancing or some other shit, or to grab her and shag her senseless.

He enjoyed the view for a few seconds more before pulling her towards him and carrying her over to the bed. Sometimes when he felt all wired up, he wanted rough sex with a good bit of slapping, biting and gouging, while other times he liked it smooth, like the lyrics of the R Kelly song they were listening to before they left the pub. Not tonight though. There was something he needed her to do and it was important for her to remember him in a good way, and not as the mad bastard who left deep bite marks on her neck and black bruises on her arse.

He entered her fast and furious, causing her eyes to open wide in surprise, giving him a mental slap on the face and telling him to take it slow and not get too carried away; he might be tempted to do something he would regret. Self-control wasn't a word that appeared in his lexicon, but when he wanted something as he wanted it now, even he was capable of reining in his wilder desires for a short spell.

Ten minutes later, he got up to fix them both a drink. He came back with a beer for him and a vodka and lemon for Jasmine. The beer was for show, he only sipped it, but he wanted her to take the full hit as he had added a little something they weren't offering in the cocktail bars. They smoked a little dope and supped their drinks and it wasn't long before he was starting to feel horny again; but held back until he was sure she had drained the lot.

He took her empty glass, placed it on the dresser and pulled her in close. She was biting his ear and scraping long nails against his balls, saying the dirtiest things, and it was with reluctance he flipped her over and spread her legs, as he was enjoying her touch so much. He spent a moment admiring her arse, a true Jamaican rear, giving women like her a different shape from white girls and making it erotic just watching them walk.

He was about to slip into her warm, tight space once again, when she went limp. Anger swept up like a tide, as he hadn't known the drug would work so fast.

For a moment he was tempted to carry on regardless, but with a groan he rolled away, feeling disgusted with himself for even considering it.

He lay still for several minutes, gathering his thoughts and trying to calm down, before rolling off the bed and putting his clothes back on. In the kitchen, he drank a glass of water to clear his head and removed his chib from a cupboard in the hall. A few moments later he closed the door and headed outside. There was no need to be quiet on account of Jasmine, as she was out for the count and would be like that for most of the night. In the morning she would wake up late with a woozy head, feeling as if she'd had too much to drink, with no recollection of what happened when she was out.

While Jasmine wasn't a worry, his neighbours were as some of them were night owls. Damien on the floor above would be itching to have his revenge for being smacked around. Miriam on the ground floor was a former Royal Air Force officer who didn't need much sleep and spent most of her time in a chair by the window watching the world go by, as if still on sentry duty, scanning the skies for Russian spy planes.

It wasn't cold, but McGovern walked with head down and collar up, not wishing to attract the attention of the drug-addled muggers and layabouts who hung around Clapham Station. He wasn't frightened of being attacked, as he could handle himself, but he was in no mood for hassle. The beating he would give any punk stupid enough to try their luck might attract some attention, and would be recorded on a multitude of CCTV cameras dotted all around the building.

He passed under a railway bridge and walked into the Lancaster Estate. This was an act a sane man would be hesitant to undertake during daylight hours and only a nutter would contemplate at night, but Rab McGovern was not a sane man when looking for the bastard who had conned him.

Built in the 1970's, Lancaster Estate was designed to house occupants of houses demolished during slum clearance in that part of South London. It had now become a haven for pimps, drug dealers, and stick-up gangs, and despite a number of attempts to improve the place, nothing would change until the tight little alleyways and narrow staircases were demolished and they stopped sending the dregs of society there.

He approached Henshaw Gardens, a square and squat block of flats designed by a seventies architect with a Lego fixation, and known to house more than its fair share of troublemakers and drug addicts. If this estate was one of the worst in London for knife gangs, drug dealers, DSS fraud and feral kids who sniffed glue and lighter fluid, Henshaw Gardens had the reputation of being the granddaddy of them all.

McGovern had been there on at least two previous occasions when the flats were visited by a large contingent of police, chasing the notorious McGinley brothers. They couldn't have been better equipped or prepared if operating in Northern Ireland or Beirut, as they'd brought riot vans, snipers, shields and every piece of body armour the Met could offer.

He failed to break his stride as he hit the stairs. For most of the day, the staircases around there were full of kids smoking weed, sniffing glue, or there would be some smack head sleeping off a fix. At this time of the morning the only things he could see in the weak light were empty beer and cider bottles, used condoms, fag ends, and a mangy cat searching for scraps. If the light was dim, the smell wasn't, and he gagged as the rancid aroma of piss, vomit and stale beer hit the back of his throat with the force of tear gas.

On the second floor, he stopped outside number 215 to catch his breath and make sure his chib was to hand. The chib was an old-fashioned police truncheon, not the modern, side-handled telescopic type, which was difficult to conceal and too big for close combat, but the twelve inch hardwood version, nicked from a copper in the early 90s during a riot. It had a ribbed handle and a leather strap to wrap around the wrist, and back in the day this would have been used to hold the baton in place while beating the living crap out of a prisoner.

He stood back, lifted a steel toe-capped boot and smashed it into the edge of the peeling, softwood door, close to the lock. There was no need for sledgehammers here. The door emitted a sharp, loud crack. He lifted his boot again and this time the crappy frame split and the door swung open with a loud creak, echoing around the empty balcony and across to the dark building opposite. The noise held no fear, this wasn't the sort of place where neighbours stared out of windows or were willing to help someone in trouble.

He had been in the flat a few times before and knew where to go. The bedroom was off to the right. He also knew Stephen Halliday would be sleeping alone as the useless prat couldn't attract a bird unless he put a seed box outside his window.

He kicked the bedroom door open and found Halliday staggering towards him in a soiled white t-shirt and shorts, dazed and confused, trying to make sense of the un-Godly noise that had just woken him up. McGovern strode forward and head-butted him in the face before kneeing him in the balls.

Halliday doubled over and screeched, 'You bastard, what the fuck are you doing? What do you want?' The sudden pain had obviously woken him up.

McGovern grabbed a handful of t-shirt. The only illumination in the room was a bright street lamp outside, filtered by cheap curtains. He was thankful it wasn't brighter as he didn't want to look at Halliday too closely; his face contorted in pain and with snot and blood leaking from his nose.

'Remember me?' McGovern growled. 'I'm the sucker you sold the fucking crap gear to.'

'What, *what*? Oh, it's you Rab. Wh...what are you talking about?' His voice gurgled as if blood was dripping down the back of his throat. Good. Perhaps he would choke to death and save him the trouble. 'I never doctored it or nothin'. I get it as a sealed bag from my contact. It was good gear, I swear.'

'Good gear my arse. It was full of fucking baking powder or brick dust or some other shite. I should charge you for the damage it might have caused to ma' insides.'

'There was nothing wrong with that stuff Rab, I use it myself. Nobody else has complained.'

'You'd stick any old shite up your snozzle, but no' me pal, and stop giving me your piss-bag excuses ya junkie prick, I don't wanna hear them. I want some decent stuff or I'll have ma fucking cash back wi' interest.'

'Give us a break man. This ain't bloody Tesco. I don't have any more. You pay your money and you take your chances. Now, leave me alone will ya? You've had your fun.'

A red mist descended over McGovern's eyes as Halliday's grating voice and lame excuses bounced around his head like a pinball. He couldn't believe the arrogance of the man who'd happily taken his money but now refused to sort out his problem. He was junkie scum and it was time for someone to teach him a lesson.

McGovern lifted a boot and sent him sprawling

back onto the bed. In two strides he was beside him. He pulled out the chib, wrapped the leather strap around his wrist and swung it in an arc. The junkie tried to protect his head with his hands, but McGovern swung it with such force nothing he did would make any difference. When he stopped, a few seconds later, Halliday was still; his lank, tangled hair matted in blood and grey brain matter.

McGovern left the bedroom and searched the flat. It didn't take long to find Halliday's stash of dope, squirrelled away in a tea caddy in the kitchen, and in a jar beside it, a thick roll of cash. He pocketed both, walked out of the flat and headed home.

When he pushed open the bedroom door he was pleased to see Jasmine was still sleeping. In the bathroom, he stripped off and spent a few minutes searching for bloodstains. They were hard to see on a black leather jacket but he wasn't too concerned; he'd played this gig a few times before and knew how to get the angle right without getting too splattered.

He slipped back into bed and lifted the duvet to have a look at Jasmine's naked form, warm and inviting, and stroked her hip before turning over and settling down to sleep. If she didn't feel too groggy in the morning, who knows, maybe he would give her something to remember him by.

# NINE

The cop watched in rapt attention as William Lawton's secretary poured coffee. PC 'Tommo' Rogerson was modern in many ways: he liked some of the music his teenage daughters listened to; he read a quality newspaper, not one of the red tops; his hair was styled at a ladies' hairdresser, rather than succumbing to the rough clippers of a barber; but he was old-school when it came to the boss's secretary.

Give him a tight skirt, nice legs and a low-cut blouse any day of the week. A spiky-haired bloke with a penchant for loud shirts and a wiggling arse? No thanks. He was a fan of period dramas and knew the man of the house was often in a close relationship with his male valet, sharing confidences as his shirt was being done up or having his wine sampled before he took a drink, but a man-secretary? No way Jose.

With coffee poured and Jules tucked behind the computer outside Mr Lawton's office, the tension eased in Rogerson's shoulders and he loosened the firm grip of his police hat lying on his lap.

'Thank you for coming today, officers,' William Lawton said from his seat behind a large desk. 'As I said on the phone, when Mr Young didn't turn up for work on Monday morning it didn't bother me too much at the time. I thought he might be suffering from a cold or had been called away to a meeting that none of us were aware of, but when he didn't show up for work by Wednesday I started to get worried. I sent someone around to his house. Jules couldn't detect any signs of life, and when he asked a neighbour they said they hadn't heard him coming and going as he usually did. I left it another day, and when he still didn't appear, that's when I called you.'

'You were right to do so sir,' Rogerson said. 'Has Mr Young's diary been checked?'

'Yes it has, but David wasn't the type to jet off to one of our suppliers in Japan or Malaysia without telling someone first. In any case, Jules or one of the other P.A.'s would need to book the trip for him. He's hopeless at doing those sorts of things himself.'

Rogerson watched Lawton as he spoke, not because he was a student of psychology or an expert in body language but because he was a copper and it was an automatic action. Some wag in the locker room said he did it to keep himself awake while listening to all the boring crap about their problems or the short-comings of their partner. In Rogerson's case he did it to try and decide if the words coming out of their mouths matched the expressions on their faces and if so, could he rely on what they were telling him?

Lawton looked the part, and was well-known to those who read the business pages. He was Managing

Director of one of the UK's fastest growing companies, and at one time Lawton's boss, Sir Mathew Markham, was never off the telly: receiving some award and talking up British business, or accompanying one of the royal princes on a trade mission to China or Hong Kong.

Lawton's hair was styled, but to any man who took an interest in such things it was dyed and receding a bit at the temples. He wore expensive glasses with natty red frames and a blue striped suit that fitted him perfectly, the product, no doubt, of one of the top tailors in Savile Row; not an off-the-peg job from a high street chain like the two Rogerson owned. He'd put his age at somewhere between late forties and early fifties, and talked with a well articulated, Home Counties accent.

'Can you tell me Mr Young's movements on the day you last saw him, Friday of last week wasn't it?'

'Yes, it was,' Lawton said, locking fingers together as if he was about to read the Evening News.

'As usual, he arrived in the office at seven-thirty. He worked until twelve-thirty, then had a bit of lunch at his desk before setting off for our research and warehousing facility in Burgess Hill.' He took off his glasses and rubbed his eyes before replacing them.

'I've seen the place you've got there,' Rogerson said, 'very futuristic. What goes on there?'

'The building you are in now is Markham's Head Office, but it is primarily a design studio. The people upstairs design new products or modify existing ones using all the latest software tools. When we're finished, they send the designs to the research lab in Burgess Hill where they create a prototype, incorporate it into a computer circuit, and test it until it breaks.'

'I see.'

'If the process is successful, the designs are sent to a manufacturing plant in China where the products are mass produced. When the order is complete, it is shipped to our warehouse in Burgess Hill and tested for quality, before being distributed to our customers. I'm simplifying a process that can take many months, of course, but no matter how long or complicated it gets, the basic elements remain the same.'

It was clear to Rogerson that Lawton had delivered the spiel many times, and if he'd possessed a greater understanding of what had just been said, he would have asked a further question or two, but as he couldn't tell a ring mains circuit from a central heating pipe, he didn't.

'Why does Mr Young go there?' Rogerson asked instead.

'He spends two or three days a month talking to the finance people and reviews budgets, production schedules, and anything else he's involved with. On Friday, he was there to attend a meeting about a supplier we've been having a few problems with. I'm told he left our offices about six forty-five, and not being a drinking man or anything of that nature, I assume he went straight home.'

'Where is home?' Rogerson asked.

'Shirley Drive in Hove.'

'Is he married?'

'He's divorced. Six years ago, I believe.'

'Are there children or other members of his family living in the Shirley Drive house; a girlfriend, perhaps?'

'No. He lives alone. He has no girlfriend that I know of, and I think I know David pretty well.'

'Do you know if he called anyone here before he left Burgess Hill on Friday night?'

'Yes, he spoke to Sarah, his assistant before she went home at about five-thirty, but no one else. I've checked.'

'I see. So, what do you think has happened to him, sir?'

'The obvious I suppose. He might have taken ill or suffered a heart attack and he's lying on the floor, unable to move. Mind you, it wouldn't surprise me if he's been in an accident on that motor bike he rides.'

'He rides a bike does he?' PC Eric Longman said, having sat silently beside Rogerson until now. He liked bikes and rode into work on a muddy trail bike that looked as if it had just come through an apocalyptic disaster zone. He wanted to get into the Traffic department where he was convinced he would swan around all day astride a big 900cc BMW, weaving in and out of traffic like Arnie in *Terminator*. Despite repeated attempts by Rogerson to burst his bubble, the boy's enthusiasm could not be dimmed.

'Yes, he took up motorcycling a couple of years back, and after starting off on a small thing, a Yamaha I think it was, he bought that big brute of a thing he drives now. It rattles the windows as soon as it starts up. I kept telling him it was dangerous for anyone to drive one of these things, especially a 52-year-old man whose reactions are not as quick as they once were, but he can be just as stubborn as my 16-year-old lad when he wants to be.'

Rogerson nodded. He knew the stats and had seen enough accidents to know it was a growing problem. Middle-aged guys usually got their first scrapes on a Honda 50 or a Vespa scooter, nothing more than a sewing machine on wheels, before moving up-market to a Yamaha or Kawasaki 125, zip-fast little machines which could out-accelerate the majority of saloon cars. For many, their burgeoning riding career came to an abrupt halt when a wife, children and a crippling mortgage came along, and then an ugly people carrier replaced the sleek bike.

Now in their mid-fifties and with money in the bank, they took one look at the latest bike catalogues and realised they could own a smart new machine capable of knocking spots off top-of-the-range sports cars for the same price as a Ford Fiesta.

What many of them did not realise until too late,

was that the engines and equipment on all modern bikes were faster and more responsive than anything they had ridden before, and in an emergency, all the training and perusing of manuals would go out the window when they accelerated too fast, took a corner too sharp, or braked too hard, propelling themselves into a whole new world of trouble.

'Have you a picture of Mr Young?'

'Yes I have.'

Lawton reached into the folder beside him and handed over a sheet of paper. It was copied from David's Young's personnel file and included his age, address and a list of his qualifications and medical history. The colour photograph was clear and, according to the blurb, taken only nine months before.

He was a thin-faced man with a rutted, pale complexion, suggesting he spent too much time indoors or ate a poor diet. Large gold-framed glasses and an untidy mess of thinning brown hair made him look like Rogerson's old English teacher, but the eyes were dark and owl-like, giving the impression he would be a powerful adversary in a meeting and a difficult man to face in tense negotiations.

'That's perfect, and I see we have his home address. Do you happen to have a spare key to his house?'

'No, I don't.'

'Not to worry, we'll sort something out. Ok. I think we've got enough to go on.' Rogerson placed his hands in his lap and looked straight at Mr Lawton. It was his turn to deliver a spiel he had delivered many times before.

'As you can appreciate Mr Lawton, your Financial Director has been missing for a week now, and at this stage I'm inclined to believe that as he was a fit and active man, nothing unfortunate has happened to him.'

'That's good to hear.'

'In missing person cases like this, at least ninety per cent are resolved in the first three or four days, by which time the misps, as we call them, have got over their strop or whatever has been bothering them and decided to make contact, unaware their friends and family have been worried sick and are out looking for them.'

'I see.'

'What we will do now is take a look at his house and make sure he isn't ill or lying behind a door. When we get back to the station, we'll ask our colleagues to be on the look-out and call local hospitals and other agencies. We'll ask them if they've seen Mr Young, and if they haven't, instruct them to inform us if he turns up.'

'Thank you, that sounds excellent. It's a great weight off my mind to know you are also looking for him, I can tell you.' Lawton glanced at his diary. 'This is Friday. David and I were due to play golf at West Hove this Sunday morning for our monthly match.

I've never known him to miss it, as the loser, which is more often than not me, buys lunch. He's such a mean so-and-so, he would never pass up the opportunity for a free lunch. If he still hasn't turned up by then, I think you need to treat him as a bona fide missing person and pull out all the stops to try and find him.'

# TEN

The day started like no other and DI Henderson doubted if it would get any better. He had spent the last hour at Malling House in Lewes, home of the top brass of Sussex Police, receiving a bollocking.

During a tense meeting which included his boss, Chief Inspector Steve Harris, the Assistant Chief Constable, Andy Youngman, the man with overall responsibility for CID, and a bod from Professional Standards, he tried to explain to them why the story in *The Argus* about Mrs Frankcombe was not a good enough reason to sack him.

If CI Harris had had his way, Henderson wouldn't be sitting in his office in Sussex House right now. He'd be making his way down to the Employment Office to sign on, unless, unbeknown to him, the whole system had now gone on-line. Perhaps he needed to check it out in case an incident like this ever happened again.

Harris had always had a bee in his bonnet about Henderson ever since the DI joined Sussex Police. Their relationship, according Henderson's brother, was not dissimilar to the way a raw Sandhurst officer often dealt with a seasoned platoon leader or sergeant; but even though Henderson hadn't been fast-tracked as Harris had, he wasn't the mug his boss took him for.

It was a good job the ACC was on his side and prevented Harris from saying something he would regret, as Andy Youngman understood his officers needed to have a blowout once in a while. What annoyed him though was receiving a lecture about the best way to handle the press and a proposal from Professional Standards to put his name down for a media training course. He had been working on this topic from the day he joined Sussex Police over three years ago.

Before coming south, Henderson had worked for Strathclyde Police in an undercover unit, targeting large and vicious drug gangs. In one particular tense standoff he'd killed one member of a gang and injured another. While some sections of the press hailed him as a hero for saving the lives of fellow officers, others pilloried him for killing 'an innocent man.' They forgot that the victim, Sean Fagin, had been an integral member of a gang that for years had been engaged in the importation of heroin, crack cocaine and crystal meth, bringing misery to thousands. Not forgetting he'd been about to shoot a police officer: namely, him.

Since then, he had been working on improving his relationship with the press, aided and abetted by his girlfriend. Her beat was the environment and rural affairs but she knew all the crime reporters at the newspaper, the main attendees of police press conferences and the people most likely to doorstep him or any member of his team.

It didn't mean he would be taking Rob Tremain, *The Argus's* chief crime reporter, out for a beer sometime soon, or, the way he felt now, stringing him up from the nearest lamppost for writing the Frankcombe story. He had to accept that Tremain had reported more or less what the woman had told him, and he would continue to treat him and his colleagues as allies and not adversaries.

DS Walters walked into his office, holding a thin file. It had to be the violent, car stealing gang file, as the other cases on his plate, an armed robbery in Hove and a domestic murder in Patcham, were much thicker.

'Morning sir. How are you today?'

'Not smelling of booze, you'll be pleased to hear.'

'Bloody hell,' she said, her face crinkling in shock. 'I'm sorry, have I put my foot in it?'

'Nah, don't worry about it, Carol. I'll get over it. I just hope Harris does as well.'

'Do I gather from your glum expression you've been over at Malling House this morning?'

'Aye, I have,' he said, taking a seat at the small conference table.

She waited for more, but as he wasn't offering, she gave up and opened the file.

'As I said at the last team meeting,' Henderson

said, ‘I’m changing our focus to concentrate more on the sales side.’

‘I thought Tony Haslam said he thought the thieves and the ringers were most likely two separate gangs, so nicking one might not give us the other.’

‘I’m aware of his views, but I think if we can nick someone from the buying and selling gang, in time we’ll find the car thieves. Or to put it another way, if we cut out their customer, they’ll have nowhere to go and be forced to stop their activities.’

‘I don’t think it’ll work.’

‘Putting your reservations to one side, what I want you to do now is look at all the ways the gang might be exporting stolen cars. I can think of a few, like shipping and personal export, but I’m sure there’s more. Track down whoever deals with the paperwork at Customs and at the main ports and see if we can get a look at their manifests or whatever they call them, and see if you can find any of our missing cars.’

‘I don’t imagine the car thieves are waiting around until they have ten or twenty cars,’ she said, ‘that would give them any number of problems. If they’re moving a couple of cars at a time, it’ll make it easier for them but harder for us to track them down.’

‘Did Tony tell you that too?’

Her face reddened, but he didn’t pursue it.

‘You might be right,’ he continued, ‘if we were dealing with a Ford Fiesta or Vauxhall Astra, but a Porsche or a Ferrari is a much rarer beast. I don’t imagine you'll find loads of them in containers heading out to Dubai or Beijing every day.'

'Yes, but–'

'Carol, stop bitching. We're all agreed, what we've been doing so far has yielded nothing and it's dispiriting for the troops and pissing off the top brass. If you can find the merest chink of light on the selling side, everyone will be as happy as sand boys.'

'I agree with you there. The lack of progress is getting everybody down.'

'So, we're in harmony, but I suspect not yet singing from the same hymn sheet. Now go off and get this organised; use Phil Bentley. Also, do me a favour and make sure Sally Graham follows up on the van sighting. I think Gerry Hobbs may have diverted her into interviewing witnesses on the Western Road assault, but I don't want the one reasonable sighting we've got slipping from view.'

'Right-oh, sir,' she said standing up. 'I'll get this sorted, but I better get out of your way before you give me something else to do.'

Henderson walked back to his desk and woke up his computer. He groaned when he saw all the emails received that morning, as he hadn't looked since returning from Lewes. They included one from the Professional Standards guy who had attended the meeting with a summary of his conclusions. One bit stood out:

'This should be regarded as a final warning. Any

further transgressions of the Professional Code of Practice will be met with serious disciplinary action.'

'And fuck you too,' he said out loud.

'I hope you're not talking to me.'

Henderson looked up and saw with relief it wasn't the Chief Constable or a visiting dignitary, but DS Gerry Hobbs.

'Sorry Gerry, I didn't mean you, but the sender of a snotty email I've just received.'

'It makes me feel better if I file those away so I don't have to look at them, or if it really pisses me off, I delete the bloody thing.'

'Is this the reason why you never answer any of my emails?'

'Ouch, I fell for that one.'

'Maybe I'll start doing that, or frame the bloody thing. So what brings you into the bad mood corner?'

Hobbs sat on the chair on the other side of the desk. He didn't like sitting at the little conference table as it reminded him too much of interviews and difficult discussions, he'd said. After today, Henderson had to agree.

'I wanted to talk to you about our armed robbery in Hove,' Hobbs said.

'Did you see the story in *The Argus*?'

He shook his head.

'Rob Tremain wrote something like, two women were injured when armed robbers attacked the Westchester Building Society in New Church Road and discharged their weapons. He made it sound like they were attacked and then shot by the robbers.'

'Poetic license, I suspect. Saying the villains shot a couple of ceiling tiles and two women were hit by the debris, doesn't sound half as exciting.'

'That's what I thought.'

Hobbs edged his chair closer to the desk and lowered his voice. 'I've spoken to a couple of narks I know and they told me Billy Francis was involved. I have to admit, it's the sort of thing he would do, you know, rob a building society all tooled up. A couple of hours ago I brought Francis in and I've been questioning him for most of the morning. He kept telling me it wasn't him, and would you believe, a couple of minutes ago we managed to check out his alibi and it stacks up.'

'No easy solutions then?'

'Nope, this is the good bit. He gave me some other names.'

'Like who?' Henderson asked, his curiosity aroused.

'A pair of South London villains: Sol Higson and Les Stephen. They moved to Brighton a few months back and started right where they left off in Croydon, robbing sub-post offices and building societies.'

'Record?'

'As long as your arm.'

Hobbs passed some papers across to him, a printout of their criminal records. Henderson looked through it with a jaundiced eye, career criminals who had never held down a 'normal' job in their lives. On an application form to join whatever club they fancied, they would be forced to put 'armed robber' in the 'occupation' field and their address as one of Her Majesty's penal institutions. They both had been inside Pentonville and Wandsworth so many times, these places would feel more like home than Croydon or Lambeth.

'My first question is,' Henderson said, 'why would Billy Francis give these two up? I know there's no such thing as honour among thieves, but isn't he a bit scared of one of them coming after him and sticking him with a blade? They've got form for violence as well as everything else.'

'I know, and I did ask, but I get the impression it's a risk he's willing to take if there's a chance we can take these boys off his patch.'

'It sounds like he wants us to do his dirty work for him.'

'In a way you're right, but if it gives us the opportunity to nick a couple of nasty villains, what do we care?'

'I hear what you're saying, as long as this isn't a wild goose chase, or even worse, some kind of trap.'

Hobbs tried to say something but Henderson held up a hand to stop him. 'Don't laugh it off Gerry, I mean it. Billy Francis is a nasty son of a bitch who doesn't have a good word to say about anybody. He might be harbouring a grudge against you or me, or the police in general. I for one wouldn't put it past him. All I'm saying is you need to be careful.'

'Ok boss, point made.'

'Good, I'm pleased to hear it. So what's the plan?'

# ELEVEN

The patrol car came to a halt at the junction of Tivoli Crescent and Dyke Road. There was a time, not so long ago, when motorists would give way to one of their Day-Glo painted patrol cars, but now, unless the blue light was flashing and they were burning rubber, they had no chance. Rogerson could be driving his wife's Saxo for all the notice anyone took.

'What do you think, Tommo?' PC Longman said as he prodded and picked at a red spot on the back of his wrist.

'What do I think about what?'

'D'ya think this missing guy, David Young's done a bunk with all the money from the safe, or has somebody kidnapped him?'

'It wouldn't be the first time a senior executive in a company like Markham has scarpered without so much as a by-your-leave, but I wouldn't shout too much about the second one in the canteen if I were you lad, unless you want to look a right prat. This is Hove, not Houston.'

'Ah, right boss, sorry.'

'I'm no expert in this area,' Rogerson said, 'but if our Mr Young has been dipping his mitts into the

Markham till, he'll have scarpered off like a virgin on a stag night at the first whiff of an audit.'

'I've been giving this a bit of thought myself, like,' Longman said. He paused as if trying to compose what he was about to say. 'See, maybe when he left Burgess Hill on his bike, he went back to Hove on one of the back roads and came a cropper on a pothole, or he went into the bushes as he tried to avoid smacking into a deer or something. I mean, if there's an accident on the main drag, it holds up traffic for hours and everybody gets to hear about it, but it's different on those quiet B-roads. I once heard a story about an injured biker who'd been lying in a field for days before a farmer nearly ran 'im over in his tractor.'

'Walk first, run later, as my old dad used to say. Let's do the good old-fashioned donkey work first, check his house, talk to his friends, and phone the hospitals, before we decide to go for a drive in the country.'

A few minutes later, they stopped outside an attractive Spanish-looking villa called 'Casa Solariega'. They were high on a hill overlooking Brighton. On a good day they could most likely see the Channel, the Palace Pier and Shoreham Power Station, but not today. Everything was shrouded in a damp sea mist.

To compensate for the sloping ground, or more likely, as a result of the laziness of busy owners who couldn't be bothered cutting the lawn or weeding the borders, many houses along the road, including the one they were standing outside, had jettisoned grass and covered the space with slabs or stone chips. Some had been a bit more creative and built a wider area for off-road parking, installed a Japanese rock garden, or tried to replicate a Mediterranean patio, but the absence of vegetation gave this part of the road a harsh, bleak look. It reminded Rogerson of a new housing development before the landscapers were brought in.

He peered in the windows and rattled the front door but as expected, it was locked. A high fence and a bolted gate blocked access to the rear of the house and for a fleeting, stupid moment, he was tempted to ask the ever-eager PC Longman to climb it.

Knowing the gangly, uncoordinated youth as he did, it was more than likely he would get stuck and they would be forced to call the Fire Brigade. The thought of the ribbing they would both receive back at the station changed his mind, as it would be unremitting for months. Words like 'monkey man,' 'cat boy' or 'fence' would become the boy's nickname for all time, long after its origins were forgotten.

Longman peered through the letterbox, moving his skinny arse from side to side, trying to get a better look inside, but suggesting his tie was caught or he'd spotted someone walking around naked. If he kept that up, they would soon receive a call on the radio about a Peeping Tom in Shirley Drive, as despite the unmistakable uniform and the luminescent patrol car, the stay at home 'neighbourhood watch' types were trigger-happy and dialled 999 at the first sign of anything unusual.

'Eric, do something useful. Go next door and find out if they're holding a spare key.'

'Right-oh,' he said and turned to go.

'And son?'

'Yeah boss?'

'There's an alarm. Make sure you get the code for it as well.'

A few minutes later, Longman came striding towards him displaying a small bunch of keys and wearing a smile on his face as broad as a Cheshire cat. Combined with his nonchalant gait, it made him look more like a pubescent schoolboy carrying his first jar of tadpoles or a bag of stolen apples, than a professional copper.

'No wonder Young lives around here,' he said, handing over the keys, 'you should see the bird living next door; she's an absolute belter. If I lived here, I'd be doing her garden for nothin' and giving her a lift into town whenever she wanted.'

'What, on the back of your muddy trail bike? You must be joking.'

'Yeah...well, some birds like 'em.'

Rogerson turned the key and pushed the door open. He strode past a pile of letters scattered over the carpet and went off in search of the alarm control panel. The code worked first time, and as he walked back to the front door to close it he felt a tiny bit smug for not alerting the whole neighbourhood to their presence. Providing, of course, Peeping Tom Longman hadn't already done so.

He sent the young man upstairs while he looked downstairs to save any more wear on his dodgy knees. Mr Young's mail was as unexciting as his own, with three official-looking letters from banks and credit card companies, two invoices from companies he hadn't heard of, and a couple of bits of junk mail, one for a charity and another for a pizza delivery service. The one thing he did notice were the postmarks, as they suggested the letters had been lying there since Friday. He placed them on the hall table and opened the door into the lounge.

It looked a bright, airy room with fantastic views through the large front window over the rooftops of Hove, weather permitting of course. The room contained little furniture, only a settee, matching chair, coffee table, hi-fi and television. It was tidy, with only a few magazines scattered over the coffee table to detract from the utilitarian nature of the place.

If Rogerson lived alone without his wife Julie's stern, guiding hand, he would live like a slob with pizza boxes, Chinese takeaway cartons and empty beer cans scattered all over the place; but David Young was a well-paid business executive and not a piss-poor copper. He probably spent most of his time at the office rather than slumming around at home at the end of a shift.

The kitchen was clean and tidy with no unwashed dishes, packets of cereal, or half-closed coffee jars lying around the worktops. With a few more bits of kit and some additional crockery, the house could be mistaken for a furnished rental or a house sale with vacant possession.

With some trepidation, he opened the dishwasher. In some houses this would have been an act of supreme folly, akin to sticking your head in the bin or down the toilet, but he needn't have worried as it contained only a plate, cup, and a few bits of cutlery and exuded a pleasant, lemony smell.

In the study, he stopped and leaned against the desk, trying to build a mental picture of the missing man. The kitchen was filled with a range of modern appliances and appeared to be a bright and inviting place to eat, while the lounge with its LCD television and sophisticated sound system, looked a comfortable place to relax. Neither of these rooms looked lived-in and he would bet by the appearance of the well-worn chair, scratched desk, and enough paper to start a bonfire, that Mr Young spent the majority of his time in the study.

In the Rogerson household, two teenage daughters hogged the TV as if they owned it, while his wife often held book clubs and knitting circles in the kitchen. The study, a glorified cupboard under the stairs, was the only place in the house where he could read a newspaper in peace. Once, when the house was particularly noisy, he'd gone outside and tried reading in the car. It had scored high in terms of tranquillity and comfort, but low on improving credibility with the neighbours. It also drew a number of funny looks and left him feeling like a right dork and so he didn't do it again.

In addition to the desk, there was a matching bookcase and filing cabinet, certificates and photographs on the wall, papers and folders scattered everywhere, and a laptop, sound system and printer. It looked to be a well furnished and fully functioning home office, but he wondered why Young bothered. His workplace at Markham had to be equipped with way more sophisticated gear than this.

A thumping noise above his head snapped him out of his reverie, as Longman came downstairs in the company of a couple of people he'd found up there, or at least that was how it sounded.

'No sign of 'im up there,' Longman said. 'No indications of foul play either.'

'Such as what, Mr Investigator?'

'Erm, I didn't see any blood splattered on the walls, no drawers were pulled out with stuff lying all over the room, and there were no broken bottles in the bathroom. You know, anything that might indicate a struggle.'

'Very good, son. It's not Traffic you should be

setting your sights on, it's CID. What about the wardrobes, any sign of a hasty retreat? Does it look like any of his clothes are missing?'

'Nope. There's plenty of stuff in there like suits and shirts and all that, and I spotted two empty suitcases.'

'Good lad. What I want you to do now is go outside and take a good look around the back garden. Look for any freshly dug areas and have a peek in the shed and the garage, make sure he's not in there and swinging from the rafters, or a hosepipe's been attached to a car's exhaust.'

'Blooming heck,' Longman said, his face lighting up. 'You don't think he might be in there? I've never done a suicide before.'

'Are you up for it?'

'You betcha.'

Idiot. Longman wandered off to locate the back door and garage keys while Rogerson turned his attention back to the study. If David Young didn't appear by the end of the weekend, this was the place he was convinced a search for him should start.

He was no detective, although there was a time he hankered to move there, but if CID were to send someone down he was sure they would find evidence on the laptop, from papers on the desk, or the rubbish in the bin, that would tell them exactly where their missing man had gone.

If Young had been dipping his greedy paws into the Markham honey jar, Rogerson would bet he was now holed up in Morocco or Mexico or some other far flung place where it would be difficult to extradite him. He couldn't put a finger on it, but he had a feeling in his bones that David Young was missing on purpose, as if he was a man with something to hide.

# TWELVE

For one morning at least, DS Carol Walters arrived at the office before everyone else. Since the start of Operation Poseidon, she and the enquiry team had been waiting for a forensic breakthrough that would provide them with something to help catch the car thieves; but when it hadn't come, she began to feel despondent.

To inject some life and direction into the inquiry, DI Henderson had changed what she and some others were doing to concentrate more on the selling side of the equation. It was a move that she didn't agree with at first, but she had to admit the change in work patterns filled her with a new sense of purpose.

The first of two wake-up alarms went off at six-thirty and instead of picking up the little trilling box of electronics and hurling it against the nearest wall, as she had done with three of them in the past year, she got up and headed straight into the shower. It was a revelation to be up so early, as she had time for a decent breakfast instead of a slice of toast on the run, and she could put on her make-up in the comfort of her own flat, rather than in the car or the toilets at Sussex House.

In addition, her journey from Queens Park to Hollingbury took less time than normal as she avoided the slow-moving queues that often halted her progress on the Lewes Road. Even so, not everything in the garden was rosy. At this early hour of the morning, all the rooms on their floor of Sussex House were cold and dark and she spent the first ten minutes switching on lights, tidying up the small kitchen, cleaning out the coffee machine and giving the same answers to departing night shift detectives, bemused to see her in there at all.

By eight fifteen, a familiar buzz returned to her part of the building, and by nine, DI Henderson arrived. She gave him ten minutes or so to get settled, before walking into his office and sitting down at the small meeting table. 'I made it in before you this morning,' she said, a touch self-righteously. 'There's a story for the Chief Constable's newsletter.'

'If it wasn't for this bloody tooth,' he said slurring his words and pointing at his jaw, 'my long-standing record would still be intact.'

'Got it fixed at last then?'

He nodded. 'I hate dentists. What a job they've got, staring into people's mouths all day with their bad breath, furry teeth and decay. Patients looking at them with hate in their eyes at the first twinge of pain. It makes our job look a whole lot better.'

She laughed. 'I'll have to remember that one if I ever have to interview new recruits. I brought you a coffee.'

'Are you some kind of sadist? This shirt looks better without coffee stains.'

He eased up from the chair and took a seat opposite her, his elbow leaning on the table and his hand nursing his abused jaw.

He had shaved at least, but Walters doubted if a comb had been dragged through his untidy mop of light brown hair for several days. His girlfriend had been trying for months to improve his wardrobe, but either due to a relapse on his part, or the task she had set herself was insurmountable, the shirt and jacket combination had been used before and the trousers still bore a beer stain from a raucous night in the pub over three weeks before.

'Did you enjoy the training course?'

'In summary,' Henderson said, 'I learned nothing and there were moments when it left me bored witless, but I met some interesting people, although I have to say some of these Met boys can drink. I'm glad it was only a two-day course as I could never have survived a week, not with the bar prices in that hotel.'

'I don't think anywhere in London is cheap.'

'Nevertheless, it's always a welcome relief to get away from the daily grind for a bit, even if it meant putting up with some strange people knocking on my door at one in the morning.'

'Well, it's what you get for leaving your room key where everyone can see it.'

'True, but in the last place I stayed in, they gave me one of these programmable cards with no room number printed on it and a couple of times I tried to get into the wrong room. So, what's been happening here while I've been away? Not much I suspect, as I'm sure you would have phoned if there was anything earth shattering to report.'

'Maybe earth shattering is putting it a bit strong, but I think we've made some progress. If you remember, I've been contacting ports, trying to find our exported cars and following up the sightings of the chilled food van. I'll deal with the ports issue first.'

'Refresh my memory; it needs a little jog this morning.'

'Phil Bentley and me have been talking with Customs at all the main ports on the east coast, trying to find out anything about the exportation of high-value cars.'

'I imagine it's been a fairly thankless task.'

'You might have told me this earlier.'

'In my experience, getting anything out of Customs is the nearest thing to root canal treatment.'

'So we found out. Cars and everything else that are being shipped overseas are moved inside a container and rarely get loaded aboard a normal ship for lots of reasons that I won't bore you with. Mind you, if I had to listen to a detailed explanation a couple of times, why shouldn't you?'

'No thanks. You know my next question, can you

find out what's in the containers?'

She shook her head. 'Nope. Customers rent the box and they can put whatever the hell they want inside.'

'I understand, but there must be some sort of export documentation to go with it. They can't just fill it up with whatever they like, I mean what if it's guns and drugs?'

'Customs carry out spot checks to make sure what's inside the box matches the export paperwork, but with tens of thousands of these things exported each week, millions a year, there's no way they can trawl through all those records looking for a specific car. That is, unless we can identify the port, date, shipping line, or container number.'

'Hmm, not good. I always imagined by now all that stuff would be computerised and all they would have to do is press a few buttons and out the information would pop. However, I suppose the incentive for your little team is to find just one car from our list and we're away.'

'Yes, true, but it's not as easy as you might think. We can't even identify the day of export. If you think I'm being pessimistic, then you've probably realised I'm not that hopeful on this side of the investigation.'

'I thought you said something about progress? It doesn't sound much like progress to me.'

'Hold your horses,' she said picking up another sheet of paper. 'I'm now going to tell you what we've done about the van sighting and as you will hear, it turned out a whole lot better than bloody shipping containers.'

'I'm glad to hear it. I need some cheering up.'

'If you remember, in the course of interviewing neighbours living close to the houses where cars were stolen, two witnesses came forward and said they saw a white van in the early hours of the morning, not long after raids had taken place. You sent Sally Graham to follow up.'

'So I did. Doctor Masters and Margaret Draper wasn't it? How did it go?'

'Very good. The Novocain must be wearing off.'

'Booze, more like.'

'I have to say, Sally did a brilliant job. Doctor Masters is three weeks shy of his eightieth and walks with a stick, but even though he's a bit weak in the limbs and doddery on his feet, his brain and eyes are still as sharp as a knife.'

'How could she tell?'

'The doc is a keen ornithologist, and as a little test, she asked him to name the strange looking bird she could see at the bottom of the back garden.'

'Clever, although he could have said he saw a Chinese Red Spotted Eagle or some other rubbish and she wouldn't know if he was right or not.'

She shook her head. 'No way, our Sally's a twitcher too.'

'I didn't know. Ok, we've established the old boy is compos mentis and has good eyesight. What then?'

'He said he didn't know much about commercial vehicles and so couldn't tell the make of the van or anything, but he remembered it was tall and white with no windows and he also said he saw some writing on the side.'

'Call me sceptical, Carol, but I'm not pulling in every Tesco driver in the south east for an interview.'

'It wasn't Tesco or any well-known company. He said it was, something-something Chilled Foods Ltd.'

Henderson opened his mouth to speak but she put up her hand to stop him. 'Let me finish. All this will make sense when you hear the whole story. After seeing the doctor, Sally went to meet Margaret Draper. She's a bit younger than the doc by about thirty years and with good eyesight. She often gets up at that time of the morning as she suffers from insomnia.'

'Perhaps the two of them should get together, you know, a doctor and a bad sleeper.'

'Very good, but you're starting to sound like Harry Wallop. Now without prompting or putting words into her mouth, she said she also saw a similar looking van to Doctor Masters, and she also spotted writing on the side. She could see it better than the doctor and was quite definite it read S&C Chilled Foods Ltd.'

'Are you sure she wasn't coached?'

'I assure you sir, she wasn't. She only remembered the name because it's the initials of her two granddaughters, Sophie and Charlotte.'

‘Let me think about this for a sec,’ Henderson said, rising from the chair and pacing the room. ‘Their description of the van ties up, the colour, the size, the time of the morning?’

‘Yes. Tall and white, no windows, boxy, a raspy engine, indicating it wasn’t new or had just started out on its journey, all of that.’

‘I suppose it’s possible. I assume you’ve checked this company out?’

She nodded. ‘I’m sure it’s made up. There’s a chilled foods business in Blackpool with the same name but they never venture further south than Manchester and none of their vans have been stolen recently.’

He sat down. ‘So, now we’re left with what? Reviewing CCTV pictures? Trying to find a few more witnesses?’

‘Seen it, done it, got the t-shirt. Now for the mega interesting news.’

‘There’s more? I should go away more often.’

‘If you remember, car number seven, an Audi R8, was nicked at the end of last week from a house near Handcross.’

He sighed at the memory. ‘Don’t remind me.’

‘There aren’t many white vans moving around Sussex at three in the morning, so we searched for it on CCTV, about the time the owner thought his car had been taken, and we found the van.’

‘Bloody hell, Carol, you’ve done some great work.

Where did it go?'

'We first picked it up travelling north on the M23 and then tracked it all the way into Croydon where, with better lighting and higher resolution cameras, we could see two occupants inside and confirmed the name on the side was indeed S&C Chilled Foods.'

'Bloody excellent. Did you get anything on the reg?'

She shook her head. 'The number is registered to a Ford Focus, owned by a woman in Doncaster.'

'Well there's another offense we can get them for. How far did you take it?'

She reached over to his desk and picked up Henderson's well-thumbed London A-Z, last used to direct him to his training course hotel, and flicked through it until she found a map of south London. She edged her chair closer to Henderson and placed the map in front of him, tracing the route with her finger.

'We tracked them up the A23, through Stockwell, Lambeth, and across the Thames to here, Prichard's Road in Hackney. A couple of cameras were out but I wasn't so bothered as I thought I could pick them up later, but when we looked again the van had disappeared.'

'Did you wait, in case they'd stopped for a fag, or maybe to check the load?'

'Yep,' she said, but it sounded like a groan, the memory of a long and tedious job still fresh. 'We checked every street for a mile radius over the next hour, from about four to five in the morning, but found nothing.'

'Hmm. They must have pulled into a lock-up or a garage along the way.'

'We thought so too.'

'So, I guess you're now at a dead end?'

'Yep, unless we can get some manpower on the streets of Hackney to kick in a few doors and rattle a few hinges.'

He frowned in concentration. 'It doesn't sound like an easy job. There's paperwork, budgets, overtime, and a load of other stuff to consider.' He paused, thinking. 'Wait a minute, I've just had an idea.'

He got up and removed his wallet from the jacket hanging from a hook at the back of the door.

'I'm sure I've still got it ...ah yes here it is.'

He pulled out a business card, marked with the familiar blue logo of the Metropolitan Police.

'This guy,' he said holding up the card, 'knows everybody in the Met. If he can't find someone to help us, nobody can.'

# THIRTEEN

With a whoop of delight, she threw her pen into the air. It landed on the back of the *Daily Telegraph* where, for once, the Quick Crossword was complete. Now Rebecca Walker's husband, Marty, could no longer accuse her of being thick and refuse to take her with him to the pub on quiz night.

She put her empty coffee cup on the drainer and reached for the dog lead. At the sound of the rattling metal, Holly, the golden retriever roused from her slumber, stretched, and walked towards her wagging her tail. If the dog could smile, her face would be plastered with a big grin, as she loved her walks. Rebecca took a quick look out the window and for once it looked dry, but there were heavy black clouds massing in the distance, leaving her in two minds: fleece or rain jacket? She clipped the lead on to Holly's collar, put on a waterproof, and headed outside.

They lived in Woodmancote, a sprawling village on the edge of the South Downs, an affluent place of large detached houses with multiple cars, burglar alarms and piss-off gates. They didn't live in a normal house like other people because Marty liked 'character' and instead their house was a creaky old cottage with leaking windows and mice in the loft. A place any children's writer worth their salt could base a thousand scary stories upon.

It took only a couple of minutes to reach the path leading over to the big field, the place where she often walked the dog. On the far side of the field there was a copse of trees where Holly would run around, and behind it, a stream. On warmer days than this the silly pooch would jump in and have a good splash about.

However, there had been heavy rain over the last few days and Rebecca didn't want to be dealing with a sodden, dirty dog. In any case, the field where they were walking was boggy, so it was likely the stream would be in spate and fast enough to carry Holly away. She called the dog over and, when close enough, grabbed her collar and clipped on the lead.

They crossed the lane and headed into Shaves Wood, a place where she knew would be drier than the field as the trees were tightly packed and provided a dense canopy. The change of venue proved to be a hit as Holly was in one of her 'wood-moods', when she preferred rooting around the base of bushes and digging holes to galloping across the grass.

Twenty minutes later, Rebecca felt tired and in need of a cup of tea, and even Holly looked as though she'd had enough. She didn't fancy walking back through the woods and decided instead to make her way over to the road, as the tarmac surface would be easier to walk on than crunching through broken twigs and mushy, slippery leaves. Blocking the way was a wide strip of overgrown foliage. She selected a place where the vegetation was less dense and waded in, the dog following hesitantly behind.

Halfway through, something caught her eye. It was large and shiny, more colourful than the old beer cans and milk cartons selfish motorists often chucked out of their car windows. Why couldn't they take it home and put it in their own bins without messing up our back yard, she would moan to Marty whenever the subject came up.

She moved towards it, her heightened curiosity supplanting any fear that it might be something dangerous, such as an old fire extinguisher or a can of toxic chemicals lobbed out at night by odious fly-tippers. Her heart did a little flip when she realised she was looking at a bike. Not any old bike, a Ducati Panigale.

She knew something about bikes. Marty had lusted after a new one for months, when he wasn't lusting after the barmaid with the broad smile and tight blouse in The Wheatsheaf. Hoping to wear her down and let him buy a new one to replace their aging Honda, the shallow chancer had begun leaving brochures for new machines all around the house, including one for this bike.

She wasn't stupid enough to think it had been abandoned by some dissatisfied owner and all she had to do was take it home, clean it up and gift-wrap it for her ungrateful husband, but owners of stolen bikes often posted rewards in magazines and on the web, and even if they hadn't, the insurance company might have written it off and allow them to buy it at a knockdown price.

On closer inspection, the bike displayed no signs of rust, but the front wheel and forks were twisted, there were scratch marks all over the paintwork and the lights were smashed, all indications that it had been in a collision. The damage looked bad, but from her knowledge of bike mechanics, nothing a few hundred pounds' worth of spare parts and matching paint job couldn't fix.

The newness of the bike, the damage it had suffered and the fact that she hadn't heard any reports of a local bike accident, left a niggling doubt in her mind; maybe it hadn't been reported and the rider was still here.

With no regard for her own safety, she fought through an almost impenetrable barrier of four-foot nettles and brambles, bearing long runners that either scratched her skin or tried to trip her up as she made her way in the direction she thought the bike had been travelling.

Ten minutes later, nursing multiple lacerations on her hands and face, and dozens of little lumps where she had been stung by nettles, she considered giving up on what was becoming a fruitless pursuit. Then she spotted a blue helmet. Moving closer, she realised it wasn't the whole helmet, but only part of it. Rebecca Walker failed to find the other piece of the helmet, but what she did find was the lifeless body of a man, his head smashed to a pulp.

# FOURTEEN

Jason Ehuru guided the car slowly up the bumpy driveway. When Cahill had told them this mark lived on a remote farm, he wasn't joshing. There were no streetlights, no villages or houses nearby and no cars passed them on the narrow B-road receding back into the night behind them.

It had been raining during the day, with thick clouds blocking the afternoon sun and turning the streets of South London grey and miserable. Even now, at two-thirty in the morning, it hadn't shifted, blotting out the moon and stars in this part of East Sussex, leaving the land all around as black as the colour of his hand.

Jason Ehuru's family were from Nigeria. His elderly relatives still talked of wide open spaces, the endless blue skies and the calm, still nights when distant galaxies could be spotted with the naked eye; but even though he looked and spoke like a Nigerian fresh off the boat, he was a London boy at heart.

He was born in Faskari, close to the Kwiambana Game Reserve in northwest Nigeria, where the body of his father lay, but he had been raised since the age of twelve by his uncle in Clapham. He would never admit that he hated the countryside, too small-minded for a thinker and street philosopher like him, but he despised the peace and tranquillity and the darkness which enveloped him, like the inside of the wardrobe where his uncle used to lock him up as a kid whenever he was becoming too noisy.

Not long after he arrived in the UK, his elder sister Monifa and her boyfriend Kosoko would take him to Clapham Common or Hampstead Heath and let him play on his own while they disappeared behind some bushes to do whatever teenage kids did together. One time, he got lost and wasn't found until a search party stumbled upon him, shivering and crying at the base of a tree.

He swore he would always stay in the city and never venture out into the countryside again. So, what was he doing here? Why did he keep coming back again and again, like a character in some Faustian nightmare?

Beside him in the passenger seat, Rab McGovern seemed to be enjoying himself. He knew the dark, open spaces spooked Ehuru and as they approached the driveway of the target house, the mean bastard lowered the window. He said someone had farted and he needed fresh air, but Ehuru knew it was bollocks; he was trying to wind him up. They had been friends for years, but a couple of months ago McGovern had beaten the crap out of a friend of his, and while he never said anything for fear of spoiling their nice little earner, he didn't forget. Perhaps McGovern saw his inaction as a sign of weakness, hence he was taking the piss, but Ehuru didn't care. His time would come and McGovern would regret crossing him.

The outline of the farmhouse came into view, its gloomy silhouette looming at the summit of a slight rise. McGovern stopped playing silly buggers and closed the window. He turned in his seat and hissed, 'balaclavas.' To the team, it was their signal to shift into action mode, put all the negative thoughts swimming around everyone's heads to one side and concentrate on the job at hand. This meant everyone doing what they were told, with the minimum of fuss, and the least amount of talking.

For the second time in a fortnight there were no gates. It always took Rooney some time to open them with his electronic bag of tricks, and it was hard to sit still in a car with a couple of jumpy blokes, hands clutching sledgehammers, all ready to leap into action at a given signal.

Once on level ground, Ehuru cut the engine and the car coasted to a stop close to the house. Using night vision goggles, Cahill searched for the phone line. They all exited the car, careful not to clunk the head of the hammer against the side of the car and wake the dog, the householders or a neighbour if they had one. Cahill carefully removed a ladder from the boot and ran to the side of the house to undo the work of an overpaid BT engineer.

On such an isolated property, it was no surprise to see the people inside had installed a burglar alarm, but without a telephone line it was like cutting the balls off a Lothario like Cahill: they might have the kit, but it was no bloody use.

Some systems could generate a 'line cut' call through a mobile dialler which in return would generate a call from the security centre to their mobiles, but by the time it reached them, the gang would be inside. In addition, the home CCTV system which could provide a video replay of their night time activities would soon be a heap of smashed up electronic circuits and broken plastic, along with their phones.

On a prearranged signal, Cahill climbed the ladder as Ehuru and McGovern moved into position on either side of the front door. McGovern nodded. Ehuru swung first, aiming at a point near the side of the door where the lock and handle were located, its weak spot. He brought his hammer back and was still leaning forward when McGovern's hammer swished past his ear. Christ, it was close. He looked over but the balaclava was inscrutable.

He swung again and this time pulled back quickly, but still McGovern's sledgehammer swung close. The bastard was again trying to bait him. He was sweating hard under the balaclava, his mind racing through the argument they had last week, trying to determine if McGovern was still upset by it. Ehuru whacked again and this time he heard the tell-tale creak from the frame as the door moved.

He leaned back to allow McGovern to swing, and all thoughts of revenge and retribution went out the window as he squared up for the 'door opener'. With a mighty lunge, the sledgehammer crashed into the door a few centimetres below where they had been bashing. The frame buckled and split and the door limped open. They were in.

Without hesitation, McGovern ran upstairs while Ehuru searched the hall. In an ideal world, the key to this guy's Ferrari 458 would be in a drawer or hanging on a peg behind the door, but not this time. A few seconds later Cahill came into the house, moving so quietly he hardly heard him.

Ehuru made a phone shape with his fingers.

Cahill nodded.

They waited. He couldn't hear any trilling of mobile phones, so either McGovern had got there first and smashed them, or the silly buggers had switched them off for the night. They didn't have long to wait before the pyjama-clad figure of a guy came half-tumbling, half-staggering down the stairs, the sole of McGovern's boot helping him along the way. When he was near the bottom, Ehuru grabbed him by the lapels and growled, 'Car keys.'

'No way.'

Ehuru punched him in the stomach. The guy convulsed in his grip and screeched something inaudible.

He raised his fist to punch him again.

'Kitchen drawer,' he coughed, 'nearest the door.'

He nodded to Cahill who headed there.

Still holding the helpless owner in a tight grip, they listened as Cahill hauled out one, then two drawers before walking back into the hall and lifting them up for all to see, the distinctive Ferrari prancing horse visible. Ehuru imagined Cahill sporting a stupid grin under his balaclava.

He released his hold on the man, who fell to the ground nursing his gut, and turned to leave.

'You can't take my car you thieving bastards, it's not even paid for.'

Ehuru reached the door, McGovern in front of him. Without a word, McGovern pushed past, back into the hallway and strode over to the semi-prone figure. He swung a boot at his chin, causing his head to snap back where it whacked against the leg of a small sideboard with a crack that resonated in the still night air. He flopped on the floor, motionless.

McGovern spun round and stopped when he realised Ehuru was watching him. He strode over and pushed him outside.

Ehuru staggered out and climbed behind the wheel of a non-descript saloon and waited with the engine ticking over until Rooney got the Ferrari started. The engine burst into life with a throaty roar, the firing up of twelve cylinders with a rich mixture of petrol and air, shattering the silence, a similar sound to his old uncle clearing his bronchial chest but sweeter.

The Ferrari shot off down the bumpy drive, rear lights dancing over the uneven surface, leaving little red tracers behind Ehuru's eyes. If he was being picky, the Maserati Quattroporte, a car they nicked a week ago, might not be as good looking as the Ferrari but it had a beautiful, sporty sound; much more aggressive than this car, but he wouldn't say 'no' to a Ferrari.

The door of the car snapped shut as McGovern climbed in. Without a word, Ehuru accelerated, his mind seething with yet another example of McGovern's uncontrollable violence as he headed after Rooney. They reached the end of the drive and turned left. Up ahead, about fifty yards further on and out of sight of the house, the van was parked under the shadow of a line of tall trees. Ehuru pulled in behind the van, and as soon as McGovern got out he sunk his foot to the floor, sending the back wheels spinning and the back-end fish-tailing as if in snow.

Ehuru drove like a rally driver along unlit, twisting roads where trees cast dark shadows and headlights picked up the glow of many small eyes peering at him from the undergrowth. This time he was too fired up with anger and resentment to be spooked.

Up ahead, he could see the bright lights of the main road, the A23. He joined it and headed north to London, keeping the car at a steady seventy-five miles an hour, hogging the inside lane as much as possible.

His caution was perhaps unwarranted as the cops wouldn't know anything about the robbery yet; the house he was driving away from didn't have a working phone or any close neighbours to run over to.

The murder of scag drug dealer, Stephen Halliday, had been in all the local newspapers and television news. He was a well-known figure in the area, an eccentric character who coached the neighbourhood football team and had a little side-line dealing in drugs, but he wasn't as bad as some. The papers said he had been killed by a rival dealer, or one of his customers after being short-changed on a deal. Whatever the reason, Ehuru knew the killer's name was Rab McGovern.

It was a risky piece of information to know. McGovern was a dangerous man. On the other hand, if used well, it could be the little nugget he needed to get the violent, unpredictable bastard out of his face forever. Now wasn't that something worth thinking about?

# FIFTEEN

At one thirty, Henderson walked into Sussex House bearing an Asda egg and cress sandwich and a bottle of cranberry flavoured mineral water. As a consequence of Rachel's assault on his wardrobe, many of his new clothes were designed with a neater cut and felt a bit snug around the waist and legs, with none of the 'give' of his previous outfits. Trying not to exacerbate the problem, he only bought the sandwich and ignored the mini pork pie and apple Danish, the usual accompaniment to a cup of coffee later in the afternoon.

Rachel would claim it wasn't the fault of the new and better styled clothes, but his expanding gut on account of his love of Harvey's Bitter, salted peanuts, and the occasional Chinese takeaway, often in the same evening. Being a canny Scot, he couldn't see the point of spending a load of money on new clobber and not wearing it, hence the lighter lunch; but no way was he going on a faddy diet, as life was for living and not for counting calories or watching the readout on a set of bathroom scales.

He had spent the morning at a house in Framfield, on the outskirts of Uckfield in East Sussex. For the twelfth time, he had met with a distraught householder, seen a door smashed to bits, and been shown the empty space where their pride and joy used to be. This time, the gang had upped the ante. The owner of the car, Grant Basham, an insurance actuary in the City of London, had been hit on the head with something hard and he was now in a coma.

The car, a red Ferrari 458 Spider only two weeks old, was to have been taken on its maiden journey the following week: a five-day drive through the Dordogne. The car had been a present to self on Mr Basham's fiftieth birthday, as up until then he had owned a succession of small cars used for the short drive between his house and Uckfield railway station. Now, it was touch and go if he would ever walk again, never mind drive a demanding car like the Ferrari.

At one of their team meetings, someone suggested the gang might end up killing someone as a consequence of their escalating violence, and at the time he'd dismissed it as scaremongering because, after all, it was only a car. A big lump of metal, glass, and plastic that could be replaced. Now, he was not so sure. It wasn't only the violence but the nature of it: brutal, nasty and incapacitating, way beyond what would be deemed necessary to extract the keys from a reluctant owner.

Their resident car thieving expert, DS Tony Haslam of the Traffic Department, assured them the gang were receiving anything from five hundred to a thousand pounds per stolen car, but was this a good enough reason to take a man's life and spend the next twenty years in jail for murder when they were finally caught?

He didn't think so, and because it wasn't what might be termed in a police operational manual or a quality newspaper, proportional violence or systematic persuasion, he had to face the prospect that they were dealing with some irrational or psychotic characters. If this wasn't enough to keep him awake at night, he didn't know what was.

The edge of his appetite was curbed by all these negative thoughts, and when he started eating, it was with less enthusiasm than when he'd first walked over to the supermarket. A couple of bites in, the phone rang. He was tempted to leave it in case it was Chief Inspector Harris with part two of the, 'You better catch them soon or we'll all be out of a job' speech, but with a groan he picked it up.

'Detective Inspector Henderson? This is Sergeant Billy Hardcastle from the Met Stolen Vehicle Unit. Eddie Robinson said I should give you a call.'

'He did, did he? Well done to you, Eddie. So Billy, how much did he tell you?'

'Not much. I understand you need some footsloggers around the streets and alleys of Hackney.'

For the next few minutes he told Billy about the sighting of the chilled foods van and its disappearance somewhere in Hackney.

‘So what is it you want them to do?’

‘I need some people to knock on doors until we find the garage they’re using.’

‘I don’t think that’s such a good idea, sir.’

‘Why not? Do you think they’ll scarper if we do?’

‘Without doubt. As soon as they get a whiff of something going on, they’ll vamoose These sorts of characters seem able to up-sticks in minutes and disappear into the wild blue yonder. A few weeks later, they’ll buy some new gear and tools and start up all over again. One of the costs of being in this sort of business, I suppose.’

‘Can you suggest anything better?’ Henderson said, feeling slightly deflated. ‘I mean we know they’re around there somewhere, it’s just a case of finding where they are.’

‘We’re talking about how many streets?’

‘Hang on.’

Henderson opened his tatty A-Z, now marked at the page he and Walters had been looking at earlier. It wasn’t a big area, but he knew from studying satellite imagery on the web that it was densely populated with blocks of flats, lock-ups, warehouses and light industrial units. ‘About half a dozen,’ the DI said.

‘I could get a few people, three or four max so as not to cause alarm, and have them walk the streets looking for suitable places where they think your gang might have taken the van. I’m thinking it has to be more than a single garage or a lock-up. We’re talking here about a big workshop where they can switch plates, and maybe a paint shop for doing a colour change. Do you know for certain the cars are transported inside this van?'

'As much as we can be certain about anything,' Henderson said. 'Ever since we discovered it, we've seen it travelling up to London after three successive raids. I would say that's pretty good odds.'

'I'd be forced to agree with you. Tell me, is there any regularity in the timing of the raids?'

'Nope, none whatsoever. Sometimes a week goes by, ten days, five days. If I could find any pattern to it, I would put a couple of cars on the M23 and a few more in Hackney and tail them.'

'I was thinking the same. You see, I can see another problem with all this.'

'What?'

'Well if we do put men on the streets and they find, say, five or six suitable places where someone could hide a big van and a few cars, we'll need to watch all six locations for a few days, or even a few weeks to identify which one they're using. I mean, we just can't ring the bell and ask if we can come inside and take a look around, can we?'

'We're into surveillance then. Mind you, if the gap between raids is only four days, we might not have long to wait.'

'Yeah, but you said it yourself, the time between raids could be up to ten days, and who knows, maybe now they'll decide to take a break and bugger off on holiday.'

'Yep, and knowing my luck on this case, you could be right.'

'Hang on a sec though,' Hardcastle said. 'I've just thought. There's something we could do and it might save us a lot of time. Let me make a few phone calls and I'll call you right back.'

# SIXTEEN

Slowly, slowly, he panned to the right. With the crosshairs lined up, a little behind its left ear, Dominic Green let out a brief smile. The Bambis had broken through the fencing close to a planting of three hundred ash, beech, and silver birch trees, part of his commitment to the environment as a responsible land owner, not to mention getting some free loot from the government; but the little buggers were in there and chomping for all they were worth.

In truth, his interest in the green agenda was to silence the 'friends of the environment' bitches from Brighton who were forever haranguing him in their vegetarian sandals about the way he was raping the green belt to make way for new office or shopping developments. If governments listened to them and implemented what they were proposing, the country would go back to the Stone Age with no power stations, no cars, no airports, and nothing else to pollute their precious countryside. As a result, everyone would starve to death, and instead of the tight planning controls in place at the moment which stopped him constructing whatever he pleased, the landscape would be littered with decaying corpses, rusting cars and crumbling buildings. No wonder everybody thought they were crackpots.

With over twenty acres of rolling countryside at Langley Manor, planting a few trees was an easy commitment for him to make. The plants, the fences and the protective sheathings were cheap. In addition, Kevin the gardener was already on the payroll and as happy as a dog with two tails to be doing something different.

The shot was a good one, and with the help of John Lester, Green's driver and bodyguard, they loaded the lifeless body into the back of the trailer. The big American freezer in the kitchen and the chest freezer in the shed were heaving with venison, so the three bagged today would be sold to a local butcher.

At one time, he'd considered donating the meat to an old folk's home or an orphanage. However, a bloke from the council told him he thought the old dears would turn up their noses at the strange tasting food, and the little snotty-nosed buggers would have a hissy fit when they found out where their juicy steaks were coming from.

He had been lying on wet grass and his shirt, trousers and socks were muddy, so before Lester went off into town to take care of some business, he dropped him back at the house. Green showered and changed and, as his kids were at school and his wife Natalie was out shopping in Brighton, he set about preparing his own lunch.

He was thin and ate frugally, as he hated fat people and the slothful way they moved. A chopped up apple, a bit of Brie and some bread was enough to fill him up for the afternoon. After lunch, he strode into the small sitting room, poured a whisky from the decanter and took a seat in his favourite armchair beside a roaring fire.

He loved the look and smell of a log fire, but if Maria the housekeeper didn't do it, he would be sitting in here freezing his nuts off. He could never get the bloody thing to light. A petrol fire at the warehouse of a rival, or a gas explosion in an old building he was trying to redevelop were a piece of cake, but starting and keeping a log fire alight was a mystery beyond his comprehension.

From lowly beginnings and more than a few brushes with the law, Dominic Green had built up a multi-million pound property development business, responsible for swanky housing estates, luxury apartment blocks, and up-market shopping centres. In addition, he also owned several entertainment businesses, with two casinos, five pubs and numerous illegal gambling dens. Why then did the Managing Director of a microelectronics company, albeit a business much larger and more valuable than his own, want to see him?

At two, Maria showed William Lawton into the room. They shook hands and chatted about the weather and the general state of the economy for a few minutes before Maria came into the room once more, carrying a tray of coffee and biscuits. She departed, closing the door behind her.

Green picked up his cup and sat back in the chair. 'So Mr Lawton, what did you want to see me about?'

At a touch over six foot, Green towered over most people, the bald head giving the impression he was taller still, which was just the way he liked it. Lawton only came up to his chin, and while his tubby demeanour might lose him a point or two in the prominence score, he was impressed by the hand-made suit, tailored shirt, silk tie and snazzy leather shoes. All the same, he expected nothing less from the Managing Director of a jewel of a business. If the corporate world did not feather the nest of their senior management, what the hell was the point?

'You may have read in the business press, Mr Green,' Lawton said in a measured way, 'Sir Mathew Markham retired from Markham Microprocessors over a year ago; but perhaps you didn't know that he now intends to sell all his interests in the company. In order not to cause an unseemly rush to the altar, as he would put it, he decided not to put the company up for sale in a public auction, but to flush out all those companies with the necessary wherewithal and invite them to make a bid.'

Green re-filled his cup and added a little skimmed milk. Lawton's dapper red-framed glasses and modern hair style might make him think he was dealing with an East End bond salesman, or a glib poker shark, but his speech was articulate and precise. 'I'm following you so far.'

'Good. To date, eleven companies have shown their cards, but none have met Sir Mathew's criteria. Now, there's been another little twist in this tale.'

'Do tell. I like twists.'

'Sir Mathew has been in talks with some Koreans and I believe if no action is taken soon, the deal will be done and dusted and they will become the new owners of the business.'

'Tsk, tsk, that was naughty of him.'

Lawton started banging on about how the Koreans would be bad for employees, suppliers, and anyone else connected with the company, but Green had been around long enough to know self-interest was playing a big part here; Lawton was fearful for his own position. He wasn't without sympathy as he would feel the same antagonism towards his employer if he were sitting in William Lawton's expensive shoes.

Green put his cup and saucer on the table. 'What you've said is all very interesting, Mr Lawton, and I must say, it's a difficult situation you find yourself in, but I fail to see how this could be of any interest to me.'

'Ah, but it will be Mr Green, you'll see. As a result of Sir Mathew's actions in talking to the Koreans, I intend to put together a consortium to buy the company from under their noses. My aim is to have a group of five or six big hitters who can raise the necessary capital to make Mathew an offer he would be stupid to refuse. I'm here because I would like you to become a member of this consortium.'

Green stroked his chin, a habit that surfaced whenever he was thinking seriously about something and not shooting from the hip as he often did. 'I'm flattered that you would think of me, but I know nothing about your business and I have to tell you, I never put money into something I don't understand.'

'The inner workings of the microprocessor industry are a mystery to most people, Mr Green. If I may, I'd like to tell you something few people know which will, I'm sure, change your perception of what we are talking about here and help you appreciate the scale of this opportunity.'

Words like 'electronics' and 'microprocessors' were an anathema to him, but words like 'scale' and 'opportunity' succeeded in piquing his interest. This discussion was starting to warm him even better than the fire. 'Call me Dominic,' he said.

'Thank you, Dominic, and please call me William. Now, you may think Markham Microprocessors is a fine company in its own right and one in which you would be wise to invest, and you'd be right. In fact, if you'd bought one hundred pounds' worth of shares two years ago, they would be valued at almost six times as much now, and if that isn't enough to tempt you, this might.'

Lawton shifted to the edge of his seat.

'What I'm going to tell you, Dominic, is top secret. None of the other bidders know anything about this yet, and it's the main reason Sir Mathew didn't want an all-out sale. When you realise what this means, it will enable our consortium to bid higher than anyone else, safe in the knowledge that we can reap rich rewards for our boldness.'

Like a poker player about to play a trump card, Lawton paused before placing his triumphant hand down on the table.

'We have developed a new enhancement to battery technology which will wipe the floor with every existing battery solution.' He pulled out one of the latest smartphones, a device that Green detested. Time robbers he called them. To Green, who only used a basic mobile for making and receiving calls, it looked like a small computer and the sort of thing Spike, his fixer and fully-qualified hard-nut, spent all his time playing with when he wasn't bashing people's heads in.

'This is the latest Apple iPhone, courtesy of the company and not available to the general public yet. It has all the latest gizmos you would expect: web access, video playback, emails, video calls and so on; but the battery will only last ten hours during normal use and perhaps three hundred hours when it's on standby doing nothing. In addition, all battery operated devices lose power even if they're not switched on, and the ability to recharge the battery diminishes over time. After three or four years, they're dead and need replacing.'

'Humph,' Green said with obvious disdain. If he had his way, the batteries would last no more than fifteen minutes and they would be incapable of being replaced. It would stop the obsession people had for looking at their phones and ignoring the person sitting beside them, behaviour he noticed was becoming more prevalent, particularly amongst women.

'We have developed a completely new technology that will change battery use forever. All around us, even as we sit here in your fine drawing room, are radio waves generated by a whole range of equipment: radio and TV transmitters, your home Wi-Fi network, garage door openers, all manner of things.

'If we could see them,' Lawton continued, 'we wouldn't be able to see over to the fireplace in this room, or to the garage outside the window because they are so numerous and all pervasive. These waves are carried on small amounts of energy, and some clever people in our labs have found a way to collect this energy, suck it into the phone, and convert it into low-voltage electricity that will keep the battery fully charged all the time.'

'What a bloody ingenious idea,' Green said. He was a keen reader of science fiction, in particular the novels of Ray Bradbury and Isaac Asimov, and loved whacky, left of field ideas. 'But why bother with a battery at all? Why not use radio waves to power the phone directly? Cut out the middle man, as it were.'

'A very good question, Dominic, and one we debated long and hard in our development meetings. We decided to opt for the battery-based solution as even though our new device will absorb radio waves from all directions and squirts electricity out in a nice, even flow, there will times when a user is in a remote location with little or no radio wave activity around them. I'm thinking here about a beach in the Caribbean or a secluded hillside in Scotland.'

'Fair enough,' he said.

'Now that I've explained the technology side, let me tell you how it will impact our business. The battery companies are not going to like it, hence we are making strident efforts to keep it a secret, and therefore I advise you not to buy any shares in their businesses in near future.' A rare smile creased his face. 'To prevent copies and industrial espionage, we will manufacture the device ourselves and license the technology to one or two other microprocessor chip makers.'

He stopped for a few moments and drained his coffee cup. Green leaned over and refilled it.

'When it's released, I can see this tiny device being incorporated into every phone, laptop, satnav, and ereader, every mobile device on the planet. I'm telling you Dominic, it will revolutionise the world of electronics and the way we use mobile devices. For Markham, the effects will be massive. We will make millions, hundreds of millions.'

The thought of millions absorbed Green's thoughts for a few seconds before he spoke. 'Two questions: the first is, did you think this idea up all by yourselves or could you find, sometime in the future, half a dozen companies filing patent infringement lawsuits against you?'

'The basic outline was dreamed up by a maverick radio genius called Gary Larner, but all the practical development work was done by the team at Markham, led by two brilliant engineers, Marta Stevenson and Sanjay Singh.'

'I take it they are, and will be, well compensated for their efforts?'

'Yes indeed. We look after our key employees.'

'What of your clever radio engineer, Gary Larner? Is he still part of the set-up?'

'No. He no longer works for the company.'

'What happened to him?'

'He had a bit of a breakdown and went crazy for a while, so we were forced to let him go. In truth, it was just what the project needed. He was going nowhere with the idea, and only when Marta and her team picked it up did we see any progress.'

'Was he sacked or did you pay him off?'

'The latter. He and his assistant received a generous pay-off.'

‘Is it likely they will cause trouble?’

‘Oh no, not at all. It’s all done and dusted now.’

Green looked at his face. This was an important point and he had to make sure Lawton wasn’t telling him porkies. Bad things happened to people who told lies to Dominic Green.

‘Fine. My second question is, how well developed is this technology? I mean, if it was up and running, I’m sure you would have brought along a working model to show me.’

‘You’re quite right. At the start of this month all we had were drawings and computer models, but last week we had a major breakthrough. We’ve built a prototype. And it works.’

# SEVENTEEN

The squad room on the first floor of Hackney Police Station was bursting at the seams. DI Henderson and DS Walters couldn't find a seat, so they stood at the back to listen to the briefing.

It was being conducted by Detective Inspector Gary Wallis, a gung-ho, 'lead from the front' type, a description often used by Henderson's brother Archie to describe some of his commanding officers in Afghanistan. When he mentioned this to DS Billy Hardcastle, Henderson's contact in the Metropolitan Police, he was told Wallis was a former member of the Parachute Regiment but a number of years ago left the Army to join the police after receiving a bad shrapnel wound in his right leg.

Henderson and Walters were in London only as observers, as there was no question in Henderson's mind or that of Inspector Wallis that this was a Met operation. The garage where the car thieves had hidden their van had been pinpointed by a Met surveillance team and it's location was very much on their patch.

The Sussex officers were there as the car thieving gang had put five local residents in hospital, one still

still in a coma with a fractured skull, and Henderson felt responsible until the gang were apprehended. It was a difficult situation for them to be in because if any of the Met officers were injured, they would receive flak for calling the raid, but they had no influence as to how it would be conducted.

It was all thanks to Billy Hardcastle they were there at all, as he had taken a greater interest in the case than they might have expected. Not only did he set up a small team to do the legwork around the area where they thought the chilled foods van had disappeared, he also used some of his people to pose as telephone engineers while they rigged up surveillance cameras across the road from the four possible sites that had been identified.

They'd struck gold two days ago when a Jaguar XK-R Coupe was stolen from a house in West Grinstead. Billy's cameras spotted it being unloaded from the chilled foods van at 3:45am, outside a dilapidated building, formerly a furniture wholesaler, in Pritchard's Road. However, it was not good news for the car owner, as in line with the gang's trend of escalating violence, he had been beaten unconscious.

Wallis had decided against a night raid, despite the obvious attractions. He believed, and Henderson concurred, there was a good chance the car they nicked last night was still in the garage, and if left any longer, it would be moved to another location. He also said he hoped no one would be naive enough to believe they would find the big bosses sitting around drinking tea and reading car magazines when they all piled in; but grabbing a mechanic or an electronics expert would put a big spanner in their operation and, with a bit of luck, could eventually lead to the top dogs as well.

Unlike similar operations mounted by Henderson in Sussex, many of Wallis's officers were armed. It was a tough call and one Henderson would not have made, as the car thieving gang had used only boots and sledgehammers so far. Not once had they deployed or threatened to use guns. However, the occupants of the garage could well be from a different gang and DI Wallis knew this part of London better than he did. Henderson had no option but to keep his mouth shut and defer to his more considered judgement.

To his surprise, Wallis then asked Henderson to come up to the front and say a few words. He didn't mind speaking in public, but would have preferred a little more notice. He liked to be well prepared and well rehearsed when making speeches at places like this, or at press conferences. In the short walk to the front of the room, he was racking his brains, searching for something useful to say that hadn't already been said by Wallis.

'Good afternoon everyone,' he said, looking around at all the inquisitive expressions. 'I am Detective Inspector Angus Henderson of Sussex Police, and my colleague standing at the back is Detective Sergeant

Carol Walters. Take a good look at our faces, I don't want any of you arresting us or shooting us by mistake.' The laughter sounded easy, but lingering behind he could feel the tension.

'I have no idea the kind of the people we might meet inside the garage, as my intelligence suggests the car thieving gang we are chasing are delivery boys, and the people today are likely to come from some other crew. The gang operating in Sussex have been responsible for a number of vicious attacks on innocent householders, gratuitous some might say. Several car owners were beaten even after they'd handed over their car keys, but I do stress neither guns nor knives were used. It just leaves me to say, good luck to everyone and I hope and trust this raid is a complete success.'

Henderson returned to his former position to polite but muted applause. Wallis made a few closing comments, dropping the 'Brigadier addressing the troops' tone and replacing it with a more street-based jocularity, as he wished everyone happy hunting and a safe return.

It was pleasing to see none of the sour faces that ended some of Henderson's briefings, when asking them to head out into a cold, miserable night to take over the surveillance of a warehouse, or to drive into a run-down estate and arrest a suspect. This lot were joking and smiling and despite the anxiety attached to any job of this nature, he was sure many of them regarded this as a cushy number.

They caught a lift to the rendezvous in the back of a grubby Ford Mondeo. It would have been acceptable in Sussex as a pool car, but he expected more from the Met's Stolen Vehicles Unit. They had to have better cars than this in their garage. Billy Hardcastle was driving. Unlike the deep, sensuous voice on the telephone, giving Walters the impression she was dealing with the English Antonio Banderas, he was small, rotund, mid-forties with a large bald patch on the crown of his head and a squashed, fat nose that had been punched too often, and, he suspected, not all in the line of duty.

In the passenger seat, Hardcastle's companion was a taciturn Geordie by the name of Adam Ledbetter, whom they were told would make a better car thief than the people they were chasing as he knew every trick in the book. However, Henderson suspected the main reason for his inclusion in the raiding party was not for his under-the-bonnet skills, but his intimidation value. He was a giant of a man and as a result Walters, sitting behind him, could only see out of the car's side windows.

Not that there was much to see. It was five-thirty on a damp Wednesday afternoon at the end of April, a long month without a break as Easter had been early this year and memories of Christmas were long forgotten even if the bills were not. Local streets which no doubt looked fine on a good day, were depressing in the pissing rain, with shoppers scurrying from shop to shop under broken umbrellas, cars splashing past long queues at bus stops and the tops of high-rise flats were blanketed beneath thick, grey clouds.

They turned off Pritchard's Road into a side street. They exited the vehicles and a large group of fourteen officers made their way up the road to the garage without further conversation. Henderson and Walters were bringing up the rear, in part due to their lowly status as observers, but also to avoid being clobbered; the Met team were wearing stab-proof vests and helmets with anti-spray visors, carrying door bangers and riot shields, and armed with side-handled batons and Heckler & Koch carbines.

Wallis had emphasised in the briefing that the close confines of a garage was not the ideal place for indiscriminate fire, and Henderson hoped all of them had all been listening. Their instructions were only to fire if they were fired upon, and the moment guns were raised, neither Henderson nor Walters needed telling twice that both of them would make friends with the floor.

The officer with the door banger smashed the door open. Once inside, Wallis shouted in a deep baritone that could grace the stage of a television talent show: 'This is the police! Stop what you're doing and make yourself visible. Put your bloody hands out where I can see them.'

Henderson and Walters squeezed in behind the last officer. The building looked small from the outside but it was huge on the inside, with two inspection pits, banks of electronic testing gear, a couple of overhead hoists and several large trolleys of tools.

In one bay Henderson saw a blue Range Rover Vogue with its bonnet raised, looking a lot like the car taken from a house in Horsham over a week ago. All doubts about the origin of these vehicles were cast aside when he spotted the car beside it: a gold Jaguar XK-R Coupe. It was the car stolen from a house in West Grinstead a few days ago, easily recognisable by the colour, distinctive wheels, and side body stripe; the car they had been tracking on CCTV yesterday morning.

There was a loud noise and a moment later, all hell broke loose. A huge black guy with an American marine's haircut started swinging a baseball bat and coppers began dropping like ninepins. Two coppers got a grip on him and grappled him to the ground while two others ran off in pursuit of another guy who'd dashed out of the door in the confusion.

The thudding of boots on the inside staircase dragged Henderson's eyes away from the scene unfolding before him. It wasn't gang reinforcements coming down to assist their beleaguered colleagues, as expected, but three coppers and Wallis racing up. A few seconds later, he could hear scuffling and shouting from the floor above.

Henderson edged between the cars to help an officer who had been smacked by the bat, leaving him disoriented and with a bloody gash on his forehead. From the corner of his eye, he noticed movement coming from a glass-fronted office at the rear of the garage. He was sure no member of the Met team had yet ventured in this direction as they were all occupied out here. Sidestepping the injured officer and dozens of scattered tools, he made his way towards it.

At the back of the office and partly hidden by a large table, a man was on his knees, scooping papers out of a scratched, blue safe and stuffing them into a metal bin. Henderson kicked the door open. The man turned, panic written all over his features. He stood up and pulled a cigarette lighter out of his pocket. Realising he wasn't heading out for a quick smoke, Henderson ran towards him, placed a hand on the table and vaulting over, and aimed a kick at his head.

He didn't get the height he needed. Instead of knocking him cold on the canvas, like a professional wrestler executing a perfect drop kick, he only caught him on the shoulder, knocking him backwards. The guy dropped the lighter, stumbled back and tripped over the bin. He tried to break his fall by grabbing the armrest of a small stack of surplus chairs piled up in the corner, but as soon as he touched it, the stack rolled away.

Chairs collided with one another and the man, now

off-balance, executed a theatrical scissor kick, good enough to be added to Cristiano Ronaldo's repertoire before losing his footing and falling into the morass.

Henderson was first to his feet. In a couple of strides, he reached over and grabbed his opponent by the back of his jacket, hauling him up from the jumble that was once a neat stack of surplus furniture. He appeared groggy, but as he turned, he swung a wooden chair leg and caught Henderson on the side of the face, causing him to jerk back in pain.

Henderson lost his grip and the guy sprinted for the door, but before he could reach it, Henderson leapt on his back and brought him down. They rolled on the floor, trading punches, and more by luck than judgement Henderson landed a good right hook under his chin. He followed it up with another rammed hard into his gut. All resistance collapsed. Henderson flipped him on his face, knelt on his back and applied the cuffs.

With all the cacophony of crashing furniture, he didn't realise Walters was now in the room behind him, rummaging through papers from the opened safe and retrieving discarded items from the bin.

'Good of you to help me,' he said, rubbing the side of his face. It ached like hell but it didn't feel like anything was broken.

'There was no need, you were doing so well on your own. You should see what I've got here. No wonder lighter-boy was so keen to burn them. I've only flicked through a bit. I don't think they were exporting the stolen cars as we thought.'

'You're making that up so you don't have to talk to Customs again.'

'Ha, I wish. No, there are emails here from a car recovery outfit in Holland. They've been supplying this lot with details of insurance write-offs for the exact make and colour of the cars our gang have been nicking. I recognise just about every car in this part of the list as cars stolen in our region.'

'Bloody hell.'

'I'll bet the mad mechanic out there has been altering the car's electronics to set up its new identity, and wait for it,' she said pulling out another piece of paper, 'they've got a goon at the DVLA who enters the cloned car's details on the national vehicle database.'

'So, the cars out there,' Henderson said, jerking a thumb towards the workshop, 'will in a few weeks' time appear in *AutoTrader* and on various websites as bona fide UK-registered cars?'

'Yep. It's an ingenious scheme if you ask me.'

'Too true lady,' the prisoner said in a broad Essex twang, 'and trust you lot to fucking spoil it.'

# EIGHTEEN

'Thirty-love,' William Lawton said aloud, hoping his voice didn't betray the smugness he felt. He hadn't been ahead much in this game and part of him wanted to savour it. He served again, but Suki's return landed well away from his racket and the failed attempt to reach it left him panting. The same thing happened with the next three balls and sealed her victory. It hurt him to admit it, but he had been beaten by a better player.

He could run Suki close, but she always seemed to have an extra reserve to draw on. Even on those odd occasions when he played well, she could always go that little bit further. After two sets, Suki still looked gorgeous, and when she released the sweaty headband and shook out her curly, golden locks, a younger man than him might interpret such a gesture as a come-on.

She had always been a good tennis player and had received coaching from the age of eight. Now about to turn thirty, and having spent too many years as a London socialite partying hard and staying out much later than was good for her, he'd hoped it would slow her down, weaken her game, and give him half a chance. But alas, not today.

Her father, Sir Mathew Markham, cheered heartily from his seat beside the net. It was a good place to spot any cheating, he'd said, but Lawton suspected it was to admire his daughter's play and follow every shot she made. The old man was convinced his daughter walked on water.

It was not unreasonable to expect the recipient of such unstinting adoration, not to mention a haloed place in industrial history with the first million selling, British-made microprocessor named after her, to be an arrogant prig or a spoiled brat, but Suki Markham was neither of these things.

'Well played Suki, yet again,' Lawton said as he shook her hand across the net.

She leaned over and kissed him on the cheek. 'Bad luck William, you ran me close a couple of times, especially at the start of the second set.'

'Yes, but not close enough,' he said as he flopped down on a hard metal chair beside Sir Mathew. He reached for a glass of barley water.

'I'm pooped, Mathew,' he said putting the glass to his lips and taking a long gulp. 'Thank God I don't play Suki every day of the week.'

'You need to think more about your opponent, William. Seek out her weaknesses and exploit them. It's just like business.'

'Yes, but as we know, Suki doesn't have any weaknesses.'

'Yes you do darling, don't you?'

‘Well–’

‘She doesn’t like the ball coming towards her face; she hates receiving a backhand slice that’s bouncing awkwardly; and you can always lob her as she’s not so tall.’

‘Don’t give away all my secrets, Daddy, William might win and it won’t only be me who’s devastated.’

Lawton listened as they moved into one of their little father-daughter exchanges, she playing the old man but not wanting to hurt him, while he tried to avoid questioning her lifestyle, as one wrong word could send her into a strop for the rest of the evening, or away to her car and back to London.

Lawton often visited the Markham household on a Sunday afternoon, although not as often as in the early days when the company was growing rapidly and they would spend every waking hour discussing issues and strategy. Nowadays, they would sit in the garden with a glass of chilled wine, or have a genial discussion in the library while drinking fine whisky and listening to one of Mathew’s Mozart CDs.

Mathew was too old to play now, so whenever Suki came to Ditchling and stayed for the weekend, Lawton made a point of being there and giving her a game. He tried to get his son Ben interested, but not even the attraction of appearing on the same court as a celebrity ‘it-girl,’ wearing only a short, frilly skirt and a tight polo shirt could persuade him. He was beginning to think the boy was gay.

Being the beautiful and sexy daughter of one of Britain's leading entrepreneurs who at one time was never away from television screens, she had become cannon fodder for the red tops for close on ten years. When she wasn't being photographed falling out of a taxi pissed as a newt, she was on the arm of the latest movie sensation, pop star, or God-forbid, a tattooed footballer with more brains in his boots than between his ears.

By four o'clock, it was beginning to cool, but it was still an effort for Lawton to rise from his seat and help pack everything away. He carried the balls and rackets to the little pavilion at the far end of the court where the old man used to find himself in the evening, as his second ex-wife couldn't stand the smell of cigar smoke. Lawton was at pains to point out that it was made from varnished wood and would go up like the Ariane Space Rocket if ever he fell asleep and dropped a lit cigar. The annoying bitch, who took an instant dislike to Lawton at their first meeting, ran off with her hairdresser before the old man ever succumbed to such a doomsday scenario, and now he could smoke wherever he damn-well pleased.

Suki busied herself in the kitchen, preparing the evening meal while the men made their way into the library. Lawton poured two whiskies while Markham slumped into his favourite chair, as if it was he who had played two sets against a semi-pro tennis player. He was getting plumper by the week, which wasn't surprising as he had little to do now he was retired, whereas at work he had buzzed around like a queen bee, fearful a new development would take root and grow without his input.

'Make mine a large one, William, I always feel more relaxed when Suki's around.'

He picked up the drinks and handed one to Markham. Before sitting, Lawton walked behind the small settee and nudged it a little closer to his host, to save him raising his voice or repeating his last comment. The old boy was in vain denial about his growing deafness.

He took a seat. 'Have you had any interest in the house yet?'

'Funny you should ask. Do you remember the author who viewed the house a week or two ago, the one I said didn't seem interested on account of the garden being too large or something...'

'Yes, I do, the guy who writes all those gory crime novels. What's his name again...ah yes, Phillip Jones.'

'Yes, him. Well, he came back to see it. I've never read any of his stuff, have you?'

'Never seem to find the time to read books myself, but Stephanie devours them, the more gruesome the better.'

'Perhaps I could get his autograph for her.' He paused for a moment. 'Do authors do that sort of thing, you know, sign autographs? I don't think of them as celebrities. Are they?'

‘I imagine such a sobriquet is restricted to pop stars, movie and television actors, and footballers. If you really want to know, I would ask Suki, she knows more about those things than you or I.’

Markham gave him a reproachful look which seemed to say, ‘Don’t go there.’

‘This author fellow came back to see the house on Friday afternoon and said he liked it. Then, this morning out of the blue, his estate agent phoned to say he’s putting in an offer.’

‘That’s great news. Is he part of a chain?’

‘He’s much too rich to bother about a chain. According to the agent, if he can’t sell, he’ll move anyway.’

‘I’m pleased for you. This place is much too big for one person. Has he agreed to pay your asking price?’

Markham nodded into his whisky glass. He was happy to talk about the results of the business, or intimate details of the company’s strategy on national television but became coy and defensive when the conversation turned to personal things like money. He seemed to forget that sitting opposite was someone he had known for twenty-odd years, a person fully aware of what his salary and bonuses were while he was working, and indeed, the size of the pension he received now.

‘Will you be sad to leave this house?’

His eyes darkened. He’d bought Stavely House as a wedding present for his second wife, Olivia, as it was the one house in the village she really loved. He saw it as a convenient way to make a fresh start after the break-up of his 23-year relationship with his first wife, Lucinda. The newly-weds took to their new house with gusto, demolishing walls, extending rooms, and building the tennis court. For over six months, they couldn't entertain visitors due to the amount of rubble and dust and instead, relied on the kindness of friends for a decent evening meal.

'I don't know,' he said, turning the glass around and around in his hand. 'I love this place and have many happy memories here, but I don't think I can say the same for Suki, Jackson, and Hamish. They were all grown up by the time I bought it and living elsewhere.'

'Yes, I know.'

'You see, when they talk of 'home' or recall favourite childhood memories, it's Lavender Cottage they mean, not this house.'

'So why don't you try and buy Lavender Cottage? It would suit you better than a big house like this.'

His face lit up under his well-trimmed beard. 'What a great idea, William. I think I might just do that.' He raised his glass in salute. 'Well done. It looks like I'm not the only ideas man in the company after all.'

They chatted a while longer before Lawton decided he needed to go. His wife always made a roast on Sunday evening, and life wouldn't be worth living if he arrived home late.

He arrived back at Lawton Towers, or Beechwood Farm, as the Post Office called it, at six. After kissing his wife and complimenting her on the delicious aromas coming out of the kitchen, although they were no match for the ones that had been coming out of Suki's, he climbed the stairs to check on the kids.

Ben was in his room playing Xbox and grunted a greeting as he dismembered four aliens, scattering body parts all over the place with a monstrous gun. Haley gave out a hysterical shriek when he opened her bedroom door, and barred him from entering, as she was having a girlie get together with two friends.

He ambled downstairs to find the Sunday papers when Gizmo, their Border Collie, padded up, tail wagging, a signal that she wanted to go out for a walk. He always walked the dog on Sunday evenings, but for once he'd hoped one of the kids might have done it. He felt tired and listless after his earlier run-around on the tennis court, and all he wanted to do now was disappear into his study and read the papers or surf the web, a cool beer by his side. It was true what they said in the education pages of the *Daily Telegraph,* teenagers were a selfish lot, and once inside their bubble, there was nothing he or anybody else could do to get them out.

He picked up a warmer jacket than the one he was wearing earlier, as the weak sun had disappeared behind a big cloud over an hour ago and it wasn't coming back. With some reluctance, he removed the dog's lead from the coat stand in the hall, called a general 'goodbye' to anyone listening, which was no one as even Stephanie had the television volume up so loud she couldn't hear him, and headed outside.

Beechwood was set in five acres, most of which was woodland, a large field with stables and paddocks for Haley's horses, and a stream reputed to contain trout. He didn't know for sure as he had no interest in fishing, and wasn't convinced he could tell the difference between a trout and a salmon, unless it was being served up to him in a restaurant or lying on a slab at the fishmonger counter in Sainsbury's.

This evening, he needed a long, slow walk to exorcise the negative thoughts swimming around his brain like the aforementioned trout. Rather than taking a leisurely meander through the grounds as he often did, he climbed the fence at the back of the property and began walking through a working forest belonging to the Forestry Commission.

He hoped a long walk would get the comment Markham had made earlier in the library out of his system, but it didn't. Sir Mathew would always think *he* was the brains behind the company and he, William Lawton, was nothing more than his sidekick, the warm-up man whose job it was to get the audience in the right frame of mind before the arrival of the great man.

When he met Dominic Green, he was told that

Green would only participate in his consortium if he could buy Markham House for redevelopment. He'd always wanted the building, he said, ever since Sir Mathew out-bid him for it all those years ago. It was located in a smart residential street in Hove where a block of Green's executive flats would not look out of place.

When Lawton first heard his terms, he was appalled and told him it was a step too far, as they had spent enormous amounts of time and money remodelling the building to suit their specific requirements. Now, thinking about it, he realised the building was not the ivory tower he once thought. They could still do their top-quality work in a purpose-built unit on an industrial estate on the edge of Brighton, or in Burgess Hill beside the rest of the Markham workforce. With all the money pouring in from Project Kratos, perhaps it was even time to move to Cambridge and be among their rivals in the industry and bask in the glory of peer envy.

Well, he was going to show Sir Mathew Markham what he was made of. 'He might think he's the brains behind this business,' he said aloud to the trees, 'but soon he's going to find out that actions speak louder than good ideas alone.' He pulled out his phone and called Dominic Green.

# NINETEEN

Suki cleared away the dinner plates and carried them into the kitchen. It had been remodelled at a cost of one hundred-thousand pounds, leaving no trace of the old country kitchen that had been there for over seventy years. In its place, wall-to-wall Neff appliances in brushed aluminium, a central isle topped with thick, Thai mahogany, a huge cooker, a built-in flat screen television, and a complicated coffee machine which would not look out of place in Aeronautical Monthly. Now, it all looked as though it had been hit by a rogue Predator drone.

It was recognised by many of her friends that Suki Markham was a marvellous cook, the culmination of several Cordon-Bleu courses, a former boyfriend who was an expert pastry chef with his own cooking show and a strong affinity for the subject, meaning she only had to use a recipe once and it was memorised. However, even her strongest supporters would have to agree, no matter what food she was preparing, she was guilty of using every dish in the house.

She loaded the dishwasher, piled all the dishes which wouldn't fit inside onto the worktop and put the leftovers in the bin. The rest would have to wait until morning. She would have made a better fist of the whole thing if she hadn't drunk so much wine at dinner, but having raved about the 2000 Chateau Haut-Brion, it would have been rude to protest when her father continually re-filled her glass.

If only William had elected to stay, he was partial to a good wine and could drink a bucketful when in the mood; but his horrid wife, Strychnine Stephanie, demanded his presence for Sunday dinner. Instead, her father enjoyed his customary two glasses and she had to drink the rest all by herself.

One of the reasons she liked coming to Ditchling was to give her liver a rest from the assault it received in the wine bars and clubs of London, but this weekend would go down as a write-off. This was the second night in a row she had drunk far more than she intended, as yesterday morning she'd received a call from Grace Drake, an old friend from Roedean, the boarding school both girls had attended.

Built high up on chalk cliffs on the outskirts of Brighton, the austere stonework and windswept colonnades always reminded her of Colditz Castle, and not Hogwarts School as kids in the Lower School referred to it. They hadn't seen one another for many years and decided to meet up.

Using hair extensions and dark glasses to disguise her face from groups of leering lads and peripatetic snappers who might recognise her, they had relived Saturday nights from their youth, crawling from pub to pub around the Lanes in Brighton. Too wired to go home, they'd rounded off the evening with a three-hour dance session at Liquid Space, a sweaty nightclub on the lower Esplanade, only a stone's throw from the pebbles on the beach.

It had felt so good to dance to music she liked and in any way she wanted without thinking how it would appear the following morning in the Sunday papers, accompanied by catchy headlines such as: 'Sexy Suki Sozzled'; 'Suki Sizzles Sussex'; or the plain nasty 'Suki Parties After Dumping Alex' (or Jon or Caleb). They soon lost track of time and how much they had been drinking and by the time she'd rolled into Ditchling in the back of a taxi at three-thirty in the morning, she was well plastered.

Tonight, she had drunk a fair amount of wine but didn't mix her drinks; it was a high quality wine, and drunk on top of a large Sunday dinner, so even though she did feel tipsy, she felt a whole lot better than she did last night. She walked into the library carrying two strong coffees, a feeble attempt to sober them both up, and found Daddy sitting in his favourite armchair, a large whisky in one hand and a book in the other. She placed a cup beside him and took a seat on the settee.

'What are you reading?'

'It's a book by Phillip Jones, the guy who wants to buy the house. It's called *The Death of Reason.'* He held it up for her to see the cover. 'I bought it on Saturday after he came round. I wanted to find out what sort of guy I will be dealing with.'

'Well, you won't find it there, for sure.'

'Why not? I've read the biography at the start of the book. I know, for instance, which school he went to and what he studied at university, and the jobs he did before becoming a full-time author. The main character of all his books, this limping detective, Inspector Rob Gresham, I'm sure is modelled on him, now that I've met him.'

'Daddy, it's fiction, you won't find out anything about anybody in there. It's all made up. I've met a few authors and let me tell you, they're a quirky bunch.'

'This is what everybody thinks, but where does he get his information from? He gets it from here,' he said tapping the side of his head. 'He can't conjure this stuff out of thin air. It must be based on his own experiences, his life, and the people he's met, but twisted around to make it interesting for people like you and me to read.'

For the next twenty minutes he launched into one of his mini-lectures, this time about literature and its contribution to society. To the unwary who strayed on to one of his favourite topics of modern art, computer technology or house conversion, they would be there all night.

She kissed him goodnight and climbed the stairs. She undressed, got into bed and picked up her phone from the bedside table. She called her agent, Bethany

Myers, who was arranging a photo shoot for her to model an up-market chain store's new summer range for publication in a well-known fashion magazine. Even though it was eleven-fifteen on a Sunday evening, Bethany would be there as she didn't sleep well and never put her phone off.

Suki was one of her regular and more lucrative clients and, as usual, she charmed her like a long-lost sister with assurances about the photo shoot, telling her she was looking forward to seeing the resultant photographs, as they would be marvellous. Suki didn't need such a level of ego stroking and only called to make sure the job was still on, as she knew the photographer they were using and for the last few weeks he hadn't been well.

After the call, she put her phone off, as the expensive Bordeaux was making her feel carefree and lightheaded, and if she phoned some of the people she was thinking about she would regret it in the morning. For once, there was no need for sleeping pills. The country air and the wine did the trick and not long after putting out the light, she fell sound asleep.

She woke with a start. She levered herself up on one elbow and peered at the clock. She looked again; yes, it was two-thirty-five. She had been asleep for over three hours, although it felt like only a few minutes. She was about to snuggle under the duvet and go back to sleep, when she heard dull banging coming from downstairs.

Her brain felt fuzzy from the wine but her memory was clear. When she came to bed, she left her father downstairs in his favourite armchair reading the novel by the guy who said he wanted to buy the house. Why was he making all this noise and, more to the point, why hadn't he gone to bed?

Suki slipped out of bed and reached for the dressing gown hanging at the back of the door. It was made of black silk with the design of a Chinese dragon on the back, and had once belonged to her frivolous ex-stepmother, Olivia. While it felt soft and silky and would be ideal for swanning around the bedroom in the middle of summer, it proved little or no use on a cold spring night like this.

She padded three doors along to her father's room and opened the door. It was obvious as soon as she walked inside that it hadn't been occupied, as not only was the bed neatly made, but the window she'd opened earlier in the afternoon hadn't been closed, leaving the room feeling like the interior of the big American fridge downstairs.

She shut the window and, for a moment, felt a pang of guilt. She imagined he had fallen asleep on the chair and had woken to find the house in darkness, before wandering into the kitchen to fetch a drink of water and tripping over a piece of detritus she had forgotten to move away. The guilt soon blew away like hot breath on a cold night as she remembered the house was equipped with more lights than the London

Palladium. If the old fool was stupid enough to wander around in the dark, it was his own fault.

The thought of getting on her hands and knees to clear up a basting pan full of greasy water tipped all over the kitchen floor by someone too drunk to open their eyes, almost made her puke, and on cue her head started to throb like a David Guetta soundtrack. She turned around and headed back to her room, walking quietly so as not to alert her father to her presence, as she hoped he would clear up any mess he created all by himself. She closed the door and slipped back beneath the warm duvet.

A few minutes later and on the point of dozing off, she heard voices. She sat up, not sure if it was part of a dream until she heard them again, and now she was in no doubt. She listened hard, trying to tune in, trying to hear what they were saying, but then they fell silent. She lay there for several moments, her mind beyond sleep and now buzzing with all manner of conspiracies and possibilities.

She jumped out of bed, angry, and headed towards the door. If this was the way he was living his life now, with the radio or television blaring out full-blast at three o'clock in the morning, she was going to put a stop to it right now. Retirement was supposed to be relaxing and enjoyable, and wasn't meant to turn him into a curmudgeonly old night owl.

She opened the door and stopped in her tracks. The voices were there again, but they were not babbling radio or dramatic television voices, they were human voices. Someone was in the house. In the early days of the business, her father often invited customers, suppliers, staff and academics to the house, often after a boozy outing to a restaurant or a pub nearby; but he always warned her in advance and in any case, he no longer worked there in any meaningful capacity. He was retired; he didn't do meetings.

She crept to the top of the stairs and peered over the banister. She was tempted to go down, but the voices were angry and she didn't like to be around when her father was telling someone off. She tried, but could not make sense of the words and sounds. In truth, any sounds in this house were alien to her, as she had never lived here. Lavender Cottage, by way of contrast, was the place where she grew up and she knew every squeak and scrape, from the identity of the person moving around upstairs, to the cat trying to sneak in through the back door flap.

Three men appeared in the hallway at the bottom of the stairs. They were all dressed in black gear and pulling balaclavas over their heads. They were heading towards the door, but before stepping outside, one of them who was holding a knife stopped and turned round. My God! It was those damned car thieves she had read about in *The Argus*.

She clapped her hand over her mouth to stop the noise of her breathing, which was coming out in short, rapid pants, the first signs of a panic attack. She tried to think of something to calm her, and thought of her boyfriend Pierre, now tucked up in bed at his parents' farmhouse in France, far away from her and her father's strange visitors. When her breathing returned to normal, she started to think about an escape plan. Her phone was still on the bedside table and at the first sign of footsteps on the bottom step, she would make a dash for it and hope she could get there before they worked out which room she was in.

Her senses were wound up tighter than banjo strings and she almost jumped out of her skin when the silence of the night was broken by the noise of car engines starting. It took her a few seconds to realise the men she saw a few minutes ago were no longer in the house and about to drive away. She crept to the landing window, opened the smallest chink of the curtain, and peered out.

Two cars were making their way over the short driveway, through the gap between two pillars where a rusty, wrought iron gate once stood. The first car was a light-coloured, boxy saloon, the second a Bentley, like the one her father owned.

She dashed downstairs. The front door was wide open, the area around it bitterly cold. She was tempted to close it and call the police, but instead she stepped outside. It was pitch black, the moon obscured by thick cloud but enough light to see her father's Bentley had gone but her Mini Cooper was still there. She ran back into the house and this time slammed the door shut.

She headed straight for the library, but when she looked inside, he wasn't there. She headed back to the hall and opened the striped-oak door leading to the lounge. She expected to see him fast asleep in a chair and was ready to give him an earful for snoozing through a visit from the car thieves, but the reprimand would have to wait, as this chair was also empty and cold.

She decided the time for stealth was over and set about switching on all the lights and pushing open all the doors and shouting, 'Daddy, Daddy! Where are you? Car thieves have stolen your car. Your beautiful Bentley has gone. Where the hell are you hiding? You can come out now, they've gone.'

She pushed open the kitchen door, but her eyes were not drawn to the mess of pots and plates on the mahogany breakfast bar, or to the cups and glasses gathered untidily around the sink, but to the prostrate body of her father. He was lying on the floor, blood slowly pooling around his lifeless body.

# TWENTY

'I have no doubt Sir Mathew's death will affect the takeover.'

'From what you've said Mr Lawton, I would imagine you'll have to call it off, for now at least,' DS Hobbs said.

'You're right. Sir Mathew was the principal shareholder in the business with over seventy per cent of the equity, and his opinion is...was...crucial. It all depends now on the terms of the will.'

'Who are likely to be the main beneficiaries?' DI Henderson said. To Lawton, it sounded an innocent enough question, a simple progression of the little probes into his life and the workings of the company and its founder; but to the DI, his suspicions were mounting.

In his experience, there was nothing like money to make people do things they wouldn't normally dream of doing. From what he had found out up to now, Sir Mathew's passing could involve millions of pounds, and he imagined there was no limit to how far some people would go to get their hands on that amount of money.

They were sitting in William Lawton's large office

overlooking Eaton Gardens, on a warm and pleasant May afternoon. If it wasn't for the fact they were discussing a murder, and if Henderson wasn't beset by his own problems for not resolving a car-thieving case that could have prevented it, he might have enjoyed it.

DI Henderson was accompanied by DS Gerry Hobbs, a man with a gentle manner who didn't often raise his voice or get angry, strange for someone married to a volatile Colombian woman and father to two young kids, but he guessed they did all the shouting for him.

The death of Sir Mathew Markham had caused apoplexy in the upper reaches of Sussex Police. He was not only a prominent figure in the town and well-known in circles frequented by the Chief Constable and the Police and Crime Commissioner, but he'd been killed by a car-thieving gang Henderson had told them he was close to capturing.

After attending the murder scene early on Monday morning, he again found himself at Malling House, ordered to explain to the Chief Constable, the Assistant Chief Constable and his own boss, Chief Inspector Harris, what the hell he was doing to catch the scum who did this. This time at least, a bod from Professional Standards wasn't there taking notes and marking his card.

They were in no mood for platitudes or excuses, but despite all the anger directed at him for his team's lack of success, Henderson was told he could ask for whatever he needed to catch them. It was a trap better men than him had fallen into, as the more resources at his disposal, the faster they would expect a result. With this in mind, he requested DS Gerry Hobbs be reassigned to assist with the murder inquiry, along with six additional detectives who would be used to pull out all the stops in the hunt for the car-thief killers.

If this wasn't enough to give him sleepless nights, the media coverage was. They were having a field day. Yesterday, *The Argus* spouted forth in a four-page spread how Sir Mathew single-handedly conquered the modern electronics world with his brilliant innovations and a strong dose of true, British bulldog spirit. If Henderson didn't know better, the article would have created the impression that he had founded a major global empire to rival Apple or Microsoft, and not just a successful UK business that had cornered a small, but nevertheless profitable slice of the electronics market.

'Mathew has three children,' Lawton said. 'Suki, who is twenty-nine and someone you might have read about in the papers,' he said with a slight sneer. 'She's a part-time model, an it-girl if you will, and a darling of the tabloids. If any of that constitutes a career, please let me know. However, she's a charming girl, utterly delightful, but she can't seem to settle down and do something worthwhile. '

'I've read about her,' Hobbs said. 'Wasn't she in rehab for alcohol and drug problems?'

If Lawton heard him, he didn't acknowledge. 'The youngest member of the family is Jackson who is twenty-four. He's a software engineer and works upstairs in this building. In case you think his job is a sinecure, I assure you it's not. He's a bright lad, went to Cambridge University and worked for a couple of electronic companies in the town before coming here. We're lucky to have him. He's a very talented designer, and even if he wasn't the chairman's son, we still would have employed him.'

He stopped to take a drink from a glass of water.

'And finally there's Hamish. He's thirty-two and also works in the business, but in our Burgess Hill warehouse facility as a packer. Now, if you think *his* appointment smacks a little of nepotism, you'd be dead right. He is the veritable black sheep of the family.'

'How so?' Henderson asked.

'Where do I start? He was the first-born son, so Mathew had high hopes that he would eventually take over the running of the business. He was a lovely child and grew into an intelligent adolescent, but at the age of fifteen or sixteen, he got into a bad crowd at boarding school and without warning, dropped out and backpacked to India where he spent three years taking drugs and getting high. A bout of malaria followed and Mathew brought him home to recuperate, but the spark had gone. He works here packing boxes and goes home at night to his television or, now and again, over to the Amex Stadium to watch the Albion. It's a pity. He had so much promise.'

'Are there any long-running disputes between any of the children?' Hobbs said.

'God no. They all loved Sir Mathew and get on well together, but don't only take my word for it, ask anyone and they'll tell you the same. No, to find Sir Mathew's killer, you need look no further than this gang of odious car thieves that I read about in the newspaper. According to some reports, their violence has been escalating over the last few weeks, making it inevitable someone would soon be killed. I wouldn't want this to happen to anyone else, but it's such a shame it had to be someone like Sir Mathew.'

'We're exploring every angle,' Henderson said.

When he visited the murder scene at first light yesterday morning, he noticed straight away how the gang had taken a different approach this time, aside from the presence of a corpse. The door had been smashed in by what looked like sledgehammers, so far so good, but the telephone line hadn't been cut, nor had mobile phones destroyed as had happened on every one of the previous 14 robberies.

In addition, Suki reported hearing a discussion between the killers and Sir Mathew that escalated into an argument, but it seemed to go on much longer than the time it took to demand a set of car keys. This was also unusual as the gang were, without exception, taciturn and rarely heard uttering more than a couple of commands. The final difference was Sir Mathew's body was found in the kitchen, but in the past, the gang only strayed from the hall to rouse the owner or retrieve the car keys.

To the media, Sussex Police top brass, and many of the detectives in his team, the raid bore all the hallmarks of a scale-up, the gang moving into a new, more violent level of activity. However, if the discrepancies were viewed separately, and in conjunction with perhaps the less significant fact that only three robbers were present when in the past they had always used four, it made him feel uneasy.

'How well do you know Suki, Mr Lawton? At the moment, she is our only witness,' Hobbs said.

'You've spoken to her?'

'Yes, we have. She is too upset to give us much more than a brief statement, but we'll try again today or tomorrow when her thoughts may be a little clearer.'

Lawton took off his glasses, rubbed his eyes before replacing them. 'Yes, Suki,' he sighed. 'I've known her most of her life. She's a beautiful, beautiful girl and one with so much vitality, but she fritters her time away setting up art galleries that don't make any money, modelling shoots that never get published and associating with men who use her for what they can get.

'Putting this to one side,' he continued, 'you should also know she has always been the light of Mathew's life, and even though she was thrown out of school for smoking dope and treats expensive gadgets like throwaway newspapers, she is likely to inherit all this,' he said spreading his arms wide.

This surprised Henderson, as he'd assumed the company would have many large shareholders, or the son working in the business would be the chief beneficiary.

'What about wives or ex-wives?' Hobbs asked, a keen student of inter-marital strife as he had been there before. So had Henderson, but his divorce had been a walk in the park compared to Hobbs.

'It's a good question, sergeant. There have been two, first Lucinda and then Olivia. Olivia will dig for all she's worth and might even contest the will if she doesn't receive as much as she thinks she deserves. Mathew was very angry when she ran off with a much younger man, her hairdresser if you can believe it, and threatened several times to cut her out. His first wife, Lucinda, is made of less volatile material, shall we say, and I'm sure Mathew would have left her a sizeable sum; but whatever it is, she won't cause any trouble, I'm sure.'

'So it could all get a bit complicated?' Henderson said.

'It could do, so watch this space. When do you think the coroner will release Sir Mathew's body? It can be a lengthy process in circumstances like this, so I understand.'

'I don't think there will be a problem in this case, sir,' Henderson said. 'There are no complications I can foresee. Will you be making the funeral arrangements yourself, or will Sir Mathew's family be doing it?'

'Oh, it'll be me making them, as I've got the experience, and in any case, they're not the sort of family who can do things for themselves; they've always had people to do things for them. In a sad way, I'm getting rather good at it, as I recently arranged one for someone else.'

'Did you?' Henderson said. 'Was it someone close to you?'

'Not close, but a valued working colleague. He was divorced and didn't have many friends or family in the area.' He took off his glasses and wiped them. 'He was our Finance Director, David Young, killed in a motorbike accident a couple of weeks back. His body lay undiscovered for over two weeks before anyone found him, the poor sod.'

# TWENTY-ONE

DS Hobbs and DI Henderson drove back to Sussex House after their meeting with William Lawton, in the Hobbs family people carrier. It was a boxy, ugly grunt of a machine exuding aromas of soiled nappies and blackcurrant juice, and the seats and floor were littered with papers and various bits of junk. If Hobbs told him it had been borrowed by four teenagers to take them away for a drunken weekend at a pop festival, he would've believed him.

It hadn't been their intention to cheer William Lawton up, but if it had they both would have received a D-minus for effort. They had left the poor bugger as miserable as sin. Hobbs reckoned it was the vision of a coke-snorting Suki using his office for drug-fuelled parties, nude photo-shoots and shag-fests with a host of her London luvvy friends that did it.

'The thought of that girl,' Hobbs continued, 'who's never out of the gossip pages of my wife's *Daily Mail,* hanging from the arm of some air-head male model, being in charge of one of Britain's leading electronic companies? It would make me feel pretty depressed as well.'

'You're just jealous it's not your arm she's hanging

from.'

'I wish. I mean, a lingerie business, party planning, or at a push, an event management outfit; but Markham Microprocessors is a tough call for anybody, never mind someone with no business experience.'

Hobbs went quiet for a minute or two as he negotiated the junction with Dyke Road. At least in the grunt machine the seats were set high so they could see over the roofs of parked cars, preventing them from pulling out into on-coming traffic.

'What do you make of Lawton's story about their Financial Director, David Young?' Hobbs said when the manoeuvre was completed.

'To lose one senior manager was unlucky, especially in the middle of a poorly disguised takeover, but to lose another so soon afterwards is nothing short of reckless. If I didn't know any different, I would think someone's got it in for them.'

'I don't know about you, but I didn't hear anything about Young's accident on the wire.'

'Same here, but why would we?' Henderson said. 'On the face of it, it's just another tragic road accident. In fact, if I did see it on the system or in a newspaper, I still wouldn't have made a connection. I'd never heard of the Markham business before.'

'Me neither, but then I never read the business news. I always get waylaid by the television or the sports pages first.'

They arrived back at Sussex House and Henderson

had only an hour to spare before his next meeting, a team briefing at six. He ignored a couple of phone messages and fifty-odd unread emails, and started researching two issues raised during the meeting with William Lawton.

He began with David Young's accident, first looking on the police reporting system, and then on a number of news sites on the web. He assumed the story would be difficult to find and would merit no more than a footnote in most newspaper pages, another traffic accident to add to the many occurring in Sussex every week. To his surprise several national newspapers carried longer and more detailed articles, on the basis that Young was an important figure in the business community.

Having now read the story a couple of times, Henderson suspected another reason for its prominence might have been because the poor man had lain undiscovered in a field of nettles, brambles and weeds for weeks, only to be found by an attractive woman out walking her dog. It had enough of the macabre and a touch of glamour to garner the interest of even the most casual of readers.

One article went on to say how he'd lived alone in a large house in Hove, had been divorced for twelve years, liked motorbikes and golf, but socialised with few people outside work. This dash of the banal atoned for the ghoulish nature of some of the narrative, but it made him wonder, and not for the first time, what sort of people worked in newsrooms and enjoyed scaring and sickening the general public. Perhaps Rachel would know.

The other topic he wanted to examine was the proposed sale of Markham Microprocessors. It was a task made more difficult than the one before, as even though he was skilled in the minutiae of dead bodies, road traffic accidents, and to a lesser extent, motorbikes, the very mention of share prices, yields, dividends or any other sets of numbers for that matter, left him cold.

At fourteen, Henderson had been a keen but challenged schoolboy, forever lambasted by his teachers at the Lochaber High School in Fort William for failing to understand the rudiments of times tables, algebra and the gobbledygook they called trigonometry. His failure to grasp the subject almost stopped him joining the police force, but following a fortuitous and amorous relationship with a young schoolteacher from Strontian, he started to master what he needed to know and ignored the rest as best he could.

He found an article on the BBC website summarising the reaction of the business community to the sale in layman's language, and section by section, waded through the technical jargon, writing down unfamiliar terms to look up later. At the bottom, it included a link to another article dealing with the effect on Markham's share price, and he found to his amazement that the company's value fell by ten per cent following the death of Young, and had now fallen twenty per cent after the demise of its founding father. In a takeover situation someone would save hundreds of millions of pounds. Now wasn't that enough motivation to get rid of the chairman?

He'd done all he could do and needed someone with a financial brain to interpret this stuff for him, but he would have to leave it for now, the briefing meeting he was supposed to be chairing started five minutes ago.

'Apologies everyone,' he said as he entered the Murder Suite and walked towards the sectioned-off area reserved for his team. They had moved out of the small meeting room as this was now a murder enquiry, and moving into the suite helped focus minds away from the travails and tribulations of the day-to-day. And in any case, the meeting room was too small for this lot.

It was not a surprise to find that nobody wanted to talk about the car thefts; the murder was at the top of everyone's agenda and without much preamble, he asked DI Hobbs to deliver his initial report.

'DS Harry Wallop and I attended the post-mortem of Sir Mathew Markham at Brighton Mortuary this morning. It should come as no surprise to anyone in this room when I tell you he died from multiple stab wounds from a large bladed knife, such as a hunting knife. What may come as a surprise, as we know many of the other car owners were beaten up, there wasn't any additional bruising on Sir Mathew.'

'Interesting,' Henderson said as he made a note and added it to his 'differences' list.

'I thought so too,' Hobbs said. 'He had high levels of alcohol in his system, which is consistent with the brief statement given to DI Henderson and myself by his daughter, Suki Markham, and may explain why neither of them had the sense to call us when they first heard the front door being sledgehammered. The forensics team are still at Stavely House, and door-to-door enquiries are continuing. I hope to interview Ms Markham more fully soon, from which discussion, we should have a better idea where our priority targets lie. That's it for the moment.'

'Thanks Gerry. Pat, if I can move on to you. How's it going at Stavely House?'

DS Pat Davidson, the Crime Scene Manager, was aged early forties and unfazed at speaking to a large group such as this. He put down the can of Red Bull he was cradling, this week's 'fad,' before addressing them.

'Yet again, the gang wore balaclavas and gloves and left nothing but a few navy blue fibres. We haven't been able to locate the murder weapon as yet, but I can say without fear of contradiction the victim received all his stab wounds in the kitchen and died in the kitchen.'

'Why there?' Henderson said. 'It's different from

all the other robberies. The car owner never moved out of the hall.'

'I think it makes sense when you look at the layout of the house,' Walters said. 'He was most likely accosted in the hall, perhaps as he went to investigate the noise at the door, and backed away into the kitchen.'

Many in the room agreed with this theory. 'Could be,' Henderson said, 'but it still doesn't explain why the gang changed their MO.'

'They wore gloves,' Pat Davidson said, 'so we haven't picked up any fingerprints or DNA from the door or the kitchen, but we'll continue to look.'

'Thanks Pat,' Henderson said. 'Let me say,' he said addressing the room, 'There are elements of this case which concern me. In none of the previous robberies, and I'm appalled to say the number of stolen cars now stands at fourteen, although their activity does seem to have tailed off since we nabbed their customer, have the gang changed their MO. The gang stay in the hall while one guy goes upstairs to find the car owner and another heads into the kitchen to pick up the keys if they've been left there.'

'Maybe they're throwing caution to the wind,' DS Wallop said.

Again, many agreed with this hypothesis, leaving Henderson sounding like a lone voice, so he let it go for the moment.

'Carol, do we have anything on CCTV?'

'There's nothing much in the way of cameras in the village, as you can imagine, and little in surrounding areas since it's quite rural, so no, we didn't pick them up. We didn't find a white chilled foods van heading north either, not surprising as we've closed down their customer.'

The meeting ended at seven-fifteen and Henderson returned to his office, despondent at the lack of progress and irritated by his inability to pull together all the disparate strands swimming around his head, and well as not being able articulate something to the team which would have helped build consensus.

He would now go home and kick the cat, if he had one, or punch the wall, but knowing his luck he would find it was made of plasterboard and cause hundreds of pounds' worth of damage. He decided instead to settle down for a quiet night in, with a take-away from Izzi's, as he didn't feel like cooking, accompanied by a glass of the good stuff if his local off-licence had any left on their shelves. His whisky cupboard was bare.

He woke up his computer, intending to shut it down without looking at anything. A large number of emails had arrived in his inbox since the last time he looked, and he resolved to look at them in the morning when he would be in a more positive mood. The way he felt now, he could delete the lot.

Reaching for the mouse, he noticed one from DI Wallis of the Met Police. He double-clicked to open it.

*DI Henderson,*

*I hope you are well and your jaw has recovered. We've interviewed the five suspects nicked at the Hackney garage as part of Operation Poseidon.*

*Dwain Harrison – a car electronics expert*

*Brian Lockhart – in charge of paperwork and the one you apprehended in the office at the rear*

*Barry Phillips – a car mechanic*

*Thomas Holt – a guy we found upstairs and a mechanic*

*Haden Jamieson – the other guy we found upstairs and probably the tea boy.*

*We've interviewed each of them three times and their story hasn't changed - they admit nothing and deny nothing. You're welcome to have a go, but I think it would be a wasted journey.*

*They will be charged with resisting arrest, police assault, and reset of stolen vehicles and with a bit of luck, conspiracy as well, once we've analysed their paperwork. I'm afraid I can't help you with the names of the car nicking gang or for that matter, the name of the person behind it.*

*Sorry not to be the bearer of better news.*

*Gary Wallis (DI)*

# TWENTY-TWO

DS Carol Walters parked her car outside the newsagents and locked it. A week ago, she would have left it with the engine running while she nipped inside to buy a newspaper and some milk, as it wasn't far from her flat and the engine hadn't yet warmed up. However, there had been a spate of car thefts in this part of Queens Park from owners leaving their engines on while in a shop or sitting at home, waiting for the car to generate some heat and demist the windows, and she decided not to risk it.

DS Carol Walters could never claim her old VW Golf was worth much, or was the love of her life, despite it being part of the booty in a hard-won divorce settlement. It was the car which transported her from A to B without too much drama, but it would be a bugger to live without.

She arrived in the office early and soon got stuck into a batch of reports about the theft of Sir Mathew Markham's Bentley. Half an hour later, DI Henderson approached.

'What's wrong with you, sir?' she said. 'I thought you had your bad tooth seen to?'

'I did...ach you cheeky mare. I don't look so

miserable, do I?'

'I beg to differ.'

'If I do, it's because of this bloody case. One step forward and two steps back doesn't cover it.'

'Let's not forget we did bring down the selling side of their operation.'

'I know, I know, or at least we caught some of the workers, but it's obvious with the Markham attack it hasn't stopped them. It looks like they've set the whole thing back up again.'

'I don't know. It was quite a sophisticated set-up. It would take time to piece something as good as that together again.'

'What annoys me is, I was hopeful that if we caught either the thieving gang or the selling gang, one lot would rat on the other; but I got an email from DI Wallis last night and he says the people we nabbed at the garage in Hackney are saying not a peep.'

'Bloody hell, another dead end.'

'Yes, but no sooner does one door close than other one opens.'

'Is this another one of your cryptic clues that I have to decipher, or have you got something else to tell me?'

'When we met William Lawton yesterday, he told us all about his Finance Director, David Young. He was killed in a motorcycle accident in March but his body wasn't discovered for another two weeks, by a woman out walking her dog.'

'Sounds gruesome, I'd hate to be the person who found him. First the chairman and now the Finance Director. Either somebody doesn't like them, or that company is cursed.'

'There's something strange going on there for sure. What I want you to do is go over to David Young's house and take a look around. See if you can find anything linking his death with Sir Mathew's. Young lived alone, so there aren't any friends or relatives we can ask.'

'Why, do you think there's a link between them?'

'Don't you?'

'I know it seems too much of a coincidence for two senior people of one company to be killed within weeks of each another, but Young died in a bike accident and Markham was killed by the car thieving gang. It's hard to see how they could be connected.'

'Nevertheless, go to Young's house and see if you can find evidence of, I don't know, death threats, gambling debts, drug usage. Anything you think looks suspicious.'

He handed over a report and a set of keys.

'What's this?'

'It's a report done by uniform at the end of March, when they were treating Young's disappearance as a missing persons enquiry. They entered his house but didn't examine it in any detail, just making sure he wasn't lying on the bathroom floor with a bottle of pills in his hand, or in the garage swinging from the rafters.'

'That's a relief. So, you want me to do what? Go over there and have a root around?'

'No, to use your womanly wiles to uncover what remains hidden to us mere mortals.'

She gave him a quizzical look. 'When?'

'Now would be a good time.'

'I suppose it gets me out of the office for a while. See you later.'

*

David Young lived in a large four-bedroom property in Shirley Drive, Hove, which in Walters's estimation was worth about eight hundred thousand pounds and even though she knew Young hadn't died in the house, somehow the empty rooms felt desolate and creepy.

DC Phil Bentley checked upstairs while she, after taking a look in all the rooms downstairs, took a seat in David Young's study, as recommended by budding detective PC Tommy Rogerson in his comprehensive report. She would make a start with Young's papers and afterwards, take a look at the laptop.

An hour later, tucked away in an anonymous blue binder she found a small pile of bank statements. She thought this odd, as she had seen a pile already, neatly filed in a blue Barclays Bank folder, and decided to take a closer look. The statements bore the logo of UBS, a bank in Switzerland, and into the account had been posted a number of large deposits. The account wasn't in Young's name as the Barclays account was, but in the name of a company called Branso Manufacturing Ltd.

Before getting too excited at the large amounts, she first confirmed the currency was Swiss Francs, and used her phone to find out the current conversion rate. She would feel a right wally blurting out to Henderson that she found massive amounts of money salted away in a secret bank account, only to discover that the exchange rate was thousands of francs to the pound and this lot were worth only a few hundred pounds.

She jotted down the amounts: one point two million pounds, seven hundred and seventy-five thousand pounds; three hundred thousand pounds, and on it went. In total, it came to a whopping eight point three million pounds.

She knew Young had been a well-paid executive in a successful company, and no doubt he was in line for large bonuses, but the timing of the UBS payments were irregular and looked larger, in her opinion, than would be payable to a senior employee in a medium sized company; but hey, what did she know?

She called Markham Microprocessors and a nice lady in the Human Resources Department confirmed the company did not own a company called Branso Manufacturing and did not deal with a business by that name. Also, that they operated a profit-related bonus scheme and payments were made to all eligible staff, including David Young, once a year. Share options were calculated after the annual results were announced and only redeemable if the recipient held them for five years.

None of the deposits in the Swiss bank account matched the steady drumbeat of salaries, bonuses or share options, either in their frequency or payment dates. It came as no surprise when the HR woman refused to tell her the amounts paid to David Young, but when Walters told her the date and amounts she was investigating, she confirmed they did not match the payments made and couldn't suggest what they might be.

Walters switched on Young's laptop and, as expected, it demanded a password. She was confident of gaining entry as her search had also uncovered Mr Young's little black book of website passwords and usernames. A password used throughout the book was 'Daniel,' which she now knew was the name of his sixteen-year old son living in Dorset. It did the trick and Windows started to execute its boot-up routine.

She was savvy with computers as she'd spent a fair amount of her leisure time on social networking sites such as Facebook and Twitter, and often late at night she could be found updating a blog she was writing about the life and experiences of a female detective. This was a secret kept back from her colleagues, as some of them were mentioned in the cases she wrote about, and unflattering nicknames were used throughout. It wouldn't do her career prospects any good if any of it leaked out.

With the laptop ready to use, and armed with the suspicious bank statements, she was tempted to use a search term such as 'Swiss' or 'deposits,' or even the date of the deposits to search the machine for all references. She decided it would be boring to watch the little egg timer spinning round and round only to return a long list of irrelevant rubbish, and instead opted for a more methodical approach and would interrogate the machine, program by program.

She double-clicked Outlook. In a matter of seconds it became clear that this particular machine was David Young's personal laptop, as none of the emails related to Markham and the single email address he used was a personal one. This made sense as his rucksack had been recovered at the accident scene and inside they'd found another badly damaged laptop. It bore a sticker proclaiming 'Property of Markham Microprocessors'.

For the next hour, she read through a succession of emails from the secretary at the West Hove golf club, his partner at the bridge club, several terse money-related ones from a stroppy woman she assumed to be his ex-wife, and a series of mushy ones from his son wishing him much fun on his new bike.

In the email 'filing cabinet' she found a flurry of emails between him and the place where he bought the bike, a large Ducati dealership in Croydon. Far from identifying a fault that might have resulted in the crash, Young was complimenting them for the quality of service he received, booking the bike in for some modification work, and enquiring whether a particular accessory was back in stock.

The spreadsheet and word processing programmes made her feel sad as she could tell by the date and time stamps that he often worked late into the night and at weekends. She found spreadsheets on bridge and football, and documents relating to the personal projects he was working on, but nothing about UBS or the large deposits.

She closed every program and sat staring at the screen. A few minutes later, DC Bentley arrived at her shoulder. He reported finding nothing odd upstairs, outside or in any of the outbuildings.

'What are you doing, sarg?' he asked.

'I found these large deposits,' she said pointing at the UBS statements, 'but I can't find any reference to them on his pc. I've looked at Outlook, Word, Excel and the rest of his programs, but I can't find any reference to them anywhere.' She blew a puff of frustrated air. 'I'm out of ideas.'

'They are large,' he said bending over to take a look. 'I wouldn't mind having a piece.' He looked up and pointed at the screen. 'If you can't find anything about them in his normal email program, it might be because he also used a web-based email account.'

'Bloody hell, I hadn't thought of looking there.' She picked up Young's black book, and after flicking through every page, found it on the last one, listed under Google.

'Well done, you,' she said as she fired up the web. She loaded Google and clicked on 'GMail'. 'Daniel' didn't work this time and she went back to the little black book where '899pan' did the trick, a truncated version of the name of his Ducati motorbike, a Panigale 899.

The emails in this account were all from Branso Manufacturing and tied up with the name on the UBS statements. Attached to every email were invoices for a variety of goods and services, many described in the woolliest of terms such as, 'Marketing Services' or 'Consultancy.' Adding them up and converting them to Swiss Francs matched up more or less to the timing and amounts of the deposits in the UBS statements.

She sat back, feeling tired and brain dead after her intensive two-hour workout.

'What are you thinking sarg?'

'If I'm not mistaken,' she said turning to face Bentley, who looked equally tired from watching her, 'our late Mr Young was involved in a massive fraud.'

# TWENTY-THREE

William Lawton shifted in the chair. The floor was his. In the cosy and comfortable surroundings of Sir Stephen Pendleton's house in Westerham, Surrey, he didn't feel the least bit nervous at being in this august company. He had spoken at many conferences, supplier meetings, and press briefings, and had been involved in multi-million pound negotiations many times before; but for the first time in his career, he was unsure what he was going to say.

He'd called this meeting of the partners in his newly formed consortium as many had expressed concern at having thrown their hats into the ring with him: that it was beginning to look like a fixed horse race. Following the recent death of Sir Mathew Markham, press speculation was rife about Suki taking over the running of the business, and to add a little zest to the tale, some suggested she had already agreed to sell her stake to a major Japanese electronics corporation.

Lawton had called them one by one and told them in no uncertain terms, anything they read in the newspapers was nothing but speculation, as no decisions had been made yet and it wasn't even a done-deal that Suki would inherit the business. Despite the reassuring phone call, he decided to have the meeting as he wanted every member of the consortium to understand the ball was still in play as far as he was concerned, and he still required their full support.

On his left, seated on the sofa was their host, Sir Stephen Pendleton. He'd created the UK's largest electrical conglomerate by buying the last remaining UK video machine, radio and television manufacturers for a song, then turning them into a well-run outfit making electrical components for the defence industries, badging up consumer electronics for many big retailers and manufacturing control systems for industry.

Before he retired, the group was sold to a French conglomerate for over a billion pounds, and as Sir Stephen was the company's largest individual shareholder, he now had a thirty million-pound investment pot. It would be hard to tell all this from looking at the house, as it could only be described as modest, but then he also owned a two-hundred-acre cattle ranch in Montana and a chalet in Verbier.

Beside him sat Fred Hallam, a car nut who had taken his large but unknown motor tuning business in Northampton into the Finnish-dominated world of car rallying, and in a matter of a few years, notched up three World Championships. Their achievements soon came to the notice of German carmaker Volkswagen who now produced a Hallam-tuned version of many of their cars, turning the lightening-quick VW Hallam Castra hatchback into the must-have choice for hardened rally fans.

Still only forty five, he was number two-hundred in the recent *Sunday Times* Rich List and interested in Markham as he believed the future of faster and more fuel-efficient cars lay not only in expertly tuned engines, quick-change gearboxes, and lean burn fuels, but in their electronics. He was confident Markham could be at the forefront of this new and exciting development.

Next to him sat the long, slim frame of Dominic Green, looking around the room with the piercing green eyes of a hawk hovering above a cornfield searching for its next prey. Earlier, Lawton asked him if he knew anything about Sir Mathew's death, as he was well aware of his reputation and knew his nose was buried in some murky troughs and that he moved around in some dark places. Rather than appear horrified, as he would be if someone asked him the same question, he'd shrugged his shoulders and asked him what he was whinging about, as in his view, the killers had done him a big favour.

Next along, and looking uncomfortable on the Queen Anne chair, was the considerable bulk of Barry King. Green had introduced him into the consortium as a long-standing friend, and if Lawton believed everything he had read about Green, the same could be said for King. He started out as an East-End gangster and cut his teeth importing alcohol, running brothels, and peddling drugs. To the world at large he was now a respectable businessman and responsible for some of the largest developments in London, including a new fifty-storey office block in Moorgate and one of the sports stadia for the 2012 London Olympic Games.

The final member was Jacques Trudeau, Managing Director of France's biggest defence contractor and a friend of Sir Stephen ever since the Frenchman had purchased his company. Like Hallam, he wanted to be involved with Markham, not so much for what they were doing now, but for the expertise they could channel into his main area of focus: defence.

His vision of the future included a Star Wars military capability consisting of pilotless planes, robotic armies, and sophisticated missiles, all controlled from a well-protected offshore aircraft carrier. In his opinion, Markham, with all its skills at shrinking electronics and making them perform complex tasks while generating low levels of heat, was perfectly suited to this market.

Lawton had been impressed by many of their pitches, but he could see a problem if they succeeded in putting in a winning bid, and that was how to satisfy all their conflicting demands. The Markham business had a full order book from mobile phone companies and they were, at the moment, in discussions with the same phone companies about the introduction of a new family of chips which would provide a range of novel services. It wasn't the sort of business which could be easily up-scaled without expensive development work and tooling, however, he was a positive person and in his mind, it was a good problem to have.

If, for any reason, the sale did not go ahead, it was likely he would still be in charge of Markham, and if so, would be interested in talking to Hallam and Trudeau about trying to grow the company organically into their business areas. He and Mathew had never considered entering the car industry, but they had been trying to crack defence for years and even Sir Mathew, with all his legendary selling and negotiating skills, couldn't get so much as a sniff.

Lawton stood up and the murmur ceased. 'Thank you all for coming. For those of you unaware of the current situation, please let me clarify.' He went on to explain the circumstances surrounding the death of Mathew Markham, the progress of the police investigation, and the reaction of the press as well as the effect of all these events on the Markham business.

'With the death of Sir Mathew, the papers are speculating that the sale will not go ahead until the contents of his will are known and everyone discovers what the inheritors of his shares intend to do. In this instance, I think the papers have got it more or less right. I have also approached the family solicitor, Mr Geoffrey Faraday, and while he wasn't at liberty to divulge the contents of the will, he did not seek to contradict my assertion that most of the shares will be left to Suki Markham.'

Up until then, whenever he paused he could hear the ticking of the grandfather clock in the hall, but at this point, everyone started talking at once.

'But she's an airhead,' King said, pugnacious and direct to a fault.

'She will ruin a fine business,' Trudeau said, throwing his hands into the air in mock horror, a gesture only the French could execute with any degree of zeal.

'Bloody hell this really takes the biscuit,' Hallam said. 'You might as well take a match to the place.'

'Gentlemen, gentlemen please,' Lawton said trying to restore calm. 'I have known Suki Markham since childhood and if anyone can influence her, it is me. I think it's safe to assume that when the dust settles and she inherits a majority share in the company, as I expect she will, she will ask me to carry on as before. I'm sure she would like to get back to her old life as soon as possible.'

He looked around and seeing several nods of agreement, he ploughed on.

'Now, in time, I will recommend to her that she sells her shares in Markham to us. If, for some reason she decides not to, or decides to put the company up for sale, we will be in the same position as we are now, ready and able to make a winning bid. I'm confident all the bases are covered.'

'How do we know, when she does inherit, Green said, 'you won't go back to your old life as MD, with Suki owning the majority of the shares instead of the old man?'

'Why would she keep shares in a business she doesn't understand and takes not a bit of interest in? If she won't sell right away, I'm convinced I'll be able to persuade her in time. From my perspective, I want her to sell it to us. I want to benefit from the riches Project Kratos will bring and the expansion in business resulting from my association with you gentlemen.' he said spreading his outstretched arm in an arc to include everyone in the room.

'At the moment, I am only a salaried hand, but as part owner I will share directly in the company's success. With the money Kratos will generate, I'll use it to expand our operations into new business areas we've never dreamed about before.'

By the grunts and nods coming from the group, he knew he was on the right track and went on to tell them how he planned to meet Suki regularly, to keep her appraised of developments and make sure no one else was feeding her a different story. He would have her ear and this was something they didn't need to concern themselves about.

The meeting wrapped up ten minutes later and

they all moved to a table at the end of the room, where Sir Stephen's wife had laid out a cold buffet and drinks. Lawton started piling some tasty-looking ham, pork pie, and coleslaw on his plate when he received a slap on the back from King and a compliment from Trudeau over his handling of the affair. From across the other side of the table, Sir Stephen told him he did well to make something positive out of what could have been a difficult situation.

He was feeling pleased with himself when Green took his arm and guided him away from the others. 'When you asked me this morning if I knew anything about Sir Mathew's death, I thought you were being a bit cheeky so I didn't give you a straight answer. Now I see you're committed to this consortium, I think I should tell you I know more than you think.'

Lawton looked back at him, shocked. He was too dumbstruck to say anything, but he didn't know if it was due to the power of Green's words or the way his intimidating presence seemed to tower over him. Those dark hooded eyes and furrowed brow gave the impression it was him being sized up for lunch, and not the mackerel fillets and salad lying uneaten on his plate.

'What I mean is, I have taken a good look at Sir Mathew's death and that of your Finance Director and I think they're related.'

'What? I've never heard anything so...so bizarre. How? What the hell do you mean?'

‘I think your company is being targeted by someone,’ Green said, a strange smile playing on his lips, reminding Lawton of his schooldays when a big bastard called Joe Barnes used to bully him. He would smile at him in the same way, seconds before punching him in the head and leaving him on the ground, crying for his mother.

‘Dominic, we make microprocessors and video chips for phones, not bloody artillery shells, nuclear warheads or cigarettes. I mean, who...who would do such a thing?’ He began to sweat, little drops gathering above his eyebrow. Green was barking and it was unnerving him.

‘This is what I would like you to tell me.’

‘I’ve told the police everything I know. Even they didn’t mention this.’

‘Phah. The police know bugger-all. Show them a body and I’ll show you an unsolved murder. They’re amateurs. Give me the names of the people you think it might be, William, and I’ll have my boys sort them out. After all,’ he said putting a hand on Lawton’s shoulder, making him flinch, ‘we don’t want the same thing happening to you when we’re in charge, now, do we?’

# TWENTY-FOUR

DS Gerry Hobbs parked the pool car beside a smart Mini Cooper S, got out and stretched, as if he had come to the end of a long journey and not a trip from Sussex House to Ditchling, with a small detour via the seafront.

It wasn't the fault of the Vectra, a comfortable enough car, but last night he'd slept in the spare room with a thin duvet and a radiator that didn't work well. The cold kept him awake. His highly-strung wife, Catalina, had been in one of her pot-throwing moods, this time about the lack of time he spent with the kids, and when she was in one of those there was no calming her down or sleeping in the same bed.

Before knocking on the front door of Stavely House, he walked across the driveway to take a look around while his colleague, DC Sally Graham, stood beside the car, texting. It was a large, imposing house with a style and elegance lacking in many of the neighbouring houses. Most of them were dull cottages with small windows and low ceilings, some of which had been extended with modern conservatories, rooms in the roof with plastic-framed, double-glazed windows and doors, and ugly ill-maintained garages.

He couldn't see the back garden, but the front was laid out as if modelled on one from the Chelsea Flower Show, with bowling green-quality lawn, edged by a broad, uneven border containing a variety of plants displaying strong colour, even though it was early May and most gardens in the area were yet to bloom. Sir Mathew's gardener had not been idle.

To one side, a wire fence surrounded an all-weather tennis court, part-hidden by a planting of mature bushes. Hobbs didn't play, but his youngsters liked the game and this place looked a much better bet than the courts at Preston Park, where even the slightest fall on the concrete could result in a skinned-knee and an abrupt end to the day's activity.

He sighed, his usual reaction when he came across a beautiful house he couldn't afford. In fact, with a sergeant's salary, two kids and a needy wife who liked coffee mornings and cakes, he couldn't afford most of the houses he saw, but it didn't stop him feeling jealous.

He walked to the door and knocked, the noise rousing DC Graham from her reverie and she strolled over to join him.

'I was enjoying that little bit of sunshine,' she said. 'There's been so much rain lately, I thought I wouldn't be seeing it again for a couple of weeks.'

'Next thing we know, you'll be asking me for a week's leave so you can rent out Wallop's apartment in Tunisia, but if this is your angle, the answer's no.

We've got a murder to solve.'

'I know, I know. It's just that I miss it when the weather turns cold. I really should have been born in a warmer country.'

The door opened and probably the most gorgeous girl Hobbs had ever clapped his eyes on stood there. 'Good morning Ms Markham,' he said hoping his voice didn't betray the sudden rush of blood to his head and the surge of testosterone to his loins. 'I'm Detective Sergeant Gerry Hobbs and this is Detective Constable Sally Graham of Sussex Police.'

'I remember you from Monday, Sergeant Hobbs, although I have to say I wasn't at my best. Come on in, but call me Suki, everybody else does.'

Hobbs hadn't forgotten Monday either, but then she'd been wearing an old t-shirt, her hair looked a mess and her face was as pale as a sheet. In fact it could have been a different person. Now, with time to get herself together, her hair was lush and bouncy, her make-up subtle and flattering, and the tight top and trousers designed to show off her amazing figure, and my God, how he appreciated it.

It wasn't that his wife was unattractive, she had been at one time, but the effects of bearing two children had adversely affected her complexion, weight, and attitude. Gone was the bouncy, happy go lucky 34-year-old who didn't drink much and could fit into a pair of size-twelve jeans, and, if he managed to peel them off, couldn't get enough sex. She had been replaced by a grumpy 40-year-old who waged a constant battle with her weight, was reluctant to go out anywhere nice or new, and was much too fond of cupcakes and cheap Pinot Grigio, a glass of which appeared in her hand almost every night.

They were shown into the sitting room. It had been four days since the murder of Mathew Markham and Scenes of Crime officers had completed their work in this part of the house and they were almost finished in the kitchen. Suki must have brought in specialised cleaners, or she and the housekeeper had been working like Trojans, as the room looked bright and welcoming and smelled fresh and airy. Gone was the musty aroma of chemicals and sweat that hung around long after a crime scene had been examined and the SOCOs had moved on to analyse someone else's misery.

They declined the offer of coffee, as prior to their arrival they had stopped at a mobile diner near the seafront for some lunch. The coffee there had been so strong, if he drank another cup he would never be able to sleep tonight, even if he was in his own bed.

'First of all,' Hobbs said, 'let me again give you our condolences on the death of your father. I know this must be very hard for you.'

'Thank you, detective. It's much appreciated.'

'How have you been coping with everything going on?'

'Better than expected. A few friends from my old

school heard about the...the murder and came over to help. They kept me company, held the paparazzi at bay, and helped me tidy the place up.'

'Whatever they did, they did an excellent job, this room looks great.' He paused. 'The reason DC Graham and I are here today is to try and flesh out some of the details you gave me on Monday.'

'I understand. I wasn't at my best on Monday, as I'm sure you would have gathered, and much of what I said didn't make sense, even to me.'

'What I'd like you to do Suki, if you could, is go over the events of Sunday one more time, in as much detail as you can remember, starting at the time you last saw your father. I know this isn't easy, so take your time.'

She blew a puff of breath, making the fringe hanging over her face flutter. It was a charming and sensual gesture, no doubt developed to impress the opposite sex or charm journalists, but he was in work mode now and more or less immune from her obvious charms.

She walked them through the events of the fatal night, from the point when she left her father sitting in his favourite chair, to the time when she found him dead in the kitchen. An officer at the first briefing of the murder team, one who hadn't visited the crime scene, said that he thought Suki could be the murderer. Hobbs rounded on him for his insensitivity, as he didn't see how heartbroken she was. Not long afterwards however, he realised it was not the dumb suggestion he first thought, and while he wasn't yet a convert, he could understand why so many of the team were beginning to come around to this way of thinking.

There were many pieces of circumstantial evidence pointing in her direction: she was the last person to see her father alive; she was the only one who claimed to have seen the car thieving gang; and financially she had much to gain from his death. In fact, many newspapers were speculating that she would inherit most of her father's shares, which were valued at anything between three and six hundred million pounds, depending on which paper he read, but neither he nor Henderson were convinced.

His counter argument would point to fresh tyre tracks found over a section of the flower border, indicating the presence of a car other than Sir Mathew's Bentley, and concurring with Suki's description of events. The issue of the inheritance was a bit of a red herring, as Lawton had told them she was already a wealthy woman with full access to a substantial trust fund set up by her father. She was also the owner of a flat in Earl's Court in London worth over a million pounds. In addition, everyone they spoke to was of the firm opinion that she loved her father, and Lawton said he'd detected not a shred of animosity between them when they'd played tennis earlier in the day.

‘Thank you, Suki,’ Hobbs said. ‘Now I’d like you to try and describe the voices you heard.’ He was treading carefully, not wanting to push her too far and lose her, but the more they spoke, the more he realised she was stronger than she looked.

‘You said you heard voices from the bedroom, and again when you were standing at the top of the stairs. Think hard; could you make out anything they were saying? I’m thinking here about accents and inflections, the words they used, how they spoke, that kind of thing.’

‘I’ve been giving it a little bit of thought myself. I’m sure I heard someone say, ‘you bastard, you bastard.’

‘Good. Could you tell anything about the voice of the person speaking? Were they young or old, black or white, deep and bellowing, thin and reedy?’

She paused a few moments. ‘Yes, one of the voices sounded young. A white guy, I think.’

‘Did he have an accent?’

‘Yes.’

‘What do you think, Irish, Scottish, London?’

‘No, I would say it was local. It sounded Sussex, maybe even Brighton.’

‘Good, well done. Now you’re at the top of the stairs and you’re listening hard. You hear shouting ‘you bastard, you bastard.’ Could you tell what they were shouting about?’

Her face crinkled up as she tried to conjure up fading memories. ‘No, I can’t remember,’ she said shaking her head.

'Don't worry,' Hobbs said. 'Did you hear one voice or more than one?'

Her face brightened. 'I know I only heard one voice and at the time, I thought it was strange, but my father has...he had a soft voice and it doesn't carry.' Tears welled up in her eyes.

Whoa. Hobbs didn't expect this; he needed to rein back.

A minute or two later, he tried again. 'Let's talk about the cars. You're peeping out of the curtain and you see two cars. One we know is your father's Bentley, but what about the other one? You said you saw a light-coloured saloon. Do you know anything about cars, could you tell what it was?'

'I should know this,' she said, 'I've owned plenty of cars. Let me think about it for a second.' She shut her eyes, her brow furrowing in concentration. Her eyes popped open. 'Hey, I've got it. The other car was a Subaru Impreza. I know that for sure as I used to have one myself.'

# TWENTY-FIVE

Henderson pushed open the door of the Shakespeare's Head and walked in. The friendly face of Maggie Roberts behind the bar would normally split into a wide grin whenever she saw him, but this time her jaw went slack as she stared first at him, and then at his brother Archie beside him.

'A pint is it Angus, and the same for your son?' she said, once her composure had been restored to normal.

'You're a cheeky bugger Maggie Roberts, sometimes I wonder why I drink in this place.'

'Oh, I think it's the lovely staff, or maybe it's the short, staggering distance back to your flat, but I'm not sure which is most important. So come on, aren't you going to introduce us? I know it's your brother, and apart from the hair and the obvious age difference, you're like two peas in a pod.'

'I can talk for myself Maggie,' Archie said, stepping forward and sticking out his hand. 'I'm Corporal Archie Henderson, and if you haven't guessed from the dickhead haircut and tattoos, I'm in the army.'

'Pleased to meet you Corporal,' she said. She finished pouring the drinks and placed them on the bar. 'For fighting for Queen and country and all that, these ones are on the house. Only the one mind, you can pay for the rest yourselves.'

'Thank you, dear lady,' Archie said sweeping two pints of Badger Ale off the bar and engulfing them in his big mitts. 'I'm sure we'll more than make up for your fine hospitality by coming back a few more times over the weekend.'

'How long are you staying?'

'I'm not sure yet, maybe three or four days, it all depends.'

'Well, enjoy yourself.'

'I will. Cheers and thanks again for these,' he said raising the glasses in salute as he walked away.

They had their choice of seats as it was still early evening, but Archie chose a table beside the window where he could monitor all movement in and out of the pub. He said it was a habit he'd picked up in Afghanistan, but his brother remembered him doing it long before then, so he could clock all the girls coming into and out of a bar.

The pub was in a residential part of Seven Dials and there wasn't much going on a Thursday night. The window looked out on a long row of tightly packed terraced houses running down the hill on both sides of the road, like a parade inspection of disciplined soldiers, with the occasional slow moving car as a driver searched for a place to park.

It all changed on Friday and Saturday evenings

when groups of young girls in their glad rags and tottering heels tried to make their way down to the bright lights of the city centre or to the railway station. They often had to hold on to one another for dear life, despite walking at a snail's pace, as they tried to descend the steep hill without making complete arses of themselves.

Whenever Archie came home on leave, he usually headed straight up to Glasgow where his wife and two young kids lived, and only if his flight was delayed or he had an early departure from RAF Brize Norton the following day, did he make a pit stop in Sussex.

Henderson didn't mind his kid brother turning up unannounced on his doorstep, as they had spent a lot of time together as teenagers, particularly when Archie was lead guitarist for a band called Blackheart. They were a competent four-piece covering seventies rock classics by Deep Purple, Led Zeppelin and Marillion, and toured dance halls and pubs all over the north of Scotland, while Archie's tuneless older brother acted as sound man, bodyguard and a poorly paid roadie.

'She's a nice bird, the one at the bar. You should get in there Angus, free booze and crisps, what more can a man want?'

'I can think of a few things, but Rachel will do for me.'

'How is she?'

'The same as when you met her last time, I suspect.

Although, since then, she's moved into her new flat in Hove. I think when you were last here she was still in the process of buying it.'

'I wouldn't mind a place like hers, high up above the street, looking down on everyone and with a pub on your doorstep, but I'd hate to be so close to a cricket ground. It's such a stupid game. The English guys at Camp Bastion were trying to teach me but I can't get my head around it.'

'Rachel's dad is a big fan and always comes to see his daughter whenever Sussex are playing at home.'

'There's a man who's got his priorities sorted. She's a journalist, right?'

'Aye, she is.'

'We had a crew from America shadowing us for a week and I can tell you, they drove us all right up the bloody wall with all their questions and stupid comments that sounded as if they came straight out of a training manual.'

Archie was not only the 'baby' of the family, but at thirty-seven, he looked it with fresh, pale skin and freckles, in marked contrast to the haggard and lined face that often stared back at his elder brother first thing in the morning. Archie didn't seem to be getting any older and even now, having completed his second tour of duty in Afghanistan with the dust, searing heat and freezing night-time temperatures, he still looked like an overgrown 14-year-old in a grown man's clothes.

'So what sort of operations have you been involved in, or can't you say?'

Archie tapped his nose and looked corporal-serious. 'Top secret.'

'Don't give me all that rubbish, otherwise we'll have to take everything we read in the papers as gospel.'

'Yer right, it's a running joke back at camp. See, the army's always telling us we can't be told this or that, as everything's on a 'need to know' basis, or it's top secret and not to be revealed to anyone outside the room. When, at any one time, there were hundreds of thousands of men all around the countryside with guns and planes. There's nothing much secretive about that, is there?'

'Is this your last tour?'

'Aye it is, I'm done with the desert. It's back to camp in the UK now for God-knows what.'

'I'll drink to that, cheers.'

'Cheers.' Archie took a long drink. 'My, the beer here's champion. The stuff we've been drinking out there is shite. So, what's new in the criminal catching business?'

'I'm working on a car thieving and murder case. Sir Mathew Markham. Does it ring any bells?'

'Markham, Markham...it does, but I can't place it.'

'Perhaps an old sergeant major that used to beat the crap out of you, or the electronics millionaire and owner of one of the most profitable companies in

Britain who was killed lately?'

'Nope, neither of them.'

'I forgot, you're one of those heathens who only looks at the pictures in a newspaper.'

'Cheeky bugger. I went to the same school as you.'

'Well, if it's not him, then it must be the sight of his daughter, Suki Markham, baring her all on page three in one of the tabloids, then.'

'What? Yer kidding. Are they the same people? Right on, Sexy Suki, the forces' sweetheart.'

'Forces' sweetheart? Tell me another.'

'No, straight up Angus. Her picture's up everywhere in the camp. Any time a new one comes out, everybody wants to see it.'

'What would it do to your credibility if you were to tell your mates your brother has interviewed her and sat as close to her as you and me are sitting now?'

'You have not? Ya jammy bastard.'

He nodded. 'She was staying with her father the night he was murdered. In fact, she's the only witness we've got.'

'Did she look as gorgeous as she does in the papers? I'll have to tell the lads.'

'Oh aye, she wore this low-cut top revealing a fair amount of flesh, and the shortest skirt you can imagine, more like a serviette. How she could walk about on those four-inch heels, I'll never know.'

'Bloody hell, I'm in the wrong job. Got any pictures?'

‘Sorry, but my mind was playing tricks. She looked pale, stunk of booze and a few minutes later, she threw up.’

‘Sounds more like it, you’ve never had much luck with women.’

‘What’s this? *Beat up a Brother* night?’

‘You deserve it. I better not pass the story on though, it’ll burst a few bubbles if they know the girl canny hold her drink.’

Archie started to tell him a story about one of his officers when he said, ‘Hey wait a minute Mr Detective. I’ve seen Morse, I’ve got the box set back in Glasgow, as a matter of fact.’

Henderson groaned. He knew what was coming. Hadn’t one of his own DCs said the same thing?

‘Morse says the last person to see the victim alive is always the murderer. If she was the only other person in the house when her father was killed, it means Sexy Suki is in the frame. Now there’s a story I can take back to the lads.’

Henderson took great pains to explain to his brother that they had investigated the Suki theory, but found it wanting on several counts. As far as he was concerned, she wasn’t under investigation.

‘Shoot my idea down in flames, why don’t you? I was about to tell you about this Captain Gainsborough.’

‘Before you do, let’s drink up. I need something to eat. I’m famished. We can get more beer at the restaurant.'

'Aye we'll go and do that in a minute, I'm starving too, but first there's something I need to ask you.'

'Ask away.'

'I think Mandy's been messing about while I've been overseas.'

'Get away, it can't be, not Mandy.' Loyal Mandy. The woman who had cared for him and helped him walk again after he was injured in the thigh and nearly deafened when a bomb exploded close to his armoured vehicle. Mandy loved army life and was never more proud of him than when he was promoted to Corporal.

'Aye it is. She's been seen in clubs and pubs with another bloke.'

'Who by?'

'A squaddie in my platoon, Andy Garston. He told me when he came back from leave about three weeks ago. He lives close to us in Glasgow.'

'Are you sure it's not something innocent, or has Private Garston been drinking too many pints of Eighty Shilling Ale and it's distorting his eyesight? We have trouble with witness statements all the time.'

Archie looked at him like he was an alien from another planet. 'Come off it, Angus. She's got two kids at home, why is she even going out on her own in the first place?'

Henderson was about to say something, but stopped. His brother might be younger, but some of his views belonged to a different generation. In any case, what the hell did he know about relationships, as he had been divorced and his little brother hadn't? 'I can't help you there, it's not an area I can claim any level of expertise.'

'It wasn't your fault you and Laura split up, it's the job.'

'You're one to talk, at least I come home at night. You're away for months at a time.'

'Aye, true enough.' He paused, fiddling with his near-empty glass. 'I was thinking, can you come up to Scotland with me and have a wee chat with her? She likes you. She'll listen to you.'

'I can't Archie, I'm the middle of a murder investigation, and in any case, what good would it do? She would think we were ganging up on her and before you know it, she'll be selling the furniture and moving to Manchester.'

'Yeah I know, but I think I might need some kind of moral support.'

For a moment the veil of the confident corporal fell away and the face of his little brother on his first day at secondary school stared back at him. He was about to make another lame excuse as to why he couldn't go, when his phone rang.

He looked at the screen. 'I need to take this Archie, it's work.'

'Aye, go ahead.'

'Hello.'

'Is this Detective Inspector Henderson?'

'Aye it is.'

'It sounds like you're in a pub. It's the place I should be right now if didn't pull another late shift.'

'How you doing Alex?'

The desk sergeant at John Street police station in Brighton, Alex Patterson, was a solidly built, former rugby prop. He could break up a fight with the force of his personality, and if that didn't work, by using his fists, which were the size of truck pistons; but he moaned about the rigours of the job like an old woman.

'Mustn't complain, but all this standing up is murder for my arthritis. You see...'

Henderson held the phone away from his ear and drained his beer glass.

'To what do I owe this pleasure, Alex?' he said a minute or two later.

'Ah, right you are. Earlier this evening we pulled in a violent miscreant from Whitehawk for affray.'

'It's only seven o'clock in the evening. It's a bit early for fighting.'

'Didn't I say all-day drinking would lead to this? He's in for knocking a taxi driver unconscious when he refused to take him back to the Wild East End, and as he's already out on bail for another assault. His next appearance in front of the beak is likely to be custodial.'

'Best place for him, if you ask me.'

‘The reason I called is because he says he’s got some information he would like to trade in return for a lesser charge, or as he puts it, if you excuse my French, no fucking charge at all.’

‘Don’t they all, but what’s it got to do with me?’

‘He says he knows one of the guys who’s been stealing all those expensive cars.’

# TWENTY-SIX

In an elegant Victorian building overlooking the well-manicured gardens of Montpelier Crescent in the Seven Dials district of Brighton, DI Henderson lived in a two-bedroomed flat on the top floor. Archie didn't mind the climb as he was as fit as a flea, but it exhausted his elder brother who arrived a few seconds later and out of breath.

'You need to get fitter, man,' Archie said. 'Join a gym or go out running or something.'

'I go out running,' Henderson said as he put the key in the lock and opened the door, 'but when I'm working on a big case like this one, I end up spending all my time at work.'

'If you can't get out as much, why don't you set up a home gym?'

'Now there's a good idea, but where would you and my other visitors sleep?'

'I take it from that remark I'm in the spare room again?'

'Just because you're risking life and limb over there in a far-flung section of the globe, doesn't entitle you to the best bed. Call it big brother privilege.'

'Spare bed it is. I've slept in worse, a lot worse if

I'm honest.'

He left Archie watching television with a four-pack of beer and a chicken curry they'd bought earlier, and drove to John Street. It could be a peculiar place to walk into at any time of the day, as it was the main police station for Brighton and Hove, a city of more than two hundred and fifty thousand souls, a number that could double during summer months and bank holidays.

Often in the afternoon, there would be a steady stream of visitors coming through the door with all manner of queries and complaints, and by midnight, and fortified with alcohol, it could be bedlam with much shouting, arm waving, and the occasional punch-up. Tonight, a large group of elderly tourists were surrounding the desk and blocking the way forward: the contents of a tour bus which had been in collision with a lorry. Henderson stood taller than many of the old biddies and the desk sergeant, Alex Patterson, soon spotted him and waved him over.

'Bloody mayhem in here,' he said, raising his voice above the noise. 'I was hoping for a quiet night so I could watch the Albion's match on the portable we've got in the back. It's the first time they've been on the box this year and the way they're bloody playing, it might be their last.'

'You'd be putting yourself through purgatory if the match I saw a couple of weeks back was anything to go by. Can I see the prisoner?'

‘I’ll call PC Carter, he brought him in.’

The desk sergeant was talking to Henderson over the ranting of an elderly lady with a fine mop of curly grey hair, who was demanding better treatment for her and her husband. They were law-abiding citizens, she said, and had contributed to taxes and National Insurance all their lives.

‘Madam,’ Patterson said, trying to control his temper as he picked up the phone. ‘I’ll deal with you in a minute. I know you’ve been hanging around here for ages, but I said I’ll deal with it. Now please let me make this phone call.’

Henderson stepped back and let them get on with it. He found it hard to ignore the animated conversations and the variety of expressions on display. They ranged from frantic anxiety, worried they would be forced to sleep on the floor of the police station and miss their favourite soaps on television, to the laid-back cool, whose only concern was what time the bar in the hotel closed and whether they would still be offered room service.

‘Hello there, DI Henderson?’

He turned in the direction of the voice. He saw a young face with a mop of dark brown hair and two rows of gleaming choppers that had never enjoyed the delights of filling-inducing Brighton Rock, or been on the receiving end of a kick or a punch from an aggressive drunk.

He said something that Henderson couldn’t hear

and when Carter started walking towards a set of double doors, the DI followed.

'That's better,' Carter said when the doors were closed and the noise level diminished below ear-splitting. 'What a commotion out there, I couldn't hear myself think.' He thrust out a hand. 'PC Bob Carter.'

'DI Angus Henderson. Good to meet you, PC Carter.'

They walked towards the interview rooms.

'What can you tell me about this guy you picked up?'

'His name is Thomas Harding. Have you heard the name before?'

'No, should I have?'

'The Harding family are notorious around Brighton for drinking and fighting, and the younger ones like Tom here are into drugs. They're a right bad lot and he's as bad as the rest of them with an arrest sheet as long as a snake, and he's still only twenty-six. Shall we go in?'

Sitting on the other side of the scratched table inside Interview Room Three was a heavy-set bloke with a round face and scruffy black hair, a vain attempt to hide sticking-out ears. He wore a practiced scowl, the like of which Willem Dafoe or Mark Wahlberg would do well to emulate if they wanted to receive another Oscar nomination; but to his surprise, no brief was sitting beside him.

This could only mean one of two things: either Harding wasn't a bright lad and didn't realise the mess he was in; or he was so confident of getting out, he didn't think he needed one. Based on what PC Carter had told him, it was possible Harding was a bit light in the brain cells department, but his body language exuded the confidence and cockiness of a man who knew exactly what he was doing.

'Tom,' Carter said, 'this is Detective Inspector Henderson, the Senior Investigating Officer on the car-thieving case we were talking about earlier.'

'Hello Tom,' Henderson said, 'how are you?'

'I'm pleased to see you mate, providing you can get me out of this fucking place. These bastards are saying they're gonna send me down for a five stretch.'

'Why don't you tell me what you know about the car thieving gang,' Henderson said, 'and we'll see what we can do about the charges?'

He laughed, although it sounded more like a sneer. 'Pull the other one mate. I've been here before and I know how this works. We'll play it my way. You give me what I want and I'll tell you what you want to know.'

'What are the charges against Mr Harding, PC Carter?'

'Assault and battery, possession of a knife, breaking bail conditions.'

'You knocked a taxi driver unconscious Tom,' Henderson said, 'because he wouldn't take you home, and you did it while you were out on bail for another serious assault. Possession of a knife is an automatic five-stretch in the eyes of many judges.'

Harding folded his arms and grunted. It irritated even the most hardened criminals when the crimes they were responsible for were laid out in front of them. Not that they saw them as crimes, more like mistakes that could cost them jail-time or give them big fines that could eat into their illegal gains.

'No court is going to look at this lot favourably,' Henderson continued, 'they'll take one look at you and see a violent thug who needs to be locked up.'

'Not gonna happen,' he said through gritted teeth.

'Let's assess the value of your information. First of all, let's see if we're talking about the same car-thieving gang.'

'Course it's the same fucking gang. It's the fuckers who've been stealing all the expensive motors like Ferraris and Porsches, the ones smashing the doors with sledgehammers, and beating up the people inside. Ring any bells?'

'I have to admit it does sound like the gang I'm after. What do you know about them?'

Harding shuffled in the seat. It was difficult for cons to rat on one another, but in the end, self-interest would prevail. 'I know one of the guys in the gang and the way he tells it, he's the leader.'

'What's his name?'

'Ha, good try,' he said pointing a finger at the DI.

'You can't trick me so easy, no fucking way.'

'How do you know him?'

'I live in Whitehawk, right, and he comes down to Brighton now and again to see this bird. We got talking and now he looks me up whenever he's in town.'

'He admitted to you that he nicks expensive cars?'

'Don't be a fucking idiot. We told him about the sort of things we're involved in and he told us what he does, fair trade. You never know, we might do some business together in the future.'

'Not if I've got anything to do with it, you won't. How does this car nicking operation work? What do they do with the cars they nick?'

'They used to sell 'em to this guy in Hackney for a grand a pop, but according to him, you lot closed it down.'

He went on to describe how a crash recovery firm in Holland would contact them with details of up-market write offs, recovered from motorway crashes across Central Europe, and the gang would be instructed to nick the same car. This level of detail had not been released to the media and wouldn't be until the trial, which meant Harding, probably for the first time in his short, offence-laden life, was telling the truth.

Henderson wrote all the charges against him on a piece of paper and scored out each one except 'assault,' and slid it over to PC Carter. To his surprise, as he expected more resistance, Carter put a tick against it. Clearly the young man realised the importance of the information without having it explained to him.

'PC Carter here will reduce the charges against you to one of common assault, for which you would normally receive a community sentence, but you'll have to take your chances with the magistrate about breaking the terms of your bail. There's nothing we can do for you there.'

He thought for a moment. 'Fair do's, it's a deal.'

'What's this guy's name?'

'He's one of your countrymen, in point of fact, a Glasgow fella by the name of Rab McGovern.'

Henderson thought for a moment, but it wasn't a name he recognised. While working for Strathclyde Police, he came into contact with numerous villains in Glasgow, but he had been away from the place for four years and by now, many young guns would have moved up to replace the old timers. In any case, it was a city of about a million people and with best will in the world, he couldn't know or remember them all.

'Like I said, he comes down to Brighton now and again to see this bird who lives on the Whitehawk Road.'

'When do you expect to see him again?'

'He's there now.'

# TWENTY-SEVEN

For the second time in a month, DI Henderson was preparing to go out on a raid. On this occasion, there were no armed cops and a former para leading from the front, only him, DS Walters and six heavily clobbered individuals. He would have liked to have had one or two more, but with a similar operation going on in Worthing, he was lucky to have any.

His boss, Chief Inspector Steve Harris, was jubilant when he'd called him last night and told him about Harding's confession and the fingering of Rab McGovern. However, his bonhomie did not extend to the CI showing up for the briefing at five-thirty this morning, as the man was fearful of turning forty and needed all the beauty sleep he could get.

It was a positive briefing, although there were plenty of yawns due to the early start, but the promise of a full cooked breakfast when they returned kept everything up-beat. Yet again, he had been in a quandary about using an armed response team, but in the end, as the gang had never used guns, it was decided for him. Several police forces who had deployed firearms in the past were now in the middle of investigations, high profile public enquiries, and in one instance, a court case over the death of a suspect. Even though this wasn't far from his mind when making the decision, operational considerations won out.

McGovern's piece of seaside candyfloss, Sarah Benson, lived on the top floor of a block of flats in Whitehawk Road. In terms of a raid, it looked like a good location as it limited McGovern's avenues of escape, but it had the disadvantage of providing the team with only one point of entry. At the risk of sounding choosey, Henderson preferred a house with a back and front door, as even though there were more exits, it restricted the area of activity, giving less opportunity for the inquisitive kid next door to be hit by 'collateral damage,' as Archie would call it. In the DI's world this was not an artillery shell or a bullet, but a flying bottle or a stray fist.

When first told of McGovern's name, he didn't recognise it, despite it being a common surname north of the border, it wasn't until he searched the Police National Computer that the realisation hit him. A younger Sergeant Angus Henderson had nicked him while working for the Football Intelligence Unit. McGovern had been spotted watching a football game at Parkhead, the home of Glasgow Celtic, while banned from doing so by the courts. No wonder they banned him, he was an archetypal football thug, running all the way from his Doc Martins, red braces, severe crew cut, to the large 'no surrender' tattoo covering most of one arm.

The second time he ran into McGovern was a couple of years later, when Henderson was working for the Strathclyde Drugs Squad. McGovern had become an enforcer for a well-known Glasgow drug dealer by the name of Jimmy Banks, and contrary to the rules of employment in his chosen profession, employees were banned from setting up on their own account.

It was a stupid and dangerous thing to do. Banks was nothing but a bigger and more violent version of his protégé, and thought nothing of slashing faces with open razors or sticking a stiletto blade in someone's gut, wounds in themselves that were not life threatening, but served as a permanent reminder of the person they once crossed.

The last he'd heard, McGovern was on the run from Banks after his little slice of private enterprise had been discovered. Word on the street suggested Banks was incandescent with rage at the insolence of the little rat, one he had lifted out of the gutter and earmarked for bigger things, for having the temerity to bite the hand that once fed him. He threatened that whenever he caught up with him again, he would blow off both kneecaps with a hollow nosed bullet and throw acid in his face, crippling injuries that even titanium replacements and years of plastic surgery could not hope to rectify.

The raid team parked around the corner from

Sarah Benson's flat and decamped from their vehicles. Henderson pressed the buzzer of an apartment on the ground floor, but it took an age for a grumpy old bugger with no love of the police to reach for his intercom button and open the communal door. They piled upstairs, the semblance of stealth and secrecy all but destroyed as heavy shields and body armour clanked and scraped along the walls of the narrow staircase, making more noise than an army of feral kids.

Without too much ceremony, the door banger moved into position in front of the door, and three strikes later they were inside. Three men turned right into what looked like the main bedroom while the rest swept through the other rooms as fast as the impediment of heavy clothing would allow.

Henderson walked into the bedroom and his ears were immediately assaulted by an expletive-loaded exchange between the commander of the assault team, demanding to know where McGovern was, and a young woman. She was wearing no more than a see-through negligee but red in the face and shouting something along the lines of, 'what the fuck are you fucking people doing in my fucking house?' Charming, I'm sure.

Even from a cursory glance, it didn't take the skills of a detective to deduce that two people had been sleeping in the double bed, and unless McGovern was hiding under the bed or cowering in the wardrobe, places where the team were checking now, he wasn't here.

'Sir?'

Henderson backed out into the hall, and at the door of the lounge, one of the lads was beckoning him forward.

'I think he might have scarpered through here,' he said pointing to an open patio door leading to a small balcony at the rear of the flat.

'How, we're three floors up?' Henderson said as he strode over to take a look. He was half-expecting to see a blood-splattered body lying on the ground below, but instead, caught a glimpse of a figure disappearing around the corner of the building.

It would be incongruous to call it a balcony, he had seen bigger coffee tables, with only enough room to position three or four plant pots. In any case, the view it provided over the backs of houses and rubbish strewn rear gardens was a good enough reason for the occupants to stay indoors.

'Help me up,' he said to the copper. He couldn't be sure who it was for all the protective gear hiding his face, but it looked like PC Fenwick.

Henderson stood on the balcony railings for a couple of seconds with one hand on the wall to steady himself, and leaned over to grasp the handrail of the fire escape with the other hand. He manoeuvred his right leg over to a rung, before shifting his weight towards the fire escape and then bringing over his other leg. It was a bit tricky and he wondered how a little old lady or someone with a fear of heights would manage it, but he guessed with flames licking at the bottom of their nightdresses, people were capable of doing extraordinary things.

Hoping his mind wasn't playing tricks on him when he saw the figure legging it around the base of the flats, he descended. If not, McGovern would be standing on the roof laughing his head off at the stupidity of the dozy cops.

He jumped the short distance from the ladder to the ground and ran towards Whitehawk Road. It didn't take long to spot McGovern, as there weren't many people running around in their pyjamas at six o'clock in the morning. It was a good job he didn't sleep in the buff, or at this moment Lewes Control would be inundated with many calls from alarmed residents as they opened their curtains.

His pyjamas were not the long, stripy cotton type, shame, as that would have made him look like the man he was, an escaped prisoner. It was shorts and t-shirt, 'Loungewear' as the marketing gurus at M&S called it, from a distance resembling loose-fitting running gear, but the illusion was spoiled as he wasn't wearing any shoes. Running barefoot might be de rigueur on the sun-soaked beaches of Jamaica or Hawaii, but it was plain stupidity on rain-streaked pavements in Brighton on a chilly May morning.

Henderson sprinted after him and as he did so,

pulled out his radio. ‘Suspect running south, along Whitehawk Road. All cars, all cars.’

McGovern was running past the Whitehawk Inn when he suddenly pulled up, holding his left leg as if he had just stepped on a piece of broken glass or a sharp stone. He glanced back to see Henderson running towards him, some two hundred yards behind. Realising he couldn’t outrun him now, he limped into the large building next door, the Whitehawk Bus Depot.

Henderson arrived at the entrance a minute or so later and peered inside. It was a large and gloomy cavernous place, designed to hold a couple of double-decker buses at the same time but at the moment it was empty; no buses, no passengers, no mechanics. The workers were probably taking advantage of a lull in operations to have breakfast, or perhaps they hadn’t started work yet but keeping well out of the way of the strange bloke who had run into their place wearing only his jim-jams in case he was an escaped nutter or a dopey student prank.

It was dull inside, partly the result of the weather, a cloudy morning with no sign of the sun, but also because it was a large building without many windows. The exception was the far end of the building, where light was pouring in through a second entrance, for buses to come in one way and exit the other. He jogged towards it, his head turning left and right, looking for the fugitive.

When he reached the end of the garage he walked outside, wary of McGovern hiding behind a wall, waiting for his pursuer to emerge. He wasn't there and he couldn't see him up or down Henley Road. This could only mean one thing: he was still inside the garage. Henderson turned and retraced his steps.

He walked through the centre of the building slowly, stopping to peer into dark corners behind pillars or the gloomy spaces at the side body of panels or giant tyres, his senses tuned for any extraneous noise. Suddenly, a figure appeared in his peripheral vision. He turned to see McGovern running towards him brandishing an enormous bus wrench.

Before he could get out of the way, he swung it, whacking his shoulder and knocking him to the ground. His shoulder felt on fire and he moved a hand to grip it, but when he looked up, McGovern was coming towards him, ready to take another swing.

This time, the crazy bastard raised the wrench above his head, intent on smashing the DI's brains to a pulp, but before it struck, Henderson rolled away. The noise of metal striking concrete filled the silent air, jarring the slim frame of McGovern. Henderson used the few seconds gained to get to his feet and scramble towards a rack of tools.

He ignored the club hammer, which would have been a great weapon if only he could swing it, and instead selected the claw hammer. McGovern walked towards him, the wrench swinging at his side.

‘C’mon copper,’ he said, raising his hand in a ‘come here’ gesture, ‘fancy your chances, dae ye?’

‘Give it up McGovern, you’re beat.’

‘I’m beat am I? Why don’t you try and prove it, then?’ He held the heavy wrench in two hands, a slugger heading up to the plate, and moved closer. ‘You’re gonna die here mate, because see me, I’m no’ going back to chokey, no fucking way.’

He lifted the wrench and swung it behind him, in readiness for making that final, deadly blow.

At the same time, the figure of DS Walters appeared in silhouette at the entrance to the garage. ‘Stop! Police!’ she shouted.

McGovern glanced round. Henderson leapt forward with the hammer and brought it down hard on McGovern’s hand, right at the point where he was holding the wrench, in what McGovern’s old drug dealer boss Jimmy Banks would have called a metal sandwich.

The garage resounded with an animalistic howl, a sound to scare the living daylights out of the fiercest Rottweiler, and the wrench fell to the floor with a resounding clang. McGovern bent double, clutching his injured hand, but before he could recover, Henderson punched him in the gut and shoved him to the floor. Despite much screeching about broken fingers and police brutality, there was no sympathy in evidence as he slapped on handcuffs and hauled him to his feet.

# TWENTY-EIGHT

'Well, if it isn't your good self, Rab McGovern, and what familiar surroundings you find yourself in.'

'After all this time to think about it, is that the best line you can come up wi' Henderson?'

'It's Inspector Henderson to you, sonny.'

'Fuck me, haven't we moved up in the world? When I first met you, it was Sergeant Henderson, but then everybody called you Haggis.'

'I recall our first meeting as well. Celtic were losing 2-0 I think it was, but you didn't get to see the rest of the match did you? You were in the back of a panda wagon, charged with drunk and disorderly and threatening behaviour.'

'Aye, those were the good old days. Parkhead was a fortress.' He leaned across the table and tapped his chest, 'oor fortress.'

'How's the hand?'

'You fucked up my chances of becoming a concert pianist for sure, but I'll cope.'

McGovern spent yesterday afternoon in the Royal Sussex Hospital having three broken fingers re-set, and by the look of the splint holding everything in place, the staff there had done a neat job. Henderson's shoulder didn't require hospital treatment but it throbbed, and the giant bruise it left could pass for a badly drawn map of Africa.

McGovern had changed little since Henderson last clapped eyes on the ugly sod all those years ago. Then, he was leading him through crowds in handcuffs at an international match at Hampden. It was huge policing operation, lines of mounted police standing easy but ready to wade in if needed, out to long columns of police cars and vans parked one behind the other in nearby streets.

Dressed in a denim jacket over a clean Megadeth t-shirt, the clothes were different now, but the lean, scarred face under short, brown hair still sneered and snarled as if the world owed him a living.

Despite a never-ending carousel of arrests and court appearances, it amazed Henderson why criminals like McGovern refused to spend the riches they pillaged and plundered from ones less fortunate and streetwise than themselves on decent legal representation. There were people in the legal profession who excelled at court petitioning and would search for a good angle to ameliorate their client's position, but somehow people like McGovern couldn't see it.

It put him in mind of legendary Glasgow solicitor John Millani, a criminal barrister who would have made a brilliant prosecutor but instead chose to defend gangsters, robbers and murderers. The waiting room in his office was often a better place to look for some of the city's criminals than any of the pubs in the East End.

Millani employed a gang of clerks to pore over ancient cases, legal directives, and law books looking for something to help their clients. He was at the centre of many high profile cases when the defendant walked free even before the trial opened, such as the man who had spent too much time on remand, another when there wasn't a judge available to take his trial, and yet another when an eagle-eyed clerk spotted a typographical error in the arrest warrant.

Instead, people like McGovern plumped for the lottery of the duty solicitor; in this case a studious-looking man called Jeffrey Watson, a fellow who said little and spent most of his time taking notes. Some of Henderson's colleagues preferred a weak or ineffective individual to be sitting across the table from them, but he didn't, as a skilful and combatant lawyer could spot holes and inconsistencies in their evidence, things he could make sure were fixed before the case came to trial.

'So, Rab, when we came round to your place, why did you start running? We only wanted a wee chat.'

'Well, why didn't ye knock on the door first instead of smashing the fucking thing to pieces? You bastards are always trying to fit me up.'

'That's a bit thick from a man who smashes doors down for a living, don't you think?'

'I don't know what you're talking about.'

'I'm talking about a car nicking team operating in my patch. Some say you're in this team and some say you're not only in it, but you're their leader.'

'Car nicking? You're joking, it's no' me pal.'

'Are you denying it?'

'Of course I bloody am, you've got nothing on me.'

'DS Walters can you please inform Mr McGovern about the email we received yesterday afternoon from our friends in the Met Police, while Mr McGovern was enjoying high tea in our fine Custody Suite.'

Walters picked up the paper in front of her.

'DI Speers of the Metropolitan Police is currently investigating the murder of a man called Stephen Halliday. At the moment, they have not yet named a suspect but they believe the motive for the murder might be drug related.'

Henderson was watching McGovern. His lip twitched at the mention of Halliday's name. If that didn't bother him, the next bit might.

'They were in the process of following up some promising leads when a man walked into Hackney Police Station and told them who the killer was. He said it was you, Rab McGovern.'

What happened next even Henderson couldn't have predicted. McGovern exploded in a volcanic outpouring of rage, causing Walters to slink back in her chair in alarm.

'The fuck you think you're playing at, you shower

of bastards? I didn't kill the skag bastard.'

'Sit down McGovern.'

'I bet that fucker Ehuru did it, trying to set me up. I should have done him in years ago.' On and on the ranting went. Henderson decided to leave the tape running despite only understanding about half of what he was saying, even he was having trouble with the strong Glasgow accent. It might pay to analyse the diatribe in more detail later, but at the moment it was doing his head in.

A minute or two more, and there was still no sign of an abatement and little chance they would get much out of McGovern the state he was in. Henderson called for a recess and for once McGovern's brief looked grateful.

Rather than head for the coffee machine at the end of the corridor and drink tepid river water, they walked back to the Murder Suite to make a better class of beverage in the little kitchen used by the murder team.

'Did you speak to DS Speers after he sent you the email?' Walters asked.

'I did, just before we went in to see McGovern.'

'Did he tell you anything about his informant? McGovern seems to know him. Someone he called Ehuru.'

'Speers didn't get his name. But he said he was a large black guy who looked as if he did weights or worked in a heavy manual job. Seemed to know what he was talking about. Check him out and see if he's got any form. I don't imagine there's many people on the system with the name, and I'll talk to Speers again and find out how they're getting on searching McGovern's flat.'

Henderson headed back to his office, but rather than waking up his computer only to find another flood of emails asking for money for the Police Benevolent Fund or announcing another booze-up to celebrate a retirement/new baby/promotion, he left it alone, picked up the phone and called DS Speers.

'Hello Trevor, Angus Henderson, Sussex Police.'

'Hello Angus. How's the interview with McGovern going?'

'Not well at all. He denied any involvement in the car thefts and blew a fuse when I told him you wanted to speak to him about Halliday's murder. He also denied killing Halliday, as you'd expect.'

'Well, I've got something to help loosen his tongue. We searched his flat first thing this morning and found what we think might be the murder weapon: a wooden club that looks like an old police truncheon. You know, the old type with the leather handle. Before my time, of course.'

'Mine too.'

'It looks clean but we've sent it off for analysis, and what makes me think we're on the right track is we also found a roll of money with Halliday's fingerprints on it and a black leather jacket with visible bloodspots. We managed to trace the girl McGovern had been with on the night Halliday was killed, Jasmine David, and she confirms McGovern was wearing a black leather jacket when they met.'

'I imagine this makes him your number one suspect.'

'Too right. Can you keep him in custody?'

'Shouldn't be too difficult. If I can't get anything else out of him about the cars or Halliday's murder, I'll have him for resisting arrest and attempting to murder a police officer, that should keep him banged up for the foreseeable.'

'Good. I'll use the time to finish forensics and re-analyse CCTV, now we know who we're looking for. It'll make my discussion with McGovern much more interesting.'

Henderson walked back into the Murder Suite and, after finding Walters, briefed her on his conversation with Speers.

'I got a result too about the guy McGovern mentioned, Ehuru. I think he is one Jason Ehuru.'

'What makes you think you've got the right guy?'

'This bloke lives in Clapham, a few streets away from McGovern, he's about the same age and he and McGovern were both in Wandsworth nick at the same time.'

'What was he in for?'

'Stealing cars.'

# TWENTY-NINE

The interview with Rab McGovern continued on Saturday morning. The room contained the same four players around the table as before, with the same nervous-looking cop standing guard at the door.

'While you've been enjoying our hospitality, Rab, we've been making a few enquiries. If you cast your mind back to our last meeting, I mentioned the killing of Stephen Halliday and that DI Speers of the Metropolitan Police wanted to speak to you.'

He left it hanging, waiting for another outburst, but it didn't come, so he continued.

'DI Speers has been to your flat in Clapham, giving it the once over and he's found evidence linking the murder to you.'

'I hope they didn't leave a fucking mess, the bastards.'

'I'm sure you'll have no complaints.'

'That'll be the day. But see, I've got nothing to worry about,' he said confident as a cock-sparrow, 'Jasmine will sort me out.'

'Who's Jasmine?' Walters asked.

'The bird I was with on the night Halliday was totalled. She'll tell you and that fucker Speers, I was with her all night,' he said, laying strong emphasis on the word 'all.'

'DI Speers has been trying to locate Jasmine,' Walters said, 'but so far they have been unable to find her. He thinks she's scarpered.'

Henderson remembered Speers telling him about McGovern's leather jacket and how Jasmine David confirmed he had been wearing it. So she wasn't missing. He decided to say nothing and see where Walters was taking this.

'Christ,' McGovern said, becoming agitated and bobbing up and down, wringing his hands as if he was a smack head in need of a fix. Maybe he was. 'You've gorra get me out of here, Henderson. I need to see Jasmine. She can sort this. I was with her all the time the Halliday bloke bought it, I'm telling you straight up.'

Walters leaned over the table. 'We might be able to find Jasmine for you.'

His eyes lit up. 'Would you? It would be pure dead brilliant, so it would. She'll get me oot, you'll see.'

'Now, if we do something for you, it's only right you do something for us.'

'No way, babe, I'm not doing it.'

She folded her arms. 'No car-thieving gang, no Jasmine.'

For once, McGovern's brief stepped in and whispered something into his ear. There followed a short exchange of inaudible whispers and animated facial expressions between lawyer and client, although from McGovern's mouth it sounded more like the hiss of an alley cat. On an A4 pad Henderson wrote, 'nice one' and passed it to Walters.

The huddle ceased and a grumpy looking McGovern stared back at them. 'I'll do it, but if Jasmine isnae here in the next two days, when I get out of here,' he said pointing at Walters, 'I'm coming to get you.'

'We'll have less of the threats McGovern,' Henderson said, 'you're not in a pub now.'

'It's no' a threat pal, it's a promise.'

'We'll see about that. Tell us about your team.'

Slowly, slowly as he doodled on a piece of paper, McGovern started to talk. 'There's four of us, me, Stu Cahill, Jason Ehuru and Brandon Rooney.'

At the mention of Ehuru's name, Walters gave Henderson a nudge but he'd noticed it too.

'Cahill does the telephone wires and alarms, Ehuru's the getaway driver and a bit of muscle, Rooney's great wi' cars, alarms, electronics and acts as lookout.'

'How do you target the cars?'

He huffed. The confession was hurting.

'Cahill's a bit of a smooth bastard and one night in a club, he picks up this bird who works for this big outfit called Juniper Enterprises.'

'Never heard of them. What do they do?' Henderson asked.

'Ach, they're into everything from shops tae docks and entertainment venues. But,' he said holding up a finger, 'and I knew this cause I like cars, they also own loads of car dealerships selling up-market motors.'

'I've still never heard of them.'

'That's cause there's no' a car dealer called Juniper. When they buy a dealer, the dealer keeps their original name, see? So when Stu stays over at this bird's place, he sneaks a peek at her work computer and bingo, we can get into their system anytime we like. With just a few clicks, we can find oot who's just treated themselves to a nice new motor.'

'Ingenious,' Henderson said. 'So how does this tie up with the buyer?'

He snorted. 'Piece of cake. Every now and again, the buyer gives me a list of all the cars he wants. He doesn't give a monkey's aboot the spec as long as it's the same colour and model. We look on the Juniper system and see who's bought one in this area and then we nick it. Mind, there's no' only us, there's other teams out there as well.'

Tony Haslam had told him this too but Henderson thought he was talking about a bunch of disparate, unconnected gangs and not a coordinated attempt by a 'Mr Big' to steal cars all over the country.

'Who's the buyer?'

'Hold on Henderson. Ah said I'd give you all the info about the gang and how we nick the motors, ah never said anything about the buyer. He's a bad bastard, cut up yer granny for a fiver so he would, so you're getting nothing out of me aboot him. You nicked his team up in Hackney, is that no' enough?'

Henderson shrugged. He would have that conversation later, as today's had a different purpose. 'Fair enough, but we'll find out eventually. Tell me about the robberies.'

'What can I say? We get a grand a motor and we've nicked, oh...aboot a hundred motors.'

'Bloody hell,' Walters said.

Bloody hell indeed, as he had no idea of the scale of this thing. It put the thieving in their patch of the South East into some kind of perspective. Not only would McGovern's admission clear up cases in East and West Sussex, but in about every police region within the Home Counties, with the bulk of cases being in London.

The telephone call he and DI Speers would make to their respective chief constables to clear up a large number of unsolved crimes would form the highlight of their day and give the two detectives brownie points, used to offset the inevitable slip-ups that would take place sometime in the future. It was all good stuff and Henderson felt a great weight being lifted from his shoulders, but McGovern had said not a peep about the Markham murder.

He wanted to ask, but guys like McGovern shot from the hip and would react emotionally to such an accusation. McGovern would most likely blow another fuse, ending this interview with little prospect of a re-match.

'I suppose your activities were curtailed by the garage bust in Hackney?' he said.

McGovern's eyes narrowed as he put down the large mug of milky-brown tea he was slurping. 'Put us out o' fucking business more like. Who put you lot on to it?'

'Nobody. We're capable of solving crimes without using narks. There must be other people you could work with?'

McGovern leant forward and eyeballed Henderson, his sharp, grey eyes like those of a ferret, tiny and unflinching. 'You know shag-all Henderson. Don't you realise how hard it is to set up a bloody smart operation like this? I'll tell ye matey, it takes months, no' days or weeks, bloody months.'

He was right and Henderson knew it, and his face flushed at such an obvious display of naivety. It involved a car recovery centre in Nijmegen, trained mechanics to clone a car's intimate details, and contacts at the DVLA. It was a big operation which would take time to put together, and even then, a large slice of luck would be required to make it all work.

'You couldn't just nick cars and sell them?' Walters said. 'I mean, couldn't you use the web or *AutoTrader*?'

'Nah, been there lady, got the t-shirt. You've got

them overhead gantry cameras and they can pick out a car's reg, cop cars can check the car in front of them to make sure it's insured, taxed and MOT'd, and garages have computers to tell them everything about a motor; it disnae take them two minutes to find out it's being nicked. It's a fucking mug's game, so it is, and I'd only do it again if I could have the same set-up as I've got now.'

Henderson was taken back by the implications of this. The murder of Sir Mathew had happened four days after the raid on the garage in Hackney. McGovern had to be lying when he said the closure of the Hackney garage had put them out of business, or the Markham car snatch had been carried out before they discovered they didn't have a buyer. Henderson sat back sulking. It was now or never.

'Where were you last Sunday night?'

'You taking a keen interest in my social life now, Henderson? Are you a poof by any chance?' He laughed at his own joke, as if watching a comedian at Glasgow Green rather than sitting in a CID interview room facing two possible murder charges.

'So, where were you?'

'Let me consult with my assistant here and take a gander at my busy appointments schedule,' he said, clearly enjoying himself. 'About nine, I went to The Right Place, a pub in Clapham wi' Stu Cahill. We had a few bevvies, well more like a skinful if the truth be told.'

He stopped to drink some tea. 'There was a band on, who were shite by the way, as they seemed more pissed than we were, but we stayed 'cause the banter was good and there were loads of fantastic birds around. We left the pub about one. I fancied a wee puff and Stu said he had some good gear back at his place. We went there with two birds we met, called,' he paused, snapping his fingers at the same time, 'yeah, Betsy Naylor and Debbie Thomas.

'We got there and had a good smoke and a few more bevvies.' He leaned across the table conspiratorially, his stale breath wafting towards Henderson like a bad omen. 'I would like to say I shagged young Betsy ragged and afterwards gave her a good spankin' and left her lovely arse red-raw, but I didnae. See, ah drank too much bevvy and conked out about half two. Fell asleep on the floor, we all did.'

'Maybe the gang were out nicking cars without you.' Walters said.

It was a good question as Suki Markham only reported seeing three intruders, but then McGovern had said he was with Stu Cahill in the pub, which would in fact take two gang members out of the equation.

McGovern's face darkened. 'Don't be fucking daft missus, they wouldn't dare. I tell them what tae nick and they do it. No fucking way would they do anything else without me or their lives wouldn't be worth living.'

‘Have you recently stolen a Bentley?’ Henderson asked.

‘Let me think aboot it for a sec. Recently; nope. Can’t say we did.’

‘What, is it not the sort of motor your buyer asks you to nick?’

‘I wouldn’t say that because we nicked one, oh it must have been three or four months back.’

‘You see, I was convinced you and your mates were at Sir Mathew Markham’s house in Ditching last Sunday and nicked his Bentley. Tell me I’m wrong.’

‘Oh ah get it. You’re trying to stich me up for his murder as well? I read the papers see? Two in one day, is this a record? It was done by some other crew, no’ us. We’ve never done a house in Ditchling, never been there, and I don’t know where the fuck it is.’

They carried on talking for another ten minutes but Henderson had lost heart. Even though he could see inconsistencies in the way the gang had attacked Sir Mathew Markham’s house, he’d come to this interview confident they would be clearing up the car thieving caper and Sir Mathew’s murder all in one stroke; but now his belief had all but evaporated.

He looked at Walters and she seemed to be going through the same emotional roller coaster as he was, and after a few more minutes he terminated the interview and the two detectives collected their papers. When they reached the door, McGovern, who was chewing his lip and seemed to be away in a world of his own, called him back.

'Don't forget, you find Jasmine and get her in here. She's my ticket oot o' this pigsty.'

'We'll find her, don't you worry,' Henderson said.

'Aye, fair do's, but this is no' the end of it, though. See, if she doesn't come up wi' the goods, I've got something up my sleeve, a kinda fall-back position.'

A devious smile crept across his face, making him look less human and more like a cartoon rat.

'Oh, what's that then?'

McGovern looked over at his duty solicitor but he was impassive to McGovern's little pantomime. 'I'll get him,' he said jerking a thumb at his solicitor, 'tae put up the Warrior Gene defence.'

Henderson smiled. A graduate of Glasgow University with a degree in Sociology and Psychology, he still maintained an interest in both subjects despite the passage of twenty-odd years. However, it would shame him to admit, he often didn't have the time to read the thick copy of *Psychology Today* that thumped through his letterbox every second month.

He knew what McGovern was talking about, as there had been a television programme about the Warrior Gene a few months back. At the time, it piqued his interest and so he'd dug out the relevant issue of the magazine to read and checked it out on the web.

The article and the television programme focused on a court case in America in which the prosecution in a murder case were convinced that the perpetrator would receive the death penalty as there was overwhelming evidence against him. However, the sentence was commuted to life imprisonment after a psychologist successfully argued the killer carried the monoamine oxidase A gene, or MAO-A gene.

The controversial theory behind this gene suggested there existed a direct correlation between aggressive behaviour and the presence of the gene, providing the subject had also suffered a violent childhood. It followed that it wasn't only the murderer's decision to kill, but his genes were making him more inclined to do it.

Henderson wheeled around to face him. 'You forget McGovern, I've met your mother and I know she lives in a nice house in Maryhill. Nothing you can say would ever make me believe that you've had a bad upbringing, quite the reverse in fact. If this was ever brought up in court, it would take the jury less than two minutes to realise it was you who had brought shame and humiliation on your family, and not the other way round.'

Henderson slammed the door behind him and walked back to his office in silence. His sour mood was compounded by the knowledge that it was McGovern who was battering his way into respectable people's houses and beating them up, and there was no doubt in his mind that the injuries suffered by Frankcombe, Basham and all the rest were the result of McGovern's addiction to violence.

Henderson played over in his mind key passages of the interview, but try as he may, he could not see how McGovern could be fooling him. He knew the type, poke them, prod them, shout at them and they would always react in the same way, too stupid and vain to lie. Likewise, people like him boasted about their conquests and played down their failures. No way would he nick a top of the range Bentley and not mention it.

He had to face it. What looked like an open and shut case had now spilled its guts all over the carpet. If he believed it wasn't McGovern's crew who carried out the raid in Ditchling, then they couldn't have killed Sir Mathew Markham. If wasn't them, who the hell was it?

# THIRTY

DI Henderson didn't mind Mondays as much as Bob Geldof. On this one in particular, he should have been jubilant: the car thieving gang were history, Rab McGovern was now in secure custody, and DI Speers had picked up the rest of the car nicking crew, Ehuru, Cahill, and Rooney.

There could be little doubt that McGovern murdered Stephen Halliday. Jasmine David remembered waking up in the middle of the night and noticing that McGovern was no longer in the flat. Using this information, they were able to track McGovern's movements on CCTV as he walked through Clapham to Henshaw Gardens and along to Halliday's flat, and bloodstains discovered on the policeman's baton, which they found in McGovern's flat, had now been analysed and found to belong to the victim. As promised, McGovern would be meeting Jasmine again, but he suspected she was not going to be the 'Get Out Of Jail Free' card he was expecting.

The reason for his glum disposition was despite the gang admitting their involvement in the car nicking enterprise, they could hardly do otherwise in the face of McGovern's confession, they all denied killing Sir

Mathew. This shouldn't have come as a surprise, as no one wanted a murder charge hanging over their heads, but Cahill's 'nicking' list proved the gang had never been asked to steal a Bentley around the time of Sir Mathew's death, and, as McGovern told them during the interview, the gang had never been to Ditchling.

Chief Inspector Harris was undeterred by the gang's denials and felt sure further interviews would establish their guilt, and he left Henderson to do the necessary while he prepared for a press conference to pass on the good news to the media. It was perhaps not a quirk of timing that he found a new 'cold case' on his desk this morning, his boss's way of wiping his hands of the car thefts and Markham's murder, as he believed those responsible were now in custody and it was time to move on.

The next call he made was to his brother. Archie decided on Friday that rather than stay on in Brighton for the weekend, as planned, he would go up to Glasgow and see his kids and have it out with his wife. He'd packed his kit bag and was dropped off at Brighton Station, the corporal's ears tingling with big brotherly advice.

They were both aware of several well-publicised cases of soldiers returning from duty, armed with a stolen AK47 or commando knife, and pulling it out during acrimonious exchanges, thus guaranteeing the discussion would end in tragic circumstances. Archie reassured him he was unarmed and said he had no intention of hurting her. Nevertheless, he had been counselled to take it easy and walk away if the strain was becoming too much.

'Hello Archie, how are you? How's Glasgow?'

'I'm champion Angus, how are you? Did you solve your car nicking case yet?'

Henderson went on to tell him about the arrest of McGovern and capture of the rest of the gang.

'Well, you should do the same to some people up here as they're all going nuts about the comment a Celtic player made to a journalist after a game against Aberdeen. You'd think football was the most important thing in their lives to hear them. Give me rugby or shinty any day of the week.'

'I hope for your own sake you're not sitting in a pub or standing in George Square, otherwise you might be playing jeopardy with your manhood or the shape of your face. How are Mandy and the girls?'

'They're great.'

'So, there's no strange man on the scene, then?'

'Ach no, it was all a piece of nonsense, if you ask me. The guy she's been seen with is the leader of the local youth club, a place where she helps out a couple of days a week. He's a church elder, twice her age and has been happily married for thirty years.'

'What about all this clubbing you were talking about?'

'The only club she's been in is the Labour Club with

her father, and it's hardly a den of iniquity, is it?'

'You need to have a wee word with your snitch and tell him to get his facts right before he starts bending your or anybody else's ear.'

'Aye I will, but this time I'll be armed and dangerous.'

'For Christsakes Archie don't do anything–'

'Hold your horses old man, I'm only winding you up.'

'Less of the 'old man.' I'm only a few years older than you and let me tell you, there are times when I find it hard to believe you managed to reach the age of thirty-seven unscathed.'

Henderson put the phone down a few minutes later. He was relieved that his brother hadn't gone home to a domestic car-crash, but annoyed with his so-called 'comrades' for not checking the facts, spreading such damaging rumours which Archie must have felt so powerless to do anything about so far away in Afghanistan.

Henderson dealt with the most pressing emails and phone messages and then spent a couple of hours continuing the work he'd started last week on companies interested in buying Markham Microprocessors, now keener than ever to find another motive for killing Sir Mathew. When he finished, he headed upstairs to the offices of Jamil Shirani, a DS in Fraud.

Jamil, a qualified accountant and an expert on the

dirty dealings of businesses, worked in the City of London for several years before joining the police. To some, it was a strange move as previously he was a Compliance Officer for a major US bank earning a six-figure salary. Henderson had known the young man for a few years, as he was a keen poker player and they often sat on opposite sides of the table, and had come to realise that the principles of fairness and justice were higher priorities in Jamil's book than mere money and possessions.

'I'm investigating the death of Sir Mathew Markham,' he told him when they were seated, 'and I'm thinking his death might be linked to the proposed sale of Markham Microprocessors. If so, the death of Finance Director David Young could also be linked. At the moment, I'm unsure about the motive, but maybe the reduction in share price brought about by their deaths might have been engineered by one of the buyers. What do you think?'

Jamil leaned forward, his dark eyes as impassive as they were at the poker table. His black hair was cut short and he had a well-trimmed beard and moustache. He no longer wore the five hundred pound suits he did at the bank, impractical for police work as they would be ruined after a couple of operations, but nevertheless his smart-casual clothes looked expensive.

'Nothing is out of bounds where corporate greed is concerned, Angus, and I could cite numerous takeovers that were plagued with allegations of blackmail, prostitution, bribery, drugs and of course, murder. Although I stress, murder is at the far end of the spectrum and rare, as there are so many other effective tools at their disposal.'

He tapped the keyboard on his computer before twisting the screen around for Henderson to see. 'Ever since the chairman's death, Markham's shares have fallen sharply, but in the weeks since then, they have recovered a lot of ground. However, two hundred and fifty million pounds has been wiped off the company's value and I don't know about you, but that's a lot of money to get greedy about.'

'When you put it like that, it puts post office robberies and raids on building societies into some sort of perspective.'

'Although you have to realise, the fall is likely to be temporary.'

'Why?'

'Well, the underlying principles of the business haven't changed, the fundamentals as we call them. They are still a well-run company, making great products and they have many large customers in all the main electronics centres of the globe. If there is a takeover, the new management team will need time to find their feet but when they do, they will start to woo the City with their expansion plans and profit forecasts and soon the shares will return to near enough their old level, and this particular window of opportunity will be closed.'

'That's fine,' Henderson said, getting animated now as his promising theory was beginning to make sense and standing up to Jamil's financial scrutiny. 'Maybe whoever is doing this wants to buy the company now. They'll get the benefit later, when the share price recovers.'

Jamil nodded. 'Yes, then you will see one of the great business deceptions rear its greedy head. You see, the incentive pay of senior managers is usually based on an increasing share price. So in the scenario I have outlined, they would earn fat bonuses when the share price recovers, and as we now know, they didn't do much to earn it at all.'

'Deception? It's more like daylight robbery.'

'Ha, right. Now you've come up with one motive, the falling share price, have you thought of any others?'

Henderson shook his head. 'I can't think of anything else.'

'You see, one thing you could say about this killer, if there is a single killer, he has targeted the company carefully. He has killed an old man who no longer works there, and a Financial Director with good contacts in the City and with a pretty high standing but I would argue, two replaceable men and not key players in the company's future strategy.'

'How so?'

'Markham is a specialist technology business and

what they need to drive it forward is brilliant techies making great products, and business people who can interpret such knowledge, keep them happy, and sell the products to all the large electronic companies.

'The key people at Markham,' he continued 'are Managing Director William Lawton, who is also a great salesman, and the microprocessor design team who continue to produce highly saleable products, headed up by Marta Stevenson. Marta and her senior designer, Sanjay Singh, have been responsible for developing and improving the system software which has been inside every major Markham microprocessor chip for the last twenty years. It's not too grandiose to say they are the technology equivalent of Lennon and McCartney.'

'Yeah, but can they sing?'

Jamil laughed, flashing uneven white teeth with a gap in the middle.

'I think I see what you're getting at,' Henderson said. 'If the motive of the killer is something other than a drop in share price, the murders of Markham and Young might be in revenge for something, or to remove an obstacle to progress, and if they don't get what they want, the killings we've seen so far are only for starters?'

He nodded. 'It's only a theory Angus, but in my twisted way of thinking like a copper and not like an accountant, I think he doesn't want to kill the victim yet but make him suffer. Your job is to find out why.'

# THIRTY-ONE

Henderson stood up and stretched. He gathered up a pile of papers from his desk and walked along the corridor to the Murder Suite.

It was a large, open-plan area that could be sub-divided to provide a flexible working space for major investigations. It had the added advantage of moving officers from their normal place of work into an area where they would live and breathe the investigation, free from the distractions of daily duties. However, as a place to conduct a review meeting, it lacked the formality of a small meeting room because officers swung idly on chairs, fiddled with staplers or nudged one another with sly asides, leaving him with the impression they weren't listening.

In fact, chairs were at a premium. Every detective out in the field made a point of returning to base when word got round of McGovern's confession and the gang's subsequent arrest. For some, it was the end of the school term all over again, illustrated by shirts hanging out of trousers, slouched bodies on chairs, and more smiles and a happier atmosphere than could be found at the Comedy Club. Rather than start the meeting with a roundup from each of the team leaders as he often did, there was no need today, and instead he talked them through the interview with McGovern.

His words brought gasps of relief and release from members of many small teams tasked with calling car dealers, customs officers and other police forces as they realised their jobs were finished; and dignified smiles of satisfaction from Scenes of Crime Officers and the Family Liaison Officer at yet another job well done. He knew the feeling well, but it was also tinged with a pang of regret for some when they recognised that the job on which they had spent the last few days, or even weeks, had been for nothing. The luck of the draw had given them a dead end to drive into.

It made a pleasant change to see all the happy faces instead of the glum frowns that had often dogged this investigation, as everyone was glad to see the back of a gang of savage car thieves who had terrorised the county for so long. For a few minutes Henderson said nothing as mutual backslapping spread around the room with the alacrity of a box of chocolates on someone's birthday.

'Now,' he said trying to restore order, 'for the car-thieving teams your investigation work is complete and I would like to thank you all for your efforts, so go out tonight and enjoy the celebration.'

He nodded towards DC Baldwin, a happy go-lucky lad who was often first to the bar. 'Kenny, see me after this briefing and I'll give you some money to start you off tonight, as I won't be there to celebrate with you and to pick up the tab.'

A cacophony of riotous noise burst out and only calmed when he held up his hand. 'Now for the bad news. I'm going to be an old nag and ask you all to ensure your interviews, notes and everything else are fully documented and your files are complete and up-to-date, ready to hand over to the CPS and begin court proceedings.

'This disbanding directive, however,' Henderson continued, 'does not apply to the murder team under the direction of DI Hobbs, as you guys are still working on this investigation.'

'What?'

'Why?'

'Bloody hell, what's going on?'

'The widely held belief of the media, Chief Inspector Harris, and many in this room, including at one time myself,' Henderson said, 'was that if we caught the car thieves, we would also catch Sir Mathew's killer. I have heard nothing from McGovern and DI Speers has heard nothing from the rest of the gang that leads us to believe McGovern's crew carried out the raid on Stavely House.'

One item at a time, he went through his reasons, but to his astonishment, few agreed with his analysis.

'The gang have been escalating their violence for some time and almost with every raid,' DC Stone said. 'It was inevitable they would kill somebody in the end.'

'I agree,' someone said from the back.

'Look what they did to Grant Basham,' Phil Bentley said, 'they gave him a serious beating and nearly killed him. He's still in a coma.'

'You see sir,' DS Harry Wallop said, 'one minute we're celebrating the capture of a gang we know for sure nicked fifteen cars in our neck of the woods and put several innocent people in hospital, now you're telling us it was someone else who did in poor Mr Markham. If you're suggesting we have a copycat gang on our hands, well I just don't see it.'

There were many shouts of agreement and Henderson knew, in part, this was caused by the number of new additions to the investigation team, brought in to investigate the murder who weren't so knowledgeable about the gang's methods. However, it was those who had been with him since the start that he was most disappointed with.

'Enough of all your moans and groans,' Henderson said, 'let's get on with finding the real culprits. I'm handing out to the murder team details of eleven companies who have shown an interest in buying Markham Microprocessors.'

'What for?' DC Bentley asked.

'I'm convinced the deaths of Mathew Markham and David Young are connected and were committed by someone with a grudge against the company, to remove a barrier from someone's way or to reduce the share price, giving the people who want to buy it a cheaper price. I think the answer lies with one of these eleven companies and I want you people to find out who it is.'

'How do we do it with this?' DC Bentley asked, looking blankly at the paper in his hands.

'What you all need to do is make an appointment to see a senior director. The Managing Director would be my preference, but the Financial Director or Commercial Director should do. Find out what interest they have in acquiring Markham Microprocessors and how badly they want it.'

There was screech from the back of the room.

'What's going on over there?' Henderson said.

'I've been given California sir,' DC Mat Thomas, the youngest member of the team said. 'I've never been to California.'

'You're still not going, Mat. What I want you and the other officers with foreign companies to do is conduct desk research. Look at their websites, business news sites and social networking sites to determine how well Markham fits into their future plans, and then give them a call or send them an email to get their take.'

The more experienced members of the team who had been given a trip within the UK kept quiet, knowing they would get a break away from the office for a day or two on what, on the face of it, looked to be a routine task.

'Remember,' he said, 'you're only interested in the

MD or one of the main board directors. It's unlikely a junior officer or even a major shareholder would be involved in this. It has to be someone who would receive some benefit from killing Markham and Young, so it's more likely to be the Managing Director or the owner of the business.

'I don't imagine this stage of the investigation will move too quickly,' Henderson continued, 'as many of these senior people will be hard to tie-down, but keep pressing and remind them this is a murder investigation and not a visit from the Monopolies Commission.'

'It's not likely that when we talk to them,' DS Harry Wallop said, 'they're going to admit to killing Sir Mathew, is it?'

'You're right Harry, but this is where your detective nous comes in. You'll either get the impression they are desperate to buy it and will stop at nothing until they do, in which case we'll investigate them further, or they might tell you about another interested company whose methods they regard as underhand.'

He concluded the meeting and returned to his office, subdued by this new change in direction. Like Harry Wallop, he did not believe the MD in one of the companies they visited would suddenly admit to murdering Sir Mathew, so this was effectively a first pass. The next stage of the investigation would take longer, but he was not sure he would be allowed to see it through, as the patience of CI Harris, the Chief

Constable, and the press was wearing thin. To head this off, he decided not to tell his boss and hoped by the time he was forced to confront him, he could prove motive.

He woke up his dozing computer and noticed an email from DI Speer.

*Hi Angus,*
*When we spoke earlier today, I said my guys were checking the alibis of McGovern, Ehuru, Cahill and Rooney for the night Sir Mathew Markham was killed. I've got some feedback for you.*
*McGovern & Cahill - Betsy Naylor and Debbie Thomas confirm going to Cahill's flat with Cahill and McGovern and neither men left the flat during this time. All were asleep before Ms Thomas at 4am. CCTV analysis proved no one left the flat until morning.*
*Ehuru - A bouncer at the JayCee club in Croydon. He worked there until 3am and received a lift home from fellow bouncer Ross Wilder at 3:30am. Wife confirmed he didn't go back out.*
*Rooney – Lives at home with a large family. Brought home drunk at 11:30pm by a local taxi firm. Taxi driver confirmed. His mother says he went straight to bed and didn't get up until the following afternoon.*
*I hope it helps,*
*Trevor.*

# THIRTY-TWO

For the third time in a week, Suki Markham woke without a hangover. It had been four weeks since her father's death. Without doubt she had been shaken by it, but even before, she was becoming bored with her hedonistic lifestyle. It wasn't only the drinking and the late nights, but the strange 'friends' who hung around her apartment in Earl's Court and the bizarre drugs slipped into her hand when so off her face she had no idea what she was putting in her mouth.

Jackson, who'd been staying with friends in Covent Garden the previous night, arrived at eleven.

'Hi Sis,' he said as he breezed in.

She closed the door and followed him into the kitchen.

'So what's with the new clothes?' she said. 'Jeans and t-shirt too good for you now?'

The long, untidy hair had been cut and the two-day stubble, a testament to laziness and not a desire to look sexy, was gone, leaving him looking younger and leaner than the average 24-year-old.

'Ha,' he said as he filled the coffee machine and switched it on. 'The jeans I wore to work were worth more than this lot put together, but I thought it was time to smarten up. You know, become a bit more responsible now I'm to care for Dad's legacy. I see the bug is catching on.'

She executed a little twirl to show off her new, toned-down look. Short skirts, boob tubes, see-through blouses, lacy stockings and all the rest would find a good home in the local charity shop, she was finished with it all and looking forward to a brighter future which didn't include any baggage from the past.

The electronic box close to Suki's ear buzzed.

'That will be William. Jackson, go check the living room's tidy will you? I'll let him in.'

The last time she saw William Lawton was at her father's funeral when he read a moving eulogy, summarising her father's business achievements from the start-up of the business through to the present day, before reading tributes received from many well-known business leaders and television personalities.

'Hello William.'

'Hello Suki,' he said leaning over and giving her a kiss and a warm hug. 'How are you bearing up?'

'I'm fine.'

She followed him into the living room where he strode forward to greet Jackson. 'Hello Jackson,' he said offering his hand.

It was Tuesday, a business day, and it was no surprise to see Lawton dressed in an Armani suit and pressing the flesh with his trademark smile, as if meeting contacts at an Atlanta business conference. The meeting had been requested by Lawton, pre-empting them doing the same thing, although his hasty timing left her a little annoyed. She had never worked in a commercial business and never had any money worries, so she couldn't understand the unseemly rush, but Jackson assured her it was normal. Lawton would be worried about his position and the effect the continuing uncertainty might be having on customers and suppliers.

They sat around the dining table, positioned beside large bay windows overlooking Bramham Gardens a place where Suki would often sit and read.

'As you know, Suki,' their visitor said, 'Mathew had been trying to sell the company before he died. At the last count fifteen companies have shown an interest, and I'm sure the number would be higher if he had framed the sale differently and publicised it better, but that's the way he wanted to play it.'

'He always kept Jackson and me informed.'

'Good. Whilst it would be an exaggeration to say this tragedy has affected our day-to-day operations, because it hasn't, as Mathew retired from an active position over a year ago, it has left a cloud hanging over Markham House, and it will not move until a decision over the ownership is made. Every day I seem to be fielding more and more questions from journalists and lawyers acting for potential buyers and, in their own officious way, demanding to know what is happening.'

His focus was on her, ignoring Jackson who sat silently and unperturbed to be a software engineer in the same meeting as his Managing Director.

'What I want to know is, firstly, the contents of the will and secondly, what you intend to do. I would imagine Mathew has left most of his shares to you, Suki, but did he leave them in trust or did he put some qualification on how they were to be used?'

Suki had known William Lawton for over twenty years, and with an intuition inherited from her mother, could read him like a book. He was greedy and self-serving, and while he may have liked her father at one time, latterly they did not get on and he appeared to be milking their relationship for all it was worth. He couldn't care less about the succession or whatever he was calling it, he only cared about William Lawton and the empty shell of a bitch that he called his wife.

'The will was read on Saturday,' Suki said. 'Mum received the house in Ditchling and two million pounds in cash and shares.'

Lawton's mouth fell open. 'Fantastic. She deserves it. I hope she retires somewhere warm to enjoy it.'

'Olivia received more or less what she put into the marriage, which wasn't much, and as you can imagine she isn't happy with the end result. She's threatening to sue but the lawyers say it'll be a waste of time.'

'Good.'

‘Hamish was left a large sum which will be placed in a trust to provide him with a lifetime income. Only time will tell if it makes the slightest difference, but I don’t think the business needs to recruit a new packer in Burgess Hill just yet.’

Lawton said nothing, his mounting anticipation palpable.

‘My father’s shareholding in Markham Microprocessors...’

‘Yes?’ he said, a little too eagerly.

‘He left it to me–’

‘My God, it’s happened. What was Mathew thinking? I thought he would set up a trust or something, I mean,’ his face creased in a wan smile, ‘what do you know about running a high-tech business, Suki?’ He stood up and paced the room. The glasses were pulled off as he emphasised a point, a characteristic developed to make him look more intelligent.

‘What do you intend to do about the sale, Suki? There are people, important people, waiting in the wings, expecting to be allowed to bid for the company. Some will be more than a little annoyed if the process is held up or halted.’ He spun round and stared at her, his glasses gripped tightly in his hand. ‘The sale will still go ahead, I assume?’

‘This little charade has gone on long enough,’ Jackson said.

‘Don’t interfere, Jackson,’ Lawton said as he retook

his seat. 'This is a discussion between Suki and myself.'

'What, don't interfere you lowly software engineer?'

'I mean this is between Suki and myself, so please allow us get on with our conversation.'

'You didn't let her finish. What Suki was about to say was my father's shares were left to Suki *and to me*, an even split. As you know, William, Suki has no interest in running the company on a day-to-day basis. All the voting powers of her shares will be passed to me.'

'So, what...you're the new owner? I can't get my head around all this.' Lawton's face was a jumble of emotions and it took a few seconds before he spoke again. 'Well, well congratulations are in order Jackson. Good luck to you.'

'Thank you.'

'So what are you planning to do? Are you going to carry on doing your current job?'

He shook his head. 'The first thing I'm going to do is stop the sale.'

'What? You can't do this.'

'Why not? You said it yourself, I'm the new owner, I can do what I like. It was never really a sale in any case, more an expression of interest.'

'There are people, many influential and powerful people, who believe they are in with a chance of buying a great British company. They will be extremely disappointed not to be given the opportunity to bid. There will be repercussions and some might seek redress in the courts. Others might–'

'Let them. Perhaps I should explain. You see, a part of my father wanted to sell, cash in his chips and wander off into the sunset, but there was another part of him who believed he had put so much of himself into the business he could never walk away. Hence he couldn't put it up for sale. What he was looking for was for another company to come along and take care of his baby, as well as he would.'

'He wanted to sell, I'm sure he did.'

'We could argue about the merits of a sale all day long, but as far as I'm concerned it's not going to happen. But more importantly, another part of him distrusted his Managing Director, but he couldn't persuade his children how a man who'd played them at football and tennis, let them beat him at cards, and competed as a robot on the Xbox, could in any way be crooked.'

'What are you saying, Jackson? I'm not crooked. This is scandalous.'

'So,' Jackson continued, 'he concocted the Korean bid to smoke you out, William, to show us non-believers you had no more loyalty to the Markham cause than a journeyman footballer seeking out the highest wages in the Premiership.'

'Concocted the Korean bid? I don't believe what I'm hearing, but it's a damned lie to say I have no loyalty. I would do anything for Mathew, for the business. You know I would.'

'The merest whiff of the Korean offer and you rushed out to put together a consortium to acquire the company, a consortium loaded with a couple of asset strippers and several well-known criminals.'

'You can't go around sounding off about respectable businessmen like this. You just can't.'

'But there's more. I mean there's the small matter of the scam David Young was pulling.'

'What? Yes, David, you're right. The police have started an investigation, I understand. He was fiddling invoices right, left, and centre. Pocketed over eight million they said.'

'Father knew about it months ago.'

'What? How?'

'Tania Jamieson.'

'Who?'

'Your Accounts Payable Assistant; the tall lady with the strawberry-blonde hair. She called father at home when all her attempts to bring this serious matter to your attention were ignored.'

'I'm a very busy man.'

'Too busy to investigate a major fraud? I don't think so. You didn't investigate it because,' he said pointing a finger at Lawton's chest, 'it was you who was behind it. You set it up and it was you, not David Young, who benefitted from the proceeds.'

'That's an outrageous accusation. Don't you know

who you are talking to Jackson? I've known you all your life. I would never steal from the business, I wouldn't. I understand incriminating papers were found in David Young's house, how could it have anything to do with me?'

'The documents found at Young's house were not there because he was stealing from the company, they were there because he was investigating a theft, a theft initiated and perpetuated by you.'

Lawton's face turned hard. 'You can't prove any of this.'

'I admit you've covered your tracks up well, using a bogus company and moving the money to Switzerland, but I'm sure when the police are finished, they'll come to much the same conclusion as we have and come looking for you. If this isn't enough, I wouldn't be at all surprised if they don't reopen the case surrounding David Young's death. Maybe it wasn't an accident, after all.'

# THIRTY-THREE

'Now, this is what I call impressive,' Walters said, as she stepped from the car and stood admiring the house from the top of a long gravel driveway.

'I reckon the gardener's house at the entrance is twice the size of my flat. I'm in the wrong job,' Henderson said.

'You never know, solve this case and you might get promoted.'

'I still couldn't afford the gardener's house.'

The chemical tycoon, Danislav Shalberov operated his worldwide business empire from a large country estate in Surrey. The word 'mansion' was a term often overused to describe apartment blocks in smart districts of London, the pads of Essex gangsters and many new housing developments in the Home Counties. The term 'chateau,' was used in much the same way by the French and conjured up large, dreamy spires in the Loire, but in fact it could apply to any building with a vineyard, no matter how small, ugly, or insignificant. However, neither expression could quite capture the size and stature of this place.

To the ignorant at map-reading or those befuddled by a complicated sat-nav system who came upon this place by chance, it could easily be mistaken for an up-market conference centre, rehabilitation clinic for the boozy wealthy, or a luxury five star hotel, as it looked far too large and opulent for one man, his wife and seven-year-old child.

It was one of the most expensive family houses in the south-east and boasted every extravagance a billionaire could desire, including a twenty-five metre swimming pool and spa complex, heated driveway, and a purpose-built, temperature-controlled wine cellar with room enough to store fifty-thousand bottles and enough space to have a party inside and drink some of them.

They approached the door and before Henderson's finger reached the bell, a formally attired footman, no doubt alerted to their presence by the security man at the gate, opened it. They were shown into a bright and lightly decorated sitting room with a grand piano at one end and two floral-patterned settees at the other, arranged either side of an intricately-patterned marble fireplace. The walls were painted a light yellow colour, and in combination with high ceilings and enormous windows at both ends, the room had a warm, airy feel, even if the weather outside suggested something different.

Danislav Shalberov owned several chemical plants, petrochemical installations, oil terminals and a fleet of tankers spread around the globe. They operated through a variety of holding companies based in

Lichtenstein or Liberia, but no matter how complicated these arrangements might be in the eyes of the law or tax experts, they were all ultimately owned by the Kirov Chemical Company located somewhere in this building.

He had a reputation as a no-nonsense tyrant who rewarded employees with high salaries and generous perks but he had no patience with fools or for incompetence. He thought nothing of firing anyone if they fell short of his high standards, and if they were Russian, sending them back there.

An article in one of the Sunday supplements portrayed the Russian as peripatetic, jetting around the financial and oil capitals of the world signing deals or sailing to meetings aboard his large, ocean-going yacht. This made Henderson wonder what sort of man they would be meeting, as he lived a life of unbelievable luxury, matching the moguls of ancient India or Middle Eastern oil sheiks, staying in five-star hotels, eating in Michelin-starred restaurants and acquiring whatever took his fancy. This included a five million dollar diamond necklace for his second wife, the international model and size zero stick insect, Heidi Boniface. It wouldn't take long to find out, as Shalberov had just walked into the room.

'Good morning Detective Inspector Henderson, Detective Sergeant Walters. Welcome to Grantwood, my home and the centre of my worldwide business interests.'

He spoke in crisp Oxford English with no trace of his Moscow origins. Wearing a light grey suit with a tailored blue shirt and no tie, he looked younger than his picture and younger than his reported thirty-eight years. His handshake felt firm, his presence confident, and his gaze was steady and inquisitive, qualities Henderson would have attributed to an older, more seasoned negotiator and businessman.

'Thank you for seeing us at such short notice, Mr Shalberov,' Henderson said.

'I'm happy to do what I can to help.'

Following a quiet knock on the door, a young girl walked into the room and placed a silver tray containing a coffee pot and three cups. She poured the coffee and without uttering a word, left and closed the door behind her with a soft click.

'So, Inspector, my secretary tells me you are interested in the sale of Markham Microprocessors and our proposal to buy it.'

'Yes we are. Following the murder of Sir Mathew Markham, we are interviewing everyone who knew him in an attempt to build up a picture of the man and to determine if the sale of the business had anything to do with his death.'

'This is very interesting, as newspapers are saying he was attacked by a gang of carjackers who I believe are now in jail. We have them in Russia also. They follow people when they go into smart shops and attack them when they reach their car, weighed down with many shopping bags. They can be violent too and have been known to kill the car owner if they do not hand over the keys. You obviously do not believe these people are responsible for killing Sir Mathew or you would not be talking to me.'

'In my experience, newspapers often jump to conclusions before the facts are fully laid out, I'm afraid,' Henderson said. 'Let's just say there are differences between the attack on Sir Mathew and the way the carjackers have operated in the past, and these concern me. Can I ask, what is your interest in buying Markham Microprocessors? Much of your business is in larger, heavier forms of engineering and as far as I know, Markham currently doesn't do any business with your company.'

'I see you have done your homework Inspector, highly commendable. I first met Sir Mathew at an Institute of Bankers dinner at which the Chancellor of the Exchequer, Mr Stanley, gave a rousing speech when he told us what a fine place the United Kingdom is to do business in, which I believe it is. I offered Sir Mathew an open invitation to come here to my home for a meal and a few weeks later, he came to lunch. It was then he told me all about his plans to retire and perhaps to sell the business and I must say, I liked what I heard.'

'Did you know him well?'

'I met him only twice but I have talked to him several times on the telephone and so I would say we were friendly, but not so close. The last time I spoke to him was some two weeks before he was killed. His death saddened me, he was such a fine man.'

'How would Markham Microprocessors fit into your business plans?'

'It is perhaps not so well known in the west, but I do have some interests in the electronics industry. I own component manufacturers and we supply two of the major mobile telephone companies in Russia. At the moment, none of them use Markham chips, but I see this as a big opportunity for us to make the leap into creating our own brand of smartphone. Markham is a wonderful company and not only do I want to own it, but I want to keep it out of the hands of the Japanese and the Koreans.'

'Oh really? Any particular reason?'

His face hardened. 'I hate those little yellow bastards and their dog-eating friends, the Koreans.' He then launched into a long tirade about the spread of the yellow peril from the East, the atrocities committed in the Russo-Japanese war of 1905 in which his great-grandfather and many of his family were killed, Japan's dominance of the modern electronics business and some other stuff Henderson didn't understand about finance.

It lasted a full ten minutes, but although the words were coarse and bitter, they were delivered in a crisp, articulate style.

'How important is taking over Markham to your

on-going business strategy?'

He leaned towards Henderson. 'When I want something, I am willing to pay whatever it takes. If by some miracle I do not acquire Markham Microprocessors, my acquisitions team and the head of the unit, Dmitri Usilev, will all be sent back to Russia and they will never be seen or heard of again.'

# THIRTY-FOUR

'It sounds like a threat to kill in my book,' DS Gerry Hobbs said. 'Mind you, if Shalberov does carry it out, we won't find Usilev's body lying around here so it won't be our mess to clear up.'

The senior officers in the Sir Mathew Markham murder team were sitting around Henderson's small meeting table, Hobbs, Walters and Henderson, reviewing the completed company interviews and a mass of information gathered by the web-based research team.

They had been at it for over an hour and Henderson was coming to the conclusion it had all been a waste of time. Even though many of the reports included sound examples of greed, arrogance and vanity, they found nothing to suggest any of the Markham bidders would stoop to murder.

'Well, as we haven't got an obvious candidate,' Hobbs said, 'we should make a list of the ones who strike us as being the most suspicious and spend more time following them up.'

Hobbs looked at each of their faces but found little enthusiasm. 'I'll make a start. I think Shalberov deserves to be there.'

'Why?' Walters said. 'He's just an aggressive businessman. There are half a dozen people like him in this pile.'

'True,' he said, 'but he's known to be a serial sacker of staff, and even though there may be no substance to the threat he made about murdering Dmitri Usilev and his acquisitions team for their failings, rumours have dogged the guy for years.'

'Such as?' she said, her expression sceptical.

'Well, when he first acquired his vast collection of former state assets after the break-up of the Soviet Union, he did it in collaboration with a business partner, called,' he looked at his papers, 'Christov Futerov. He put up the finance but no sooner was the ink dry on the deal than Futerov died in a water-skiing accident. This placed Shalberov in total control of all the businesses and, as you saw boss, he's never looked back.'

'Yeah but–' Walters said,

'There's more,' Hobbs interrupted. 'It says here in this newspaper report one of his mineral crushing plants in Kirov was dogged by strikes, and closed for the third time in a month by workers led by a militant socialist called Vladimir Lukyanov. While out drinking in a bar in Kirov Oblast, Mr Lukyanov was set upon by a group of men and kicked to death. Ever since then, the plant has been strike-free.'

'I'm convinced,' Walters said. 'Put him on the pile.'

'I would also add to the list,' Walters said, 'the guy

Phil Bentley and Sally Graham met in Manchester, Liam Fletcher, the Managing Director of Fletcher Electronics. His background is dodgy and there are strong rumours the money he needed to start his business came from dealing in drugs.'

'He sounds a nice fella,' Hobbs said.

'He built up the small electrical business his father used to own into one of the largest component manufacturers in the North West by lavishly entertaining corporate buyers. They moved into the big league after a couple of aggressive takeovers, including one in Newcastle when the MD who was the founder of the company and reluctant to sell, drowned in a river near his home.'

'He sounds suspicious, put him on the list,' Hobbs said.

'Any more?' Henderson asked. 'No takers? Well I would like to suggest one.'

'Who?' Hobbs said.

'William Lawton.'

'Come off it sir,' Walters said, 'he was big pals with Mathew Markham and the whole family.'

'Yeah, he's known Suki all her life,' Hobbs said.

'There are two reasons. One is this *Financial Times* report, dug up by Seb Young.' He held it up for them to see. 'It says Lawton has been putting together a consortium to buy Markham Microprocessors on the quiet because he felt sure Sir Mathew was going to sell it behind his back.'

‘I never knew about this,’ Hobbs said.

‘There’s more. One of the members of his consortium is none other than our good friend, Dominic Green.’

‘What Green? Unbelievable.’

‘You’re kidding,’ Walters said. ‘Dominic Green? ‘What the hell does he want with an electronics company?’

Green had been ‘Public Enemy Number One’ in the Sussex region long before Henderson moved there. Everyone in the building knew how the one-time slum landlord and owner of squalid bed-sits and DSS hostels became a multi-millionaire and rebuilt his public persona into a generous benefactor and friend to the rich and famous. In business, he was a shark swimming in a pool of goldfish, treating tenants, landowners, squatters, protestors and anyone else who got in his way with the same contempt and disrespect for their legal rights as any feudal landlord would have done in the Middle Ages.

‘None of his businesses are connected with the electronics industry,’ Hobbs said, ‘and as far as I know, none are even what you might call high-tech.’

‘It might be possible,’ Walters said, ‘that Lawton knows exactly what he’s capable of, and is using him to intimidate anyone who gets in his way.’

‘Let’s take it a stage further,’ Henderson said. ‘When the dust settles on the will and the inheritance and all the other stuff, Lawton could well be the main beneficiary. If Suki takes over, he'll still be Managing Director. If his consortium buys it, they would keep him on as MD but he would also own a slice of the company as well.'

The door to Henderson's office burst open.

'Good afternoon everyone,' Chief Inspector Harris said.

'Good afternoon sir,' echoed those seated.

Across one arm he held a coat and his face looked flushed, as if it was cold outside or he was angry. 'I would like to speak to Detective Inspector Henderson, in private if I may.'

'Leave your stuff here,' Henderson said over the noise of scraping chairs, 'we'll continue later.'

When the door closed, Harris turned to face the DI who was standing, leaning against the small meeting table.

'Angus, what the hell's going on?' Harris said.

'In respect to what exactly, sir?'

'I'm talking about the wild goose chase you've sent the murder team on. That's what.'

'Wild goose chase? I don't think so sir. We're investigating a murder and trying establish motive for the killing of Mathew Markham.'

'Don't give me this bloody crap. Sir Mathew's murder has been investigated and McGovern and his team are in the frame. So where's your problem?'

'They didn't do it, sir. Their alibis are sound. I sent you the email I received from DI Speers. He agrees with me.'

'Alibis my arse. It's a put-up job by their mates, that's what it is. It's a classic case of nobbling the witnesses, and given time, you and Speers will unpick their stories. This is what you should have been spending your time on, not running off to London and bloody Cambridge talking to businessmen.'

'I don't see it like that. We can't build a murder case against McGovern.'

'Now listen to me, Inspector,' he said, poking a finger at Henderson's chest. 'I will relieve you of your command if you persist with this nonsense. You've wasted enough time and resources already. I want you to charge Rab McGovern with Sir Mathew Markham's murder and let the CPS loose on the evil bastard. The media will love it and you'll be a hero. Disband the team at once, allocate them to other duties, and I'll forget we ever had this conversation. If you don't, I'll have your badge and you'll be lucky to score a security guard's job at Sainsbury's.'

# THIRTY-FIVE

'Good afternoon Detective Inspector,' the receptionist said, smiling. 'Back again so soon? Excuse me, where are you going?'

'William Lawton's office,' Henderson said, running up the stairs. 'Don't worry I know the way. Open the upper door if you please.'

Henderson didn't hear the next thing she said but he was sure she would be lifting the phone to call Lawton. He heard a click as the security door opened and without pausing, he walked past a startled Jules, opened Lawton's office door, and strode in.

Lawton was talking on the phone while a tall, well-dressed man sat in the visitor's chair at the side of his desk. Henderson paused a moment to take in the scene as Jules rushed into the office and pushed by.

Henderson moved to the desk, intending to put an end to Lawton's call or wrap the cord around his neck when he heard him say, 'got to go,' and put the phone down.

Henderson placed both hands on the desk, leaned over and eyeballed him, his face cold and angry. 'I need to see you now, Lawton.'

'I'm sorry Mr Lawton,' Jules said, resplendent in a

bright pink sweater and patterned yellow and blue spotted shirt. 'He just pushed past me, there was nothing I could do to stop him.'

'It's ok Jules,' Lawton said, 'I'll handle this. Go back to your desk.' He turned to his visitor. 'Mason, I'm sorry for this little...interruption. Could I ask you to step outside for five or ten minutes? Jules will look after you.'

'No problem, William,' he said in a Texan drawl. 'I need a comfort break, in any case.' He looked at Henderson. 'You sure you're gonna be ok?'

'There's nothing to worry about, Mason. Mr Henderson is a policeman.'

'Where I come from,' he said, raising his sizeable bulk from the chair, 'these are the very people you need to worry about.'

He walked to the door and closed it with a bang.

Henderson turned to Lawton. 'You slimy toad, Lawton, you've been keeping something from me,' he growled.

'What...what do you mean?'

'I mean, Mathew Markham wasn't murdered by the carjacking gang as the newspapers seem so fond of saying, but by someone who would gain by getting him out of the way. Someone like you, for instance,' he said pointing a finger at the Managing Director's shocked face.

'This is preposterous, Inspector. Mathew and I were great friends. I would never do anything like this to him. Your accusation is quite frankly, outrageous. I should report you to your superiors for making such wild allegations and...and to my lawyer for slander.'

'Are you denying you set up a secret consortium to buy Markham after Sir Mathew put it up for sale?'

'I...I...suppose now it has been reported in the financial press, I can't deny it, but he was going to sell it from under my nose, from under all our noses. I had to do something to stop him.'

'Like killing him?'

'Absolutely not. I had to stop him selling it to someone else, this is why I set up the consortium. There is no other reason.'

'What do you care who owns the company? It's just a job.'

He sighed. 'It's more than that. This is a prestigious British company and I couldn't let it fall into foreign hands, could I?'

'More like you were frightened of losing your job and all this,' he said spreading an arm wide.

'No, no. I...' For the first time since he had known him, Henderson saw Lawton fluster. It was not a pretty sight, but from his point of view, it was where he wanted him to be.

'Why did you team up with Dominic Green? Don't you know Green's reputation? He'll have you for breakfast.'

'He's a changed man Inspector. He's a respectable businessman, despite whatever tripe *The Argus* writes about him.'

'A respectable businessman, my eye,' he said, raising his voice. 'You're in league with a viper and you don't even know it. He'll take you places you don't want to go and before long you'll be talking to me from a seat inside one of my interview rooms.'

'I'm sure Mr Green would have something to say about that. In any case, this consortium is not only about him. There is also Sir Stephen Pendleton, Jacques Trudeau, Fred Hallam–'

'Yes, and Barry King, another crook. Mr Lawton, are you telling me an almost fifty per cent drop in Markham's share price doesn't greatly benefit your cause?'

'The share price has recovered a large proportion of those losses since Mathew's death, I'm pleased to say; but it's true, the price fall would have saved our consortium a couple of hundred million. But you need to remember, it benefits everyone else bidding just the same.' He sighed. 'This is all a bit academic, as I'm leaving Markham and the business is no longer for sale.'

'Why? What's happened?'

'Jackson Markham is what happened. He's taking over on Monday and I'm out. He now controls Mathew's shares and has decided to cancel the sale. My consortium no longer has a purpose and I imagine will be disbanded.'

*This is wrong*, thought Henderson. If Lawton

killed Sir Mathew, why would he walk away without a fight? His own well-reasoned arguments were falling away before his eyes, like a child's sandcastle on the incoming tide. He was missing something, but what? Something Jamil said to him popped into his head.

'If not the bidders, who else would benefit from a falling share price, or by killing Sir Mathew?'

Lawton blew out a long blast of air from his lips. 'I don't know. None of the staff, as they have share options and need a rising share price to profit, ditto our investors. The financial press are well pissed off as it makes a mockery of all their predictions, and our competitors are laughing their heads off at our apparent fall from grace. So in summary, there's nobody I can think of.'

'Let me rephrase,' he said, his anger bubbling up to the surface once again. 'Who else would want to see Mathew Markham dead? Who else had a grudge against him, against you, David Young or Markham Microprocessors?'

'You think David's involved in this too? Why? I thought his death was an accident.'

He slumped back in the seat but Henderson gave him no time to feel comfortable as he towered over him, ready to grab his throat if no answers were forthcoming. The answer was here, somewhere in this room.

'David could be a bit rude at times and he could be abrasive, but who isn't when the pressure's on?'

Lawton continued. 'I mean, he often fell out with Paul Davis, but then he's a rough northerner, so what would you expect? Sorry, no offence Inspector.'

'None taken.'

'Then there's Mathew, genial old Mathew. He got on with everybody, but he hasn't been a regular in this office for over eighteen months, and for a couple of years before then he spent most of his time on the golf course or playing tennis.'

'What about in the early days, when you were trouncing competitors and beating up suppliers? Could any of them be gunning for you now? Maybe you had, I don't know, copyright disputes, patent infringements, court cases.'

Lawton's face darkened. 'There is one person we haven't mentioned in all of this and now I think about it, he is perfectly capable of doing something reprehensible.'

'Who?'

'Gary Larner. His name hasn't come up before as he's a non person around Markham. The reason for saying this should become obvious when you hear the story, but not a word of what I'm about to tell you must leave this room. Am I being clear?'

'Do I need to reiterate, Mr Lawton? This is a murder enquiry. If you have any pertinent information, I want to hear it and only then will I decide how to use it.'

Lawton stared at him. 'I'm afraid that's not good

enough. I need to know none of this will end up in the public domain. This is sensitive stuff.'

Henderson was getting fed up with this little game and was tempted to charge him with obstructing an inquiry; but no, he decided to keep him on-side.

'What if I say I won't discuss anything you tell me with anyone else except where it has a material impact on this murder investigation. If it does, I'll talk to you or your successor first. How about that? It's the best I can do.'

'I suppose it'll have to do. Sit down, you're making me feel uncomfortable.'

Henderson took the seat vacated by the Texan at the side of Lawton's desk, which provided him with a good view to determine if he was lying, and his face would be within easy reach of his fists if he was.

'The story starts here in this building. The people upstairs are at the moment working on a product which will change the world of electronics as we know it. We call it Kratos, after a Greek myth symbolising strength and power. You won't see anything about this in the press yet, as we don't want our Asian cousins catching wind of it and copying it before we've recovered our substantial development costs.'

'Fair enough.'

Lawton went on to explain Project Kratos and it was only when he said that everyone in this building would become a millionaire did the DI see its significance.

‘It’s that big?’

Lawton nodded.

He explained this in a cool, neutral way, as if he was talking about someone else’s product and not a development that he had obviously worked on for many years. He was such a devious sod, Henderson wouldn’t put it past him to have the designs in his back pocket on the day he walked out of here for the last time.

‘Two quite brilliant engineers, Marta Stevenson and Sanjay Singh are currently leading the project. However, the basic idea and some of the groundwork was done by a maverick engineer called Gary Larner, a genius with radio transmissions. He, and the person working with him, James Nash were sacked eighteen months ago for gross misconduct, after a security guard caught them having sex with a couple of girls and snorting coke in the development studio we have at the back of our warehouse in Burgess Hill.’

‘An ignominious end to a promising career, and all captured on CCTV, no doubt.’

‘Quite, and the footage would have appeared on the web if David Young hadn’t grabbed it first. It was my fault. I was so enthused I gave them free reign to come and go as they pleased and spend whatever money they needed. In the end, they abused the privilege.

‘They were both very bitter,’ Lawton continued, ‘and claimed we kicked them out just to get our hands on the project. In reality, it was a blessing in disguise as they had done little beyond a basic drafting of the idea. If it hadn't been for the brilliance of the current development team, who took the rough drawings, concepts and the little bit of code they'd written and brought it up to the stage it is now, we would never have the working prototype we have today.'

'How was their bitterness expressed?'

'In every possible way. It started with letters, aggressive emails, Marta and Sanjay were hassled in the street, silent phone calls, rubbish being sent through the post; you name it. It only stopped about nine months ago after our lawyers threatened to take them to court. It was a calculated bluff on our part as they could have used the court case as a soap box to gain publicity for their grievances and blow the lid on Kratos. I suspect they had run out of money, and the prospect of a long and complicated legal battle put the wind up their sails.'

'Where are they now? Working for a competitor on a similar idea?'

With a sigh, Lawton reached into a drawer at the bottom of his desk, unlocked it, and pulled out two files. 'No, they did nothing of the sort, Inspector. They had no product to sell and neither would we without the work of Marta and Sanjay.' Lawton opened both folders and spread them out in front of him.

'I'll get Jules to make copies for you, but the last time we heard, Nash was living with his parents in Burgess Hill, and Larner on his own in a house in

Haywards Heath.'

'You think one of them might have killed Sir Mathew?'

'James Nash, no, he's really a follower. On the other hand, Gary Larner is so odd and his behaviour at times could only be described as volatile, I wouldn't put something like this beyond him. When he worked here, most people would have called him eccentric and a touch unpredictable, but when he left, I don't know if it was due to drugs, alcohol, or simple bitterness, but he seemed to become unhinged. He's just the sort of guy you would cross the road to avoid. He's definitely a man I think you should be talking to.'

Henderson walked away from Markham House a troubled man. He long suspected the hand of Lawton was behind the murders of Sir Mathew Markham and David Young, but his arguments had been demolished with the skill of a fine poker player in possession of a superior hand.

What disturbed him more than Lawton's clever wriggling, was that he, a rational, logical and dispassionate copper, was about to stake this case, his reputation and perhaps his career, on the guilt of two disgruntled ex-employees, neither of whom he knew much about. He started the car and pointed it in the direction of Burgess Hill.

# THIRTY-SIX

James Nash's house in Potters Lane, Burgess Hill, was of modern brick construction, semi-detached with white wood cladding. The small garden looked neat and tidy with mature bushes along one edge but the carport at the side of the house had a plastic roof, noisy for those nearby during a heavy downpour.

It was early evening in late spring, and even though streetlights were on, it was not yet dark. It felt good to be moving into summer. Henderson hated winter with its short days and dull, dappled light, a haven for crooks who could set about their business without impediment and a bind for people like him who never saw daylight except when working. He rang the doorbell.

A diminutive middle-aged woman with auburn-coloured hair answered. Dressed in an old cardigan and loose fitting tracksuit bottoms that did nothing to flatter her slim figure, it was clear she had not been expecting visitors. He didn't explain his reasons for being there, instead calling it a routine enquiry and asked to speak to her son.

'You better come in, I suppose,' she said.

She stood at the foot of the stairs and hollered,

‘James! There’s someone here to see you!’ For such a short person she had a loud voice, no doubt the result of living with a son, as they all seemed to go through a ‘deaf’ phase, particularly in their teenage years. She turned to Henderson. ‘He spends all his time in his room, doing God-knows what, but nothing to interest you lot. He’s a good boy.’

A bedroom door upstairs opened and another voice said. ‘Yeah, what is it?’

‘He’s awake at least,’ she said. ‘Go on up if you like.’

Henderson climbed the stairs as Nash’s mother walked back into the living room. Seated inside he could see a bald-headed man watching a crime drama on a widescreen television. If either of them took the trouble to come upstairs, they could have a dose of the real thing in their son’s bedroom, although he suspected the interview with James would involve a lot less action.

A tousled haired young man wearing jeans and a t-shirt stood on the landing, his face bland and impassive. From the DOB on his personnel record at Markham, Henderson knew he was 23, but he looked as fresh-faced as any 17-year-old he had ever come across.

‘Hello James, I’m Detective Inspector Angus Henderson from Sussex Police. I would like to have a word with you.’

‘Is this about my mountain bike?’

'What happened to it?'

'It got nicked outside Costa Coffee in town.'

Henderson shook his head. 'No, I'm not here about the bike. This is something more serious.'

Nash shrugged his shoulders in a 'what the hell,' gesture and walked into his bedroom.

There were two chairs: a low-set, fabric-covered recliner and a leather swivel chair in front of a desk. In order not to intimidate him, as some of his colleagues might have been tempted to do, Henderson ignored the swivel chair beside the desk and opted for the ugly recliner, which proved to be surprisingly comfortable.

The room was square and small, much as he would expect in a modern house, but tidy. On the wall, there were no pictures of sexy models, Star Wars characters, or the music industry's latest sensation, unless a poster of U2 at Glastonbury could be included.

The room was dominated by the biggest desk possible within the space available, and upon it sat two computer screens and several pale cream boxes, glowing with green and red lights. From his vantage position in the low seat, Henderson could see a myriad of black cables underneath, as they curled and twisted like a bowl of spaghetti. A bundle of them led over to a small storage unit in the corner, housing a laser printer and sound system, through which was playing James Blunt or Jack Johnson.

'You've got an impressive pile of kit there. What do

you use it for?'

'I'm a freelance software designer,' he said sitting down.

'What does that mean to a layman like me?'

'It means I work for myself designing whatever software is needed by small businesses and individuals.'

'Such as?'

'I get involved in website design, software installation, modification of computer code, sorting out computer problems, the works. I've just designed a website for a hardware shop in Brighton. They've been going for a hundred and twenty years, and only now, if you can believe it, have they decided to join the world of on-line commerce. It involved a fair amount of training as well.'

'I can imagine. It sounds like interesting work.'

'Not really.'

'It's not challenging?'

'It has its moments.'

'You're a fan of the Seagulls, I see,' he said nodding towards a neat pile of football programmes lying close to the window.

'Yeah, I've got a season ticket and I go to some away matches as well. Do you follow football?'

'Yes. I sometimes get to a match but more often than not I'm working Saturdays so I don't get over there as much as I'd like.'

'Bad luck, they've been good to watch these last few

weeks. I mean, we had a terrible start when a pub team could have beaten us, and I thought we were certainties for relegation, but they turned it around. There's been some cracking games these last few weeks.'

'So I've heard. The reason I'm here, James, is I'm investigating the murder of Sir Mathew Markham.' To Henderson's surprise, the inevitable, 'I thought the carjackers did it,' didn't come.

Nash nodded. 'Yeah, I remember hearing about it, but I didn't follow the story. You probably know that I used to work there and left in what might be called acrimonious circumstances, so I don't go out of my way to find out what's going on.'

'Yes, I knew about that. Tell me what happened when you were there.'

He swivelled in the chair from side to side as if dealing with difficult memories. 'I wasn't long out of university and this was my first job so I was hot on the theory but light on the practicalities. In a way, I was a glorified gopher for Gary; he was the brains of the outfit.'

'How far did you take it? The idea, I mean.'

'You've heard about it?'

'Yep.'

'Did they get it to work?'

Henderson hesitated, remembering his promise to Lawton but Nash of all people, deserved to know. 'I'm told they now have a working prototype.'

'Bloody hell, I'm amazed, but I knew it would work in the end.'

'Tell me about you and Gary.'

'Gary's a good computer programmer, but a genius with radio, and like many geniuses he's great at generating ideas but crap at implementing them. He couldn't even be bothered doing a mock-up to show the bosses what we had achieved, and given that they were funding it all, that really pissed them off.'

'I can understand their frustration.'

'Half the time, I didn't have a clue what he was on about and so in the end, when I thought we were close and we could save our jobs by demonstrating how smart we were, it was a shock to find we didn't even get to base camp.'

'Did your sacking come as a surprise? Do you think it was fair?'

He smiled weakly and shrugged. 'Define fair. In legal terms, I suppose it was. Lawton had the best lawyers behind him; but morally no way. At the time, I felt bitter and cheated, we both did, particularly at the way Lawton handled it. We thought he was trying to keep all our ideas for himself.'

'What do you think about it now?'

'Ha. It was stupid. I suppose we were behaving like a couple of Billy Bunters let loose in our very own sweet shop, and we didn't bother when it started to piss-off the rest of the staff. In a way, it was Lawton's fault for giving us so much rope and Gary's for demanding it, when what we needed was more direction. Gary, you see, was too much of an obsessive to ask for help and too disorganised to use it.'

'What's he like as a person?'

'What, Gary or Lawton?'

'Gary.'

'He can be bold, imaginative and clever, but when something doesn't please him he starts mouthing off like an ancient Roman emperor, demanding everything. He annoyed a good number of people at the company, including the chairman's son, Jackson. When the drugs and women thing went down, there was no more slack in the rope and out the door we went.'

'Did you keep copies of the designs?'

He shot Henderson a look.

'Don't worry I won't tell the lawyers.'

'I don't know why I'm bothered being so secretive, they're obsolete now. We weren't supposed to keep copies, but we did, and me and Gary tried to build a prototype. Despite blowing a load of our severance cash on computers, testing gear, circuit designing software, and spending three solid months cooped up in a rented workshop,' he said shaking his head, 'we still couldn't get the thing to work. You'd think because we were using our own money, we would have been better organised and focused, but no, if anything Gary was worse. It was a bad time for me, for both of us. I'm glad to be out and doing something more mundane.'

'What did you mean when you said Gary got worse?'

'Well, you know, when it wouldn't work it made him more morose and somehow it added to the feeling that he'd been cheated. He was supposed to take medicine for a bi-polar condition, but he stopped and was taking dope instead, so his mood swings were,' he sighed, 'at times volcanic.'

'Does he still hate the company and the people in it?'

He hesitated. 'It's not my place to speak for him, I don't want to drop him in it. You should ask him yourself.'

Henderson fielded a few more questions but soon drew a halt as he'd probably got everything James Nash had to offer. He eased himself from the chair with some difficulty, as it seemed to have moulded itself to his shape. 'I've enjoyed talking to you, James. Here's my card. If you think of anything else in the meantime, I'd appreciate a call.'

He walked to the door and stepped out, but stopped and turned. James was facing the computer screen and tapping away on the keyboard with all the finesse of a skilled typist.

'Do you still keep in touch with Gary?'

'Nah. I haven't spoken to him for about six months, maybe more. Last I heard, at the start of this year he got a job in the IT department of some financial services company in Brighton. Boring as hell, he said but it pays the bills. He's now bought himself a boat and spends all his spare time down at the marina.'

# THIRTY-SEVEN

It was a short drive from Burgess Hill to Haywards Heath, but long enough for Henderson to mull over his conversation with James Nash. Two things stood out. It was Lawton, not Markham, who was the subject of their ire.

It was Lawton who pulled them up about their bad-boy behaviour and Lawton's name that appeared on their termination letters. So if they were targeting the business, why did they kill Sir Mathew Markham and not William Lawton? Was he an easy target, an old man who rarely ventured out, or were they saving Lawton for last and making him sweat, much as Jamil suggested?

Another question annoyed him: why had James Nash lied? When he'd asked him if he still kept in contact with Larner, he'd said he didn't, but he knew Larner didn't like the new job and only did it to pay the bills, indicating that he had spoken to him since he'd started work. In another conversation he might have put it down to semantics, or the inelegant phrasing of a young and inarticulate lad, but Nash was neither of those things.

Haywards Heath was a much larger town than

Burgess Hill with its own mainline station and in close proximity to the A23. Over the years, it had shed its 'dormitory town' tag and was now home to a number of insurance and financial services companies, with a good selection of night-time entertainment in the form of dozens of pubs and restaurants.

A few minutes later, he turned into Bolnore Road, a leafy area of individual detached houses in marked contrast to the regimented and standardised semi-detached estate he left behind in Burgess Hill. Amidst mock-Tudor mini-castles, five-bedroom 'executive' retreats and small houses, extended so many times they had forfeited the right to be called a 'cottage', stood Gary Larner's place.

He parked across the street. The house was small in comparison to many of its neighbours and looked as though the exterior had not been improved in decades, with an abundance of old and paint-flaked sash windows, an original but bowed roof, and a driveway dotted with many clumps of grass and weeds that if left untended, would soon become incorporated into the untidy garden.

He walked over to the driveway, his presence shielded from neighbours by a rampant laurel hedge blocking out much of the light from nearby street lamps, giving the house a black, forlorn look. The windows were in darkness with the curtains open, suggesting there was no one at home, but he knocked on the door all the same. In his experience, IT people were a strange bunch and he wouldn't be surprised to find Larner inside, tapping away on his keyboard in a darkened back room wearing nothing but an old straw boater and flip-flops.

He knocked again, louder this time, the sound reverberating around the empty hallway, but still came no reply. The house, the encroaching garden, the stillness of the night, reminded him of a poem he first learned in school by Walter De La Mare, called The Listeners. He could still recall his favourite stanza.

*'But no one descended to the Traveller*
*No head from the leaf-fringed sill*
*Leaned over and looked into his grey eyes,*
*Where he stood perplexed and still.'*

The poem was a metaphor for a dying man knocking on death's door, and since the traveller received no reply to his knock, it meant his time on earth wasn't yet over. Henderson liked the poem, but hoped its sudden appearance in his mind and its preoccupation with death was in no way prescient.

He walked back to the driveway. After making sure he wasn't being watched by a vigilante dog walker or the Neighbourhood Watch coordinator out for an evening patrol, as it wouldn't do to try and explain his presence here to a couple of plods from Haywards Heath Station, he disappeared around the side of the house and into the shadows.

When his eyes adjusted to the gloom, he could see he was standing in front of a gate, and over to the right, blocking the way into the rear garden, the doors of a garage. The gate looked old and a good kick would most likely open it, but he was glad he didn't because when he turned the handle, he found it wasn't locked. He eased it open and could see why. Either through settlement in the house or warping of the wood, the gate had shifted a couple of inches away from where the hasp met the corresponding staple on the gate post. It couldn't be locked even if Larner wanted to.

Carefully he walked past windows at the back of the house, but his caution was unnecessary as he couldn't detect the slightest chink of light inside, no ghostly flicker of a television, no tinny prattle from a portable radio, nothing to indicate the presence of anyone. He had only the light of the moon to guide him, but it was Blackpool Illuminations next door, a light blazing in every room; no doubt the refuge of a posse of teenagers, too lazy to switch anything off. The house was far enough away not to bother him and separated from Larner's by another tall and untidy hedge.

Before tackling the back door, he decided to take a look in the garage. In his experience, crooks often hid incriminating things inside sheds and garages, things they didn't want the casual house visitor to spot. It was often the place where tools were stored and where he might find something useful to open the back door, or a window, without causing too much damage.

The side door to the garage looked as old and dilapidated as the gate, and this time the weakness lay in a rattling, loose-fitting lock. It was a disappointing discovery as he fancied a challenge, but instead he dug his fingers into the space between the door edge and its frame and eased the door closer to the hinges. It opened with an unoiled creak, a piece of cake for him or any neighbourhood lawnmower thief.

Henderson had investigated many old garden sheds and garages over the years, in search of drugs or guns, and knew to blunder inside without looking was a mistake of the naïve and foolhardy. Any number of calamities were lying in wait, such as a smack on the head from a low hanging plank, to bruising an ankle on a discarded spade, but more painful, in his personal experience, was tripping over a rake and falling headlong into a bundle of barbed wire. He reached into his pocket and pulled out his battered and trusty Maglite and switched it on.

In contrast to the neglect evident all around the house, the inside of the garage was tidy and all tools and implements had been put out of harm's way on shelves and brackets, leaving a broad open space for him to walk around in. Either that or Larner didn't own much stuff. Not having tended a garden for many years, Henderson wasn't tempted to have a poke inside a small box containing seed packets, or to take a look along the shelves at boxes of fertiliser or weed killer to see what he had been missing. Whenever he saw anyone mowing the lawn with a grumpy expression on their face, it simply re-affirmed his resolution to live in a flat.

He looked around for a few minutes, but finding nothing of interest, turned to walk outside, when the torch illuminated a large cardboard box in the corner, nestling under two rolls of nylon netting. Propping the Maglite on a shelf, he carefully removed the rolls. They were large and bulky and looked heavy, but when he went to lift one, it weighed next to nothing.

He opened the box expecting to find a stash of beer or well-thumbed porno magazines, a discovery which never failed to lighten up many a boring drugs search, but felt slightly cheated to find it contained only clothes. Slowly, as he didn't want to be assailed by a squadron of moths or have his face covered in dust, he removed a black balaclava, fleece and trousers. He grabbed the torch and aimed it inside. There were three sets of each. His heart skipped a beat. There had been three men at Mathew Markham's house, and Suki had described clothing similar to this.

His mind began racing, but like the waves at Brighton Beach, no sooner did the excitement rise, when seconds later it receded. They might well be the clothes of criminals, but equally they could be gardening clothes, building clothes or the clothes Larner used when cleaning his boat. They were simply clothes, and unless a fragment found at Markham's house could be matched to anything in this pile, it would prove nothing. Even then, a clever lawyer would be able to pick holes bigger than any moth.

The logical part of his brain was saying, leave it alone, it's nothing, but his intuition was screaming and demanding his attention. It was too big a coincidence to ignore. He spent a few more minutes searching the rest of the box but found nothing more, so he replaced the rolls of plastic sheeting back on top and walked over to the back door of the house, more convinced than ever that he was on the right track.

The neighbours had settled down for the evening to watch television and the teenagers must have gone out, as all the upstairs lights were off. If Larner's house was as modern as those in Burgess Hill, the back door would be made from uPVC, be double-glazed, and fitted with a multiple locking system, nigh-on impossible to open without a hammer and an arrest warrant; but this one wasn't.

It was made of wood with a large window at the top and an inset panel at the bottom. This offered a few choices, none of which were unpalatable or difficult for a burglar or a curious copper. He could smash the window or, less messy, kick in the bottom panel, which was in all likelihood made from something no thicker than plywood, and crawl through the gap. His personal favourite was to open the door with the key, which he could see through the window, hanging from a peg close to the door.

He went back to the garage and removed a long-bladed screwdriver, used by handymen to work in those tight, inaccessible places where a big hand and a normal-sized tool wouldn't fit. The rust on the blade suggested it hadn't been out of the tool box for a while. In his other hand, he carried a wooden stepladder and a piece of wire.

Balancing on the steps, Henderson used the tip of the screwdriver to cut away a small section of wood from the bottom of the frame of the little window above the main kitchen window, and eased the screwdriver into the gap. After a bit of wriggling about, trying to get the angle right, he pushed it under the window handle. After checking to make sure the ladder was still on a sound footing, he gave the base of the screwdriver a sharp smack with his hand and was pleased to see the handle jump from its rest.

Holding the little window open with his shoulder, he leaned inside the kitchen and hooked the loop he'd made at the end of the wire over the handle of the main window and pulled it open. A few minutes later, he inserted the key into the lock and opened the door.

# THIRTY-EIGHT

DI Henderson walked slowly into Gary Larner's house. If there had been an alarm he would have been shocked, as he couldn't see a tell-tale box outside, and given the general state of disrepair and neglect all around he would imagine an alarm would be way down on Larner's list of DIY priorities. Sure enough there wasn't, and he stepped into the kitchen confident he wouldn't be scurrying back out twenty-seconds later, trying to make it back to the car before the ear-splitting bell sounded.

Kitchens were good places to hide things; storage jars and closed food containers looked innocent enough until opened, but he didn't bother looking as he was certain what he was looking for, wouldn't be there. He didn't know what it was but he was sure if he came across something suspicious, he would recognise it.

Larner's study was adjacent to the living-room and at first glance, looked like it contained more kit than the Houston Space Centre. It was jam-packed with all manner of computer gear, including three huge screens, two keyboards, a powerful looking server, and on another table, printers, scanners and black boxes, all twinkling, all powered-up. He wanted to take a look at one of the screens, but worried that as soon as he touched it the whole room would light up like a beacon, so he kept well away from anything which would hasten such an unfortunate event.

Venetian blinds covered the window and when he looked closer, they were lined in a thick layer of dust, suggesting they hadn't been opened for a while. He pulled the cord and allowed a little light from the street to filter inside. Aside from the computer gear, he could see a bookcase, filing cabinet, cupboard, and pile of stuff in the corner which would take a four-man SOCO team a week to look through.

He closed the blinds and switched on the torch. Taking a quick look inside the filing cabinet and the cupboard, he soon realised that to make any sense out of it he would have to go through every file one by one. The normal course of action in such circumstances would be for him to obtain a search warrant, but after Harris's angry tirade earlier today, he would be reaching for Henderson's P45 faster than Wild Bill Hickok could draw his Colt Navy revolvers. He needed time to do this thoroughly, but at this precise moment, time was one commodity in very short supply.

He switched off the torch and went in search of Larner's bedroom. He'd reached the top of the stairs when heard the sound of a car stopping outside. He moved to the window at the end of the hall and peered out through grubby net curtains.

Adjacent to Larner's drive, a car was parked which hadn't been there when he first arrived. He watched and waited but the silence that followed was oppressive, as if the room was filled with thick, dense smoke, and it was a relief when the driver's door opened. It stayed open, swaying back and forth without anyone appearing, until he realised the driver was either talking to someone inside the car, or trying to retrieve something from the glove box.

A few seconds later, a man appeared. Henderson had seen Larner's mug shot in his personnel file, but with no idea if he was large or small, fat or thin. In any case, this guy was too far away and the light from the nearby street lamp too weak to tell if it was him or not.

The guy stood there looking at Larner's house. Henderson was sure he had closed the back door but did he leave the venetian blinds just as he found them? In legal terms, he was up the Red River Rapids without a paddle, canoe, or life jacket. Breaking and entering without a warrant, not even with more watertight evidence than he had, would spell the end of his career and a possible criminal prosecution.

A few seconds later, a woman exited the passenger door. She was irate and intent on carrying on with whatever conversation they had been having in the car. For a minute or so their movements were acted out in slow motion, as they seemed more focused on their argument than moving away from the car.

The guy turned and locked the car and the couple walked towards Larner's driveway. Henderson was about to leg it downstairs to the back door when they stopped, turned, and crossed the road. They passed under a street lamp and the realisation hit him. The man carried a bottle of wine and she flowers, the invitees to someone's dinner party, but with a measure of doubt as to which house they were going to. He was glad he hadn't been invited, as he was sure the warring couple wouldn't be good company, and knowing his luck he would be seated right next to them.

He waited a few minutes more, until he heard the slam of the door of the house opposite, before making his way downstairs and checking the blind in the study. The blind looked fine, but as he emerged from the study he spotted a door underneath the staircase.

If it was a cellar, it was a rarity as this valuable extra space had been phased out of UK house building over the years since the Second World War, due to cost constraints; but it was a great place to hide all manner of stuff. He turned the handle but the door was locked and instinctively he did what he used to do at his grandmother's rambling old house in Inverness, he ran his hand across the top of the doorframe.

The key was large, metal and ornate and looked more like an offensive weapon than a door entry device, but when he fitted it into the keyhole, it turned and pulled back the bolt with the same, sure snap of a modern, well-oiled mortice. He opened the door and peered inside. It was dark but he could feel a draft of cool air and knew he was looking into a cellar and not a broom cupboard.

If sheds, greenhouses, lofts, and garages held unknown calamities which could kill and maim the unwary, cellars were ten times more dangerous. One time he had fallen down a steep flight of steps, as they'd started immediately on opening the door. He switched on the torch and after making sure of his footing, ventured inside and closed the door, but not before pocketing the key. No way did he want to be locked inside by accident or on purpose.

Standing at the top of the stairs he panned the torch around the wall until he found a light switch, and using the combination of the weak light spilling up from a bulb in the cellar and the torch, descended the stairs. Near the bottom, he ducked under low-lying rafters and looked inside.

Expecting to find boxes, old books, and discarded household appliances and furniture, it took two takes to realise there was a fair amount of those but behind them, a woman was chained to one wall and a man to the other.

They were hard to spot against the grey walls as their clothes and faces were as grimy as their surroundings. He ran over to the woman and knelt down to loosen the rope around her hands, while bombarding her with a volley of questions before realising she had something in her mouth.

He removed the gag and with the only handkerchief in his pocket, wiped her dirty and blood stained face. He guessed her age at early forties, with long black hair, now tousled and matted. She sported a fat lip where dark, red blood had coagulated, and a black eye. In addition to the rope tied around her hands, her leg was secured at the ankle to a long, metal chain set into the wall, impossible to undo without bolt cutters.

'Who are you?' He said. 'What are you doing here?'

'My name is Marta Stevenson,' she said in an American accent after spitting out some gunk in her mouth. 'Who are you?'

Marta Stevenson? Wasn't she the microprocessor designer Lawton was praising earlier? 'I'm Detective Inspector Angus Henderson, Sussex Police.'

'Thank God,' she said, her face lighting up. 'You've come to rescue us.'

'I didn't know you were here,' he said, not wishing to tell her the truth, that he was there under his own initiative. He realised he needed reinforcements and reached for his phone, but when he tried to dial, he found there wasn't a signal. A cellar offered many advantages but this wasn't one of them.

'I need to go upstairs and phone for help, I can't get a phone signal here.'

'Don't go, please. Don't leave us. He says he's going

to drown us. He's only gone to get stuff for his boat and then he's going to dump us both at sea.'

'Who? Where?'

'Larner, Gary Larner says he's taking us to Brighton Marina where he has a boat and he's gonna take it out to sea and drown us. We were kidnapped yesterday.'

On hearing the word 'we' it reminded him of the other prisoner behind him. He turned and moved towards him. If Marta looked bruised and bashed, her companion appeared, to his untrained eye, to be in worse shape. He had a large cut on the side of his head that was leaking blood down the side of his face, he had a knife slash on his upper arm, and his leg was tucked to the side at an odd angle, making him think it was broken.

He looked dead, but when he felt for a pulse, he was alive but in need of immediate hospital treatment. He tried moving him into a more comfortable position and to make sure his airways weren't blocked, but stopped when he heard a strange noise. He listened, and heard it again. There was a creak on the cellar stairs.

# THIRTY-NINE

'Who the fuck are you and what are you doing in my basement?'

Henderson turned. Gary Larner stood at the bottom of the cellar stairs. He was smaller than Henderson expected, about five-nine, but solidly built. His hair was a tousled mop of long, sandy-brown strands, making him look wild, reinforced by the angry scowl and wide-eyed glare on his face.

'I am Detective Inspector Henderson of Sussex Police and I'm arresting you for the kidnap and assault of these two people.'

Larner strode towards him. Before he could react, Larner punched him in the face. He fell back but as Larner swung another, he ducked, not enough as it still made contact and knocked him to the ground and into a pile of cardboard boxes.

His head was still swimming when he felt Larner reach down, grab hold of his jacket and attempt to pull him upright. As if in a dream, Henderson pulled up his knees, planted the soles of his feet on Larner's chest and pushed with all his might. Larner staggered back and lost his footing when he tripped over the prone figure of Marta Stevenson and smacked his head on an exposed water pipe.

Henderson struggled to stand upright. It was a simple task made more difficult as he had landed on cardboard boxes, many of which were half-empty. When he tried to apply pressure, they collapsed, reminding him of trying to move around his yacht 'Mingary' on a rough sea.

He got to his feet at the same time Larner got to his. Henderson's head cleared quickly but Larner's didn't and he staggered around like a Friday night drunk, slow and lopsided, a glassy look in his eyes and with a gun in his hand. Larner shook his head and slapped his face while waving the gun to and fro, trying to maintain his balance and shift the fog clouding his brain.

'Think you can come in here and fuck everything up for me copper? Except my boat ain't so big and there's only space for these two fuckers,' he said, flicking the barrel of the gun towards the woman. 'So I guess I'll have to kill you now and dump your body overboard later. But wait a minute Gary. You're not coming back, are you? No, I'm not copper, sorry about this. So what will you do Gary?' Theatrically, he put his index finger over his lips as if thinking.

'Why don't you let these people go?' Henderson said. 'This man needs urgent medical help.'

'Medical help, eh? Ha, what a good joke. Where Sanjay's going, the little fishes will give him all the help he needs. Won't they Sanjay?'

'You could–'

'Shut up copper,' he bellowed. 'I'm thinking.'

His eyes narrowed and a devious smile creased his face, the smile of a psychopath. 'Yeah, I hear you, Gary. I know just what to do,' he said, 'Gary comes to the rescue once again.' He raised the gun.

To his surprise, Henderson didn't close his eyes as he thought he would when facing instant death. He wanted to look this madman in the eye, wanted to imprint his face as a lasting memory in the killer's brain. Slowly, slowly his fingers tightened around the handle of the gun, his face contorted in a concentrated frown. Henderson saw a twitch in the trigger finger.

Out of the corner of his eye, something moved behind Larner. The gun went off with a boom, nearly deafening him in such a confined space. Larner crumpled up in pain.

At first, Henderson assumed Larner had shot himself as he couldn't feel any pain, but he soon realised Marta Stevenson had whacked him on the shin with a slack bit of her leg chain. Henderson threw himself at his assailant, catching him in the midriff in a clumsy tackle, the two men careered into the empty void at the back of the cellar, the gun clattering to the floor somewhere behind them.

Larner tripped and fell but Henderson still maintained a grip on his jacket and they tumbled to the ground, Henderson on top and Larner on the bottom, breaking the DI's fall. They rolled together on the floor trading blows. Henderson was getting the better of him, but many of his punches were ineffective as he couldn't get a good swing and it was doing nothing to subdue the struggling Larner. Just then, Larner kneed him the groin.

He doubled up in agony, and despite tears in his eyes and the inside of his head experiencing an explosion of colour as if peering through a child's kaleidoscope, he forced them open as no way did he want to lose sight of this slippery bastard even for a second. Instead of teeing up for another blow, Larner hobbled across the floor towards the stairs, and after grabbing the banister and holding it for a second or two for support, he disappeared up the cellar stairs.

Gingerly, Henderson forced himself upright, but as soon as he did so, he felt giddy. He waited a few seconds and despite vehement protestations from Stevenson to stay with them, he headed up the stairs. The front door lay wide open, blowing in the chilled night air and making the sweat on his face feel clammy. He crossed the threshold and looked outside in time to see the rear end of a Subaru Impreza disappear over the short driveway and roar off down the road.

He pulled out his phone and this time it did have a signal. 'Control? This is DI Henderson, Serious Crimes Unit. I need an ambulance and two patrol cars to Bolnore Road in Haywards Heath.' He turned to look at the front door. 'The number of the house is...sorry there's only a house name. It's called The Cedars, that's C-E-D-A-R-S. Inside the house, two people are chained to a wall in the cellar, so they'll need cutting gear, and one of the victims is in a bad way. Have you got all this?'

'Yes sir.'

'I am now in pursuit of a grey or silver Subaru Impreza heading out of Haywards Heath to destination unknown. Try and obtain the number from the DVLA, the car belongs to one Gary Larner, L-A-R-N-E-R at the Bolnore Road address. When you get it, put it on ANPR straight away, but flag him as armed and extremely dangerous and not to be approached.'

He ran to his car and drove after Larner. At the junction of Bolnore Road and the A272, he waited for a line of cars to pass, but couldn't see which way Larner went. He knew he owned a boat at Brighton Marina, but would he still go there after his plans had been revealed? Henderson didn't know much about him, whether he had a mother in Maidstone, a brother in Bradford, or a friend in Farnborough, or if he even possessed a passport, so he didn't have a clue where he was heading. By the time he reached the A23, offering the choice of north to London or south to Brighton, his mind was made up.

He called DS Walters.

'Hello sir, how are you? Which pub are you in? Are you looking for some company to come and cheer you up?'

'What the hell are you on about?'

'I heard Harris mouthing off about the interviews we did last week. In fact, I think the whole office heard him. I imagine you're sitting in some pub drowning them.'

'What me? No chance, it's not my style. Now listen up. I've just found two of Markham's software designers chained up in Gary Larner's house.'

'Who's Gary Larner?'

'A guy who used to work for Markham but got booted out for taking drugs and entertaining women on company premises. He was working on a secret project, but thinks Markham cheated him out of the profits.'

'I'm with you now.'

'He kidnapped the leaders of the team working on this secret project, and he was planning to drown them before I turned up.'

'Mu God. Where is he now?'

'I'm in pursuit, or at least I think I am, unless he's headed off to the airport or a train station. I'm on the way to Brighton Marina.'

'Why do you think he's heading there?'

'It's the place where he keeps his boat, and after dumping the two captives overboard and shooting me, I think he was probably going to leg it across the Channel to France or Belgium.'

'I take it he didn't shoot you?'

'You're right, I'm more or less intact.'

'I'm pleased to hear it, as he sounds a right nutter. Have you called for back-up?'

'No, because I can't tell them exactly where to go. I might be wrong about the marina.'

'You'll need back-up in case you run into him again, and your hunch is as good as any. I'll set it up.'

'Cheers. Where are you now?'

'Still in the office.'

'Don't you have a home to go to?'

'We spent so much time talking about the barney between you and Harris, I didn't get anything done. I get the feeling I'll start paying for it now though, as I think you're going to keep me here all night. Hey, I've got some good news for you. Mathew Markham's Bentley has been found.'

'What?'

'Yeah. It was discovered on an access road in the Ashdown Forest, a burned out shell. An ignominious end to a beautiful car, and hardly the rational behaviour of a bunch of car thieves intent on making a quick buck, don't you think?'

He thumped the steering wheel in anger. 'Why couldn't they have found it a couple of days ago? It would have strengthened my case.'

'I think so too.'

'Does that mean you and everybody else are now coming around to my way of thinking?'

'Just about.'

‘The best thing you can do is stay where you are and coordinate everything until somebody locates Larner. Keep in touch with Lewes control and call me if he’s spotted by any camera, ok?’

‘No problem. Good luck, sir. I think you’re going to need it.’

# FORTY

DI Henderson was tearing along the outside lane of the A23. He was in his own car with no blue light, no siren, and no Day-Glo stripes, giving other road users the impression of a young tearaway, filled with his own importance and believing his two-hundred quid road tax gave him sole ownership of the tarmac.

He passed the two stone pylons erected either side of the southbound carriageway to mark the northern boundary of Greater Brighton, known to locals as the Brighton Gates, when his phone rang.

'Angus it's me,' DS Carol Walters said. 'Control have informed me they're on the look-out for a light-coloured Subaru Impreza, yeah?'

'Aye, it's Larner's car, the one he was driving when he left his house in Bolnore Road.'

'Don't you remember, this is the same type of vehicle Suki Markham told us she saw on the night Sir Mathew was murdered?'

'Bloody hell, so it was. I'd forgotten.'

'One other thing, I've been told by the petrol heads around here is that it's a fast motor, so it's not beyond the bounds of credibility to suggest it might have been used to knock David Young off his motorbike, if his death was, as you said, somehow tied up in all of this.'

'We'll know for sure once we get hold of the car. An accident like that is bound to leave a mark on the bodywork even if he's cleaned it, which somehow I doubt as Larner's a bit of an untidy sod.'

'There's our guy Locard rearing his ugly head again.'

'What?'

'You know, the criminal psychologist you're always banging on about. Criminals always leave something behind at the scene and always take something away with them.'

'I'm astounded, not because you remembered Locard, but you were actually listening to what I was saying in those meetings.'

'Cheeky beggar, talk to you later.'

Henderson didn't know too much about cars, but there were few in the CID division of any police force who didn't know about the Subaru Impreza. At one time, they were the getaway vehicle of choice in numerous jewellery shop snatches, security van heists, post office and bank robberies, in fact any crime requiring a fast getaway. Just about every modern car is capable of breaking the speed limit, but few cars could touch the Impreza for its 0-60 acceleration, including many cars found in the average police garage. This, coupled to a four-wheel drive system, meant it didn't fishtail all over the tarmac when the gas was applied.

The junction with the coast-hugging A27 lay up ahead. He shot up the slip road but was forced to brake hard as the road directly in front of him was choked with slow-moving traffic. This was not unusual in Brighton as numerous large scale-events took place all year round, up-ahead at the Amex Community Stadium, the Racecourse, the seafront and at numerous theatre and concert venues. It didn't slow him down too much, as a few minutes later, his junction appeared and soon he was speeding towards Brighton Marina.

He knew the route well as his own boat was anchored in the same place, although it was still shored-up for winter with the sails packed, the hull tied to embedded rings at the side of the harbour and tarpaulins covering all exposed areas, as he hadn't found the time to sort it out.

Soon, he eased the car down the familiar concrete-sided marina slip road, which on bleaker nights than this felt more like a tunnel. He abandoned the car on thick yellow lines close to a barrier, erected to prevent riff-raff from straying too close to the exclusive apartment blocks, some of which had their own parking space for their car and a berth for their yacht, and ran towards the boats.

He didn't have any idea what sort of boat Larner owned and wouldn't have a cat's chance in hell of finding it without some help There were almost fifteen hundred berths in the marina and even to a sailor like him, many boats looked the same. Instead, he headed towards the reception area, hoping against hope that one of the berthing masters was around.

It was after nine o'clock and dark and it was unlikely that many yachts or speedboats would be out on the water, but the berthing masters ran a twenty-four hour service. Even though the Marina was used mainly by leisure craft, plenty of commercial fishing boats sailed from there, working all-year-round to land lobster and mussels, and it was not unknown for the odd yacht to turn up part-way through a long-distance voyage, or a group of kids out on the water practising night-time drills.

He pushed open the door to the office and felt a surge of heat and coffee aroma hit his face like a warm Sahara breeze. To his relief, a man was seated behind the desk, someone he had seen several times before. He was staring at his computer screen while drinking from a large mug with the logo of one of the local yacht chandleries on the side. Given the temperature of the room, it was no surprise to see him dressed in a light coloured polo shirt and denims, but with a thick anorak hanging from the peg behind him for those times when he had to venture outside. The name badge read, 'Bill Haversome - Berthing Master.'

Henderson put his police ID on the table. 'Good evening, Bill. I'm trying to locate the berth of a boat belonging to a man named Gary Larner. Can you tell me where I can find it?'

‘No problem detective.’ He paused to look at him. ‘I’ve seen you before, haven’t I? You’ve got a boat on the west side, if I’m not mistaken. Don’t tell me.’ He looked at the ceiling for a few seconds. ‘Yep,’ he said smiling, ‘it’s a Moody 32 and named after a place in Scotland. Am I right?’

‘Well done. It’s called ‘Mingary’, a district of Ardnamurchan on the west coast of Scotland.’

‘I’ve got a good memory for boats, me,’ he said tapping the side of his head with his finger. ‘Bloody hopeless with people’s names but boats are a doddle. There’s not much else to do around here in the winter, you see.’

He turned back to the computer and started tapping away on the keyboard. ‘Ah here we are,’ he said, turning the screen towards Henderson for him to have a look. ‘Larner wasn’t it?’

‘Yes it is.’

‘I assume you know how the jetties are numbered?’

‘Treat me like an imbecile. I only know the place where my own boat is moored.’

‘Ok. There are two jetties in this Marina, they're the two floating walkways leading out from the Promenade. The place where we are now is called the West Jetty,’ he said pointing at a map of the Marina laminated to his desk. ‘You need to make your way to the East Jetty.’

‘Fine.’

‘Now, this office is four pontoons from the shore,

they're the floating walkways, perpendicular to the jetties that lead out to where the boats are located. To find Mr Larner, go down the West Jetty outside this office and head back to the Promenade, the place where all the restaurants are. When you get there, take a right and go past the apartment blocks, Neptune, Merton and Collingwood Courts until you get to Sovereign Court, and then turn right into the East Jetty. How am I doing?'

'I'm still with you.'

'Count up three pontoons and the head right, count six berths along and on the right, you'll find your Mr Larner. I passed by that way twenty minutes or so ago and there are some people about. You might be lucky.'

Henderson walked over the bouncing jetty as fast as he could, but in truth he couldn't run even if he wanted to. His ankle protested every time he put any weight on it and the swaying motion was playing havoc with his balance.

The walkways were lit by large sodium lamps as there was little else to stop the unwary falling into the water. The biggest danger lay with night-time boozers, owners who came here in the evening to sit on the aft deck of their boat and enjoy a drink, and on some of the larger vessels he had even heard the sounds of a party going on.

Henderson walked along the Promenade until he reached Sovereign Court and turned up the East Jetty. The water looked dark and murky. The restaurants and bars became smaller and more distant as he was sucked into the gloomy morass of gently swaying yachts, large and small motorboats, and all manner of rowing boats and sailing dinghies.

It was a strange sensation to be walking on the floating jetty, riding the surface of the water but despite his reason for being there, it reminded him of something he missed, as he hadn't been out in his boat for months. At the third pontoon he turned right, the noise of his approach masked by the loud ambient background sounds, ever-present in this marina and every other one he had ever visited.

It was in part caused by water slapping against hulls and boats straining against mooring ropes, but a more intrusive noise was caused by loose or ill-fitting lanyards as they smacked against hollow aluminium masts in the breeze, creating a loud metallic, clanking sound. Many travel and sailing brochures eulogised about this sound, describing it as authentic and soothing, but it was nothing but a bloody nuisance to any knackered sailor or anyone living nearby who craved a good night's sleep.

He counted six boats along and stopped alongside 'Tempest', a twelve-foot long speedboat. It had a single outboard engine and small canopy to protect the skipper, with a small cabin up in the bow for storage and the occasional overnight stay, but no sign of anyone aboard. His spirits dipped, perhaps his hunch had been wrong. He reached for his phone to call Carol and tell her the marina was a dead-end and they needed to search elsewhere, when he detected the smell of diesel.

He bent down. The smell was stronger now, meaning someone had recently filled up the fuel tank. It wasn't a smart thing to do if the boat wasn't going to be used for any length of time, as it could present a fire risk, and in time the fuel would go stale which could lead to engine problems, something not welcome when out in the open sea. This could mean only one thing, this boat was getting ready to sail.

He moved to the bow and peered through the window of the little cabin. A small wind-up light sat on the table, and he could see a zipped-up holdall bag and a box of groceries, and inside milk, bread and cheese. The food and diesel were indicative of recent activity, and providing he'd followed the Berthing Master's directions correctly, Larner was planning to scarper.

He was about to jump on-board and take a closer look when he heard a noise behind him. He turned to see the blade of an oar coming straight for him. It hit the side of his head with an almighty slap, knocking him to the ground, and more by luck than judgement he fell on the pontoon and not into the water. Unable to rise, he watched helplessly as Larner undid the mooring, threw the oar on the boat and jumped aboard.

'Bye bye matey,' he said. 'Just be thankful I don't

have time to kill you. Gary's got jobs to do, people to see.' He gunned the engine and a minute later turned the bend at the end of the pontoon and headed straight for the gap in the sea wall that led out to the open sea.

# FORTY-ONE

Henderson levered himself up. It took a few moments to realise the beautiful stars he could see were not part of the night sky, but his head's own celestial show. He shifted into a sitting position and waited until the wave of nausea passed and his personal view of the heavens melted away like summer zephyrs, before trying to stand.

A stream of blood trickled down his face but he couldn't decide what was worse, the befuddled feeling in his head, which felt like the mother of all hangovers, or the ringing in his ears. It sounded like the bells of St Michaels, a church close to his flat in Seven Dials where the spiteful campanologists of the parish always did their thing early on a Sunday morning.

He staggered over to a tap and splashed water on his face. Feeling better, he pulled out his phone and called Walters.

'You stay there,' she said, after he told her what had happened, 'and I'll call an ambulance and scramble the helicopter.'

The thought of giving up the chase when he had come so close seemed to galvanise his senses, and at that moment, he knew what he needed to do. 'No way Carol, I'm going after him. I'm off for a wee night-time sail, bye.'

He moved three berths along to a vessel he'd noticed earlier where the owner was doing a bit of spring cleaning. He was a portly man wearing a yachting sweatshirt, unbecoming jeans and wielding a large yellow duster. 'Police!' Henderson said in what he thought sounded like an authoritative voice but it must have been louder than he realised as the man jumped.

'I'm commandeering this vessel.'

'You're what?'

'Get off the boat sir. I'm chasing a murderer.'

He had a podgy face with thinning grey hair, and behind gold-framed spectacles his eyes stared back at him in shock and disbelief. Henderson pocketed his police ID and climbed aboard. He must have looked a wild sight in dishevelled clothes with heavy swelling to one side of his face, and if it could be seen in the dim light, one bloodshot eye and a blood-streaked face.

The man continued to protest but Henderson ushered him out and then spent the next few minutes familiarising himself with the cockpit layout. It was simpler than it looked as each dial and switch was labelled. He turned the ignition key and the big twin diesels of the 'Anna Mitchell' roared into life.

He didn't know too much about power boats and failed to see what enjoyment there was in bouncing over a choppy sea at thirty knots, in contrast to the pleasure gained from a leisurely cruise in a yacht which progressed through the skill of the skipper and not by the brute force of the engines. However, he was sure of one thing, this was a lot more powerful than Larner's.

'Cast off. Please.'

'Bloody hell. You'll be asking me to crew for you next.' He bent down and pulled the mooring rope away from the bollard and threw it on deck. 'Look mate, I've see the movie too when all I get back is a couple of bits of wood and a piece of the rudder. But let me tell you this, Mr Detective, I don't expect to find a scratch on her when you get back. I'm a lawyer and I'll sue the pants off Sussex Police if you do.'

'Don't worry, sir, I'll be careful,' he said easing the throttle back and pulling away from the mooring, but cursing his luck. Why did it have to be owned by a litigious lawyer and not a lottery winner or a rich businessman, someone who didn't give a toss what happened to it?

'There's not much fuel on board,' he shouted, 'so make sure you leave enough in the tank to bring her home.' He said something else but his voice was lost as Henderson opened the throttle. He ignored the five-knot speed limit as he guided the boat away from the pontoon and out towards the gap in the marina sea wall.

Out on the open sea and away from the millpond

inside the marina, the 'Anna Mitchell' started to bounce over the waves, but as soon as he opened the throttle a bit more, it sliced through them as if they didn't exist. He couldn't see in which direction Larner was headed, and now he had the choice of east to Kent, or west to Dorset. Instead, Henderson headed straight across the Channel towards France, the closest point to mainland Europe and the way he would go if he was being pursued by the police.

For a few moments, he savoured the novelty of an evening sail in someone else's boat, although well aware that crossing the English Channel was not a voyage to be undertaken by the foolhardy or the unprepared, especially after dark. Container ships as high as office blocks made their way directly across his path to Felixstowe and Antwerp while oil, ore, and grain tankers, many of them as long as football pitches, did a similar run but heading towards the giant terminals at Rotterdam and Hamburg.

Five minutes later, he spotted another boat dead ahead. It was only a speck in the distance but it was also heading towards France. He propped his knee up against the wheel, trying to keep the 'Anna Mitchell' on a steady course, and pulled out his phone. He called Lewes Control for what would be the last time as he was sure the signal would disappear in a couple of minutes.

While speaking to the operator and giving them an update of his movements, he glanced at the fuel indicator. The needle was nudging below the quarter full mark, enough to take him to France but probably not enough to bring him back, certainly not in the inefficient way he was powering those big engines. For this reason, he took the decision he would try and stop Larner soon and not allow him to travel to France.

The moon was bright and free from clouds and as he closed the gap between his boat and the craft in front, he could see beyond doubt, it was Larner's little speedboat. A few minutes later, he guided the 'Anna Mitchell' out on a wide semi circle and approached him from the port side, aiming to block his path and encourage him to return to Brighton.

Henderson was about twenty-metres away and heading for a point just in front of him, when Larner opened fire with a handgun. Henderson pulled away, less worried about a direct hit than a lucky shot; it was nigh-on impossible to shoot straight from a bouncing boat as they did in the movies, especially when trying to hit someone on another boat who was also moving in a way that was equally unpredictable.

He kept out of range but he couldn't sit out there all night, fuel or no fuel. With a determined scowl, he turned the wheel, opened the throttle and once more aimed for a patch of sea just in front of Larner's bow. Larner fired two more shots, both wide of the mark, and from the silence that followed, he was sure the magazine of the gun was empty or he was having trouble re-loading, not an easy thing to do while trying to steer a fast moving boat.

Henderson eased the engines back as the 'Anna Mitchell' rammed into the side of the speedboat. It cut through 'Tempest' like a hot knife through butter and moments prior to impact, Larner leapt overboard.

# FORTY-TWO

Henderson steered his commandeered powerboat in a wide arc as he approached the spot where Larner's speedboat had sunk, and reduced the engine tone to a soft burble. The silence that descended was oppressive; gone was the rumble of large twin diesels, the slap and bang of waves against the hull, and the shrill whining of Larner's Yamaha outboard. Now, all he could hear was the gentle lapping of waves, the bellowing of a ship's foghorn somewhere in the distance, and the garbled shouts of a man panicking in the water.

He switched on the searchlight mounted on the roof of the cabin, and scanned the sea while gently coaxing the powerboat through the waves. A few seconds later, he spotted him, bobbing in the water. Henderson smiled to himself as now the crazy bastard wasn't holding all the cards. It was fortunate for Larner that the 'Anna Mitchell' was equipped with a searchlight, as Henderson wouldn't have found him otherwise as he wasn't wearing a fluorescent life vest and there wasn't much left of his speedboat to mark the spot where it had disappeared into the blackness.

Another noise broke the silence, low and steady.

He turned to look, and in the distance he could see a boat approaching. Judging by the foam displaced by its hull, it was travelling at speed. In his head he praised Carol Walters and Lewes Control for having the sense to scramble a police launch or a Customs powerboat, boats well used to intercepting suspect ships and drug runners. Either way, they were a welcome addition to this little scene, as Larner would need warming up when rescued. Henderson didn't have a clue what safety kit was stored aboard his commandeered craft.

Larner shouted in a rasping, gurgling voice, 'Get me out of here Henderson, it's bloody freezing. I'm not...a good swimmer.'

'Why should I show you any mercy, Larner?' Henderson shouted back. 'You never showed any mercy to Mathew Markham or David Young, did you?'

'They fucking deserved it. They shafted me and stole my designs. I'd be famous and making millions if it wasn't for those thieving bastards.'

He ranted and blabbered about the injustice of it all as Henderson tied a line to a lifebelt and threw it over to him. The noise from the other boat was louder now, and he turned to see its searchlight illuminating the water two or three hundred yards behind him. Larner ducked under the lifebelt and gripped the line.

'Pull me in for fucksake. I'm freezing and I'm knackered. I've got no energy left.'

Henderson was in two minds. He could wait until

the other boat arrived and they offered assistance, or pull him in now. The English Channel could be cold, even in early summer, and there was a risk Larner could develop hypothermia. He gripped the rope and pulled. Despite the buoyancy of water, Larner was heavy, his clothes filled with water. If, as he suspected, Larner had spent time preparing for this moment, why wasn't he wearing more suitable sailing clothes? He shook his head in dismay. This was a mark of the man, sloppy, ill disciplined, and badly prepared.

Over his shoulder, the engine of the approaching boat scaled back a couple of octaves, indicating it was slowing and close by. A few seconds later, someone on-board shouted, 'Ahoy there. Are you alright?'

Henderson turned to answer and the next thing he knew, he was flying through the air. Seconds later, his world turned icy cold and the night sky disappeared.

Christ, the water was freezing. It hit him like a punch in the face and in an instant, his eyes were filled with millions of bright droplets, sparkling and jiggling before him like tiny effervescent dancers. He kicked his legs and moments later surfaced, gasping for air, more from the shock of the freezing water than any oxygen deficiency, as he had only been underwater for ten or fifteen seconds. When his vision cleared, he spotted an 'exhausted' Larner swimming strongly towards the 'Anna Mitchell'.

'Knackered my arse,' he said as he went after him. Henderson wasn't wearing a jacket and moved fast.

He reached the powerboat just as Larner began climbing the steps. Henderson reached up and seized his ankle.

Larner held on to the guardrail, trying to shrug the DI off, but Henderson had a good grip and held tight. He placed his legs against the hull and pulled. Both men fell into the water in an ungainly mangle of arms, legs and water spray. Far from being whacked, Larner was full of life. Henderson reached out to grab hold of him but he lashed out, punching and flailing.

One punch hit him full on the face, and for a moment his mind went blank. He came to, full of anger. He swam up behind Larner, seized a handful of his shaggy mop and forced his head underwater and held him there with the other hand. He could feel him flailing and punching at his body, but despite the blows and the pain, Henderson wasn't for letting go. Twenty seconds later, he hauled him up.

'Who helped you kill Mathew Markham, Larner?'

'Fuck off copper,' he gasped, spitting spray into his face.

Henderson pushed him under again. Punches were coming into his midriff but with little or no energy in the movements, and when it seemed Larner might black out, he hauled him back up to the surface again.

'Who helped you kill Mathew Markham?'

'Nicky Heath and Stevie Nolan,' he spluttered, part crying, part spitting. 'It's all on my computer at home. Get me out of here you sadistic bastard, I'm dying.'

'What about James Nash? What was his involvement?'

'Wimpy bastard. Didn't want to get involved, did he?'

'What happened to David Young?' he said, re-tightening his grip of Larner's hair, making him think he was about to duck him under again.

'Don't, don't. It was me, in my car, all right? But it was a fucking accident.'

'Pull the other one. You're an evil bastard Larner; you killed him and Markham. You're going down for both murders.'

The other vessel appeared around the bow of the 'Anna Mitchell' and Henderson could see now it was a Customs boat with a four-man crew. They edged closer and threw out two lifebelts. Henderson only used one, as there was no way he was letting Larner go until he was safely on-board and handcuffed to something solid.

# FORTY-THREE

As usual on a Monday morning, DI Henderson was seated at his desk by eight, but what was not so usual was how he had spent the weekend.

Friday and Saturday, he'd been a resident of the Royal Sussex Hospital where he was being treated for hypothermia. Despite the application of blankets, warm clothing and plenty of fluids, he could still feel the symptoms, even after being discharged from hospital on Sunday morning. Rachel made a trip into town and bought him some thermal underwear, and even if they weren't the epitome of sartorial elegance and railed against her stylistic standards, the heat generated by walking upstairs in Sussex House was enough to keep the chills at bay.

In so many ways, Larner had been a clever sod. He was being treated in the same hospital as Henderson, and although in a much worse condition than the DI, still fit enough to be interviewed by Gerry Hobbs on Sunday night. Surprise, surprise, he revealed nothing and denied everything and even had the cheek to say he would be making a claim against Sussex Police for brutality.

Henderson wasn't naive enough to believe his

'confession' out in the Channel, or think the files found on his computer would stand up in court. Larner could claim they were the components of his latest novel, a screenplay, or the fantasies of an over-active imagination. However, the kidnap and serious assault of Marta Stevenson and Sanjay Singh were real enough and not something he could wriggle away from so easily.

The Subaru had been examined and, despite the passage of several months since David Young's death, he doubted the car had ever been cleaned since. The Vehicle Forensic team found tiny flakes of red paint and in time they were confident of matching them to David Young's red motorbike. It was positive news but as Henderson stewed in the crisp, white sheets of his hospital bed, the feeling would not go away that the killers of Sir Mathew Markham were slipping away.

This feeling persisted until the arrest of Nicky Heath and Stevie Nolan. Henderson expected them to follow Larner's defence and 'take the fifth', as the Americans would call it, forcing his detectives to build a case against them, but they surprised him. They both admitted their part in the Markham attack, but said they were unaware of Larner's intention to kill and only participated in the venture to put the 'frighteners' on.

Now facing serious charges and the prospect of ten to fifteen years in prison if charged with being active participants in a murder, it didn't take long before they spilled the whole story. A good lawyer would pick apart their 'let's blame Larner' defence, but Heath told them where the knife was hidden and now it was being fast-tracked through forensics. If it proved to be Larner's knife and if Markham's DNA was found on the blade as he felt sure it would be, he would at last have his killer.

After dealing with a sudden flurry of emails, some praising his actions while others made stupid jokes about sailors, water, and boats, he decided to call William Lawton. If Larner's computer files were to be believed, Lawton was next on the hit list after the battery development team were 'recycled.' Larner had intended to kidnap him on Sunday when he would next be playing golf at West Hove, but as Larner was laid up in hospital at the time, Henderson didn't bother to tell him.

It was fortunate Henderson didn't know that Lawton was being investigated by the Fraud team upstairs in Sussex House, for a crime he'd tried to blame on David Young, as then it would have made him his number one suspect and led him up the wrong path. In fact, if it wasn't for Jackson's surprise announcement in firing him, it seemed to him he had more to gain from killing Young and Markham than Larner. Yes indeed, he needed to have another wee chat with the slippery William Lawton.

He dialled his office number but five rings later, he heard a click as it diverted.

'Mr Markham's office, Jules speaking.'

'Oh hello Jules. I'm looking for Mr Lawton. This is Detective Inspector Henderson, Sussex Police.'

'Hi Inspector. I'm sorry to say Mr Lawton has now left the company. The young Mr Markham, Jackson Markham, is now in charge. Would you like to speak to him?'

'No thank you. Do you know how I can contact Mr Lawton?'

There was a muffled rustling from the handset. 'To tell you the truth, he's persona non grata around here, if you know what I mean; but I liked him. I called his mobile on Saturday to see how he was doing and when I didn't get a reply, I went round to his house. His wife answered and do you know what she said to me? She hasn't seen him since Friday and was now so worried, she was thinking of calling you lot.'

# ABOUT THE AUTHOR

Iain Cameron was born in Glasgow and moved south to Brighton in the early eighties. He has worked as a management accountant, business consultant and a nursery goods retailer. He is now a full-time writer and lives in a village outside Horsham in West Sussex with his wife, two daughters and a lively Collie dog.

In the first three months after release, his first novel '*One Last Lesson*' was listed in two Amazon bestseller lists within crime fiction and it's been there ever since. '*Driving into Darkness*' is the second novel to feature DI Angus Henderson of Sussex Police, the Scottish detective with the calm demeanour and hidden ruthless streak.

To find out more about the author, visit the website:
**www.iain-cameron.com**

# ALSO BY IAIN CAMERON

## *ONE LAST LESSON*

The serenity of a rural golf course is shattered when a popular university student is found murdered. There are few clues, leaving DI Angus Henderson of Sussex Police angry and frustrated. That is, until he finds the victim was once a model on an adult web site run by two of her lecturers.

It's a difficult case for the DI and brings him into confrontation with two dangerous animals – *but only one of them is human.*

## *FEAR THE SILENCE*

A woman disappears without trace. She was once a famous fashion model and married to a former television interviewer, so media interest is intense. DI Angus Henderson of Sussex Police has many suspects but in time, all are eliminated except the husband.

Despite compelling evidence and pressure from all sides to arrest him, the DI has his doubts but these are dispelled when another woman goes missing in similar circumstances.

## *HUNTING FOR CROWS*

A man's body is recovered from the swollen River Arun, drowned in a vain attempt to save his dog. The story interests DI Angus Henderson as the victim was once the member of an eighties rock band. When another band member dies, exercising in his home gym, Henderson investigates.

In the search for clues, Henderson forces witnesses to delve into their past, providing pleasant memories for some and opening old wounds and grievances for others. The DI digs deeper but uncovers something he didn't bargain on.

Printed in Great Britain
by Amazon